THE SPACE
between
THE OLIVES

THE SPACE
between
THE OLIVES

{A Story of Civic Engagement}

LILY GUZMÁN

TATE PUBLISHING & *Enterprises*

Published by Tate Publishing & Enterprises, LLC
127 E. Trade Center Terrace | Mustang, Oklahoma 73064 USA
1.888.361.9473 | www.tatepublishing.com

Tate Publishing is committed to excellence in the publishing industry. The company reflects the philosophy established by the founders, based on Psalm 68:11,
"The Lord gave the word and great was the company of those who published it."

Book design copyright © 2010 by Tate Publishing, LLC. All rights reserved.
Cover design by Kellie Southerland
Interior design by Joey Garrett

Published in the United States of America

ISBN: 978-1-61739-301-3
1. Fiction / Political
2. Fiction / General
10.10.26

DEDICATION

With deep gratitude, I dedicate my story to Mr. Enrique Rodriguez Garcia, whose vision and tenacity gave birth to the Union of Ibero-American Municipalists (UIM) and to the indefatigable personnel of said organization. It has been in the core of that institution where I have come to understand the social reality of the Ibero-American peoples—united by our irrevocable Spanish legacy of deep-rooted values and noble sentiments—and to insist upon the need to reiterate to our children the commandment of respect for our elders and to recognize the immense treasure that is a clear conscience and the unbreakable commitment to personal integrity and social justice.

*Special thanks to my daughter,
Lily Garcia, for her invaluable help with this book.*

TABLE OF CONTENTS

FOREWORD

The book the reader is holding in his hands reveals, beyond its inspiration in local development processes that have happened in many Andalusian towns in recent years, and that the Ibero-American Union of Municipalists, to which the author prominently belongs, has witnessed, the story of a dreamer: one of those dreamers that make dreams possible. Let me explain in advance: I will try to dialogue with the reader and not detract one iota of interest in reading this book through the easy use of its gloss, to a greater or lesser extent, by the summary of its contents.

Faulkner said, in those phrases we find in books of quotations, that to be great, we need 99 percent talent, 99 percent of discipline, and 99 percent of work. Well, let me say that when Faulkner said this, he didn't tell us the whole truth. It is not usually the case of the few people who actually succeed in building important companies. It is not the case of Juan, even when it appears inopportune to say it, but along with these, are other keys that explain the history of our protagonist: the story of Juan.

I do not think human beings are born with a destiny planned from conception, through the work of a capricious deity who distributes skills and inadequacies among the brand-new beings. But I do not think, now and after some decades of existence, that the destiny and vocation of all is therefore solely and exclusively consequence of a free choice. If I'm correct in my suspicion, a man or a woman precociously develops a predisposition to fantasize about people, situations, worlds different from the world he or she lives in, and this proclivity, this imagination, this passion to escape the ties that bind us to the routine and fears of our past or the future that lies ahead is the hidden force at the start of a race, a project, or a vocation.

And this is the case of our protagonist. The sadness felt when, as a teenager, he watched his friends leave Alborde—imagined place where the author places the story—given that their agricultural production of subsistence was around the olive tree, forcing the emigration of many for long periods of the year.

I know it's hard to admit and repugnant to reason—and surely many of us experience it—to accept that things do not always have a secret design, a magisterial purpose out of our reach, but that gives the world an order and scheme. But strange as it may seem the wisdom in the conjunction of chance and coincidence, and this book is full of them, is more often than we would like, the real reason for the initiation of processes that can change the course of our lives.

Naturally, this tendency to depart from the real world, to imagine new scenarios, to combine the coincidences, to cross the barrier often insurmountable for our initial destination, there is a gap that most of us do not get to overcome. Those who do and manage to imagine other scenarios are the ones who go on to become creators, founders of something; they become promoters of new initiatives—dreamers. And that was, dear reader, the case of the protagonist of our story, who at first only imagined the possibility to continue playing with his friends, those he had to bid farewell, year after year, because of circumstances beyond their control.

Then, but later, comes the choice. That idea that gave impetus to a project and Juan, first with the complicity of his grandfather, imagined for his community, for his neighbors, for the institutions that served them, a better fate than the slow and onerous routine in which they were installed.

That was the moment in time when the circumstances that fate had weaved stopped commanding the course of events of that municipality and where the initial idea, humble as you can see, became the labor of everyone wanting a better future, in the community. That was the time when Alborde, with new leadership, faced his destiny with the purpose of changing it.

But I believe, and I am sure all readers will side with me after reading the book, that what made this process so great was Juan's warmth and great heart. To be great, and here is the part when Faulkner did not tell us the whole truth, besides talent, we must also have discipline, willingness to work, human quality and simplicity. And this is just what both Juan and his grandfather did not lack. Nor is the author who for those who have been fortunate to meet her, know the enormous amount of love she holds, and how with her mere presence she manages to steal something from our hearts and convey, to those of us who have come to know her, a very special affection. Only a person like her could produce the type of work I have the honor to present.

—Federico A. Castillo Blanco
Professor of Administrative Law
University of Granada
Secretary General of Ibero-American
Union of Municipalists

Excerpts of a letter from a reader:
I have twice read *El Pueblo de Juan*, in which I see a clear reflection of my life. It felt almost as if you had agreed to write my story, as if it had been destiny. With respect and admiration, I am writing to tell you that the story you have written is one of the greatest gifts I have receive in my twenty-three years of life. It is a source of inspiration, guidance, and passion for the fulfillment of my hopes and dreams for my hometown of Almoloya de Alquisiras, my own little Alborde. In your book, you write: *One cannot live a life without purpose.* And you are right. That affirmation has given me the strength and resolve to continue help-

ing the migrant workers in my town, to deal with the countless issues of the people who come to us for help. I sometimes feel overwhelmed by the sheer number of families in need, so many abandoning the quest for a better life in the United States due to limited resources. But your book has given me courage and determination. I assure you that what you wrote will touch the lives of many migrants and provide those who encounter them with a better understanding of the suffering that their families endure. I am thankful for your words and wisdom every day of my life.

—Ramiro Diaz Sanchez
Founder of *La Casa del Migrante*
(The House of the Migrants)
Director of International Affairs and
Strategic Development Plan
Almoloya de Alquisiras, Mexico

ALBORDE

Juan was born in Alborde and lived his entire life there, a small town surrounded by mountains, located in the southern region of an ancient European country, distant from other cities and somewhat isolated due to the geographical conditions of the zone.

Alborde appeared desolate and dusty, its houses cautiously watching over the deserted streets, projecting vigilant shadows over the few inhabitants who yet roamed the old neighborhoods.

The residents of Alborde were families of farmers who, after the olive harvest, which only lasted three months, initiated an uncertain journey to the north, taking them from town to town, working in the gathering of other produce, that, as if by magic, would be ready for picking precisely after the end of the olive harvest in Alborde.

The olive was the only crop that, throughout countless generations, had been commercially produced in that part of the country given that the olive trees could occupy the terrain for long periods of time without having to be replant after every harvest.

Dr. Jorge Narváez, Juan's father, was the only attorney residing in town, and his family was one of the very few that remained in Alborde year around, without needing to immigrate to other parts of the country looking for work. Only the oldest families of noble history, the handicapped, and the elderly remained affixed to Alborde, as if held by invisible nails.

Juan was extremely saddened at the conclusion of each olive harvest because, year after year, he lost his friends without hope of seeing them again. If some of the boys returned to Alborde by any chance, resuming the friendship was difficult because most of the returning children either had fallen behind in grade or dropped out of school entirely.

When a migrant family left town, nobody new for certain who would return. Many lucky ones would find permanent work in other areas or in more diversified crops or cleverly find ways of changing profession, in pursuit of the well-being and security of their families.

This time, when Juan bid farewell to Jose and Antonio, his best friends, he felt a sadness deeper than usual. Juan had been close to them since the summer of the prior year because the fathers of both friends had suffered an accident that forced them to return and remain in Alborde with their families—first to convalesce and then for an extended rehabilitation period of almost a year.

What happened was this: Antonio's father was driving a mammoth wheat harvesting machine with Jose's dad sitting in the passenger seat, going from one field to another on a rural road as part of their normal daily work routine for a harvesting company based in the northeastern part of the country, when suddenly a stampede of cattle cut in front of the heavy equipment, causing an accident where several workers got hurt.

Fortunately, there were no fatalities and, although both fathers came close to losing their hands, the agricultural company accepted all financial responsibilities for the accident, paying the salary of both men, plus workers' compensation, during the entire recuperation period. This accident retained both families in Alborde for an indefinite period of time, solidifying a tight friendship between the three boys.

Juan was heavyhearted when the boys left town. Never before had he had the opportunity to spend so many months of playful coexistence and close friendship with other youngsters his own age; for that reason, he swore to take some type of action to ensure that all minors who wished to stay in their town could do so without having to emigrate to other parts of the country. He thought about it for hours, studying how he could find the appropriate people to speak to about the subject, someone with the power to get something done before the olive harvest of the coming year.

As he walked pensively among the groves of dark green leaves, he asked himself: "Why is it that so many families do not return to Alborde? It's such a beautiful place to live."

Although some families returned, their children stayed trapped in a time warp, working as laborers, facing a future that could only guarantee social inequity, discrimination, family instability, and scarcity.

Upon returning from their migrant-work season, the youngsters inevitably found they had gradually fallen behind in their studies. The schools they attended during their travels did not keep records of migrants, or if they did, they didn't send the progress reports and final school grades to the hometown schools in a timely manner, as mandated by the education system, to be eligible to advance from one grade to another. Therefore, without documentation and final grades, the youngsters returning to Alborde were forced to start the grade all over again, unable to reincorporate with their previous classmates and corresponding age level school year. This situation took away all desire for intellectual enrichment, and they resigned to keep on as agricultural migrant workers, unable to envision a future holding the possibility of any other way of life.

Dr. Narváez was a very busy man, and every time Juan had tried to discuss the situation, investigating what could be done to resolve the issue of the migrant children, his father replied, "Everything is working fine in Alborde. The situation is evolving normally, the way it should, given the social and economic conditions of the population."

He further explained that each person emigrating to look for work in other places did so simply because he wanted to better his way of life and secure a higher income for the family, exercising his rights to a better life.

"You can't dictate to others how to live their lives, nor how to judge the opportunities before them; we all have choices, and intervening in any way is to infringe upon the freedom of action of other. In each mind lies an individual world apart from the rest, and the decision making process of each person is fundamental to the autonomy and sovereignty of the human being."

"But, Dad, many don't know there are better things for them. I believe that we could at least offer good advice."

Juan's father was convinced the existing tacit arrangement, mobilizing families, and following the rhythm of the different harvests was the best alternative for everyone concerned. The adults and the older, strong, and healthy siblings continued to support the relatives left behind in Alborde. With the money the migrants earned working the abundance of jobs found in other parts of the country, they contributed to the sustainability of their town, importing capital that otherwise would have never made it into the local economy.

Besides, according to Dr. Narváez, leaving the grandparents and those who could not work the harvests in Alborde preserved the town structure. The year-round residents maintained the homes of the migrants throughout the year and kept all local traditions alive.

Juan did not perceive the situation the way his father saw it. What he observed was a town whose essence was evaporating, obsessed with keeping all outmoded traditions intact; its inhabitants did not realize the place was crumbling and instead chose to continue on, ignoring the incessant, indisputable human escape.

The olives ripen at the end of March, when new olive flowers start to sprout. Although the flowers are in full bloom in April and May, the harvest occurs between November and February, immediately after which all families initiated their inevitable journey to find temporary work. For Juan, the farewell was too painful and the phantasmagoric abandonment in which his town lived after each harvest was slowly killing his hope of staying in the beloved town where he had grown up.

After the families left town, late in the afternoons, Juan was accustomed to visit his paternal grandfather to share the afternoon snack, known as *merienda* in the Spanish tradition. On the way to his grandfather's house one day after Jose and Antonio had left, Juan decided to unburden his heart and confess his concerns to the grandfather, thinking he would understand the pain of separation through which he lived each year when he was left without his group of friends.

It was cold, and he walked briskly, thinking about the history and impact of the olive tree, and how the Moorish people, migrating from the south hundreds of years ago, had introduced it in that part of the country. He pondered how such a simple plant could have sustained the hope of so many families throughout history, from the old Mesopotamia region to America, where the olive tree was first taken to the Antilles and later to the entire continent after Christopher Columbus's discovery of the new world.

The olive trees were in bloom practically since the beginning of the year. In June, one could see the olives well formed, increasing in size during the summer and autumn, transforming in color from green to purple to black, adorning the trees in magical splendor. Juan was fascinated with the history of his town and the lineage of its inhabitants, tirelessly reading about the development of the Mediterranean culture and the influence it stamped around the world, even in aspects apparently fortuitous.

His grandfather lived in ancient house on the outskirts of town. It was a large, rundown house with massive doors and tall windows surrounded by cypresses, birches, and pines that, like powerful guardians, unchallengeable, protected the old castle.

The house was built in two levels of ample rooms, and its floors were covered by bright mosaics that gradually crawled some three feet up on several of the walls, forming asymmetric designs in blue and green tones with white borders. On the second level, conceived in some mythical story, a spiral staircase made of iron climbed about four meters in height to reach a small surveillance tower located on the north side of the little castle; long and narrow colored glass windows framed the small observation room. On the back of each step, plaques made out of copper displayed bucolic scenes telling the ancient history of Alborde, encompassing a period of about three hundred years that had concluded some two hundred years earlier.

The people of Alborde told that the small castle was built by Omar, a noble Moor who swore eternal love to a beautiful gypsy named Lucia, who wandered the southern part of the country with the members of her tribe. After feverish promises of love, Omar started the construction of the castle with the purpose of retaining the attractive gypsy, without sparing any expense in the supplies used in the structure. He believed that, as soon as Lucia confirmed his dedication upon witnessing the beauty of the sanctuary he built for her, she would agree to leave her nomadic life behind and live with him in the castle forever.

Omar obsessed over every detail of the construction. He ordered cedar and mahogany doors and on the tall windows installed colorful glasses imported from faraway lands to illuminate each room, allowing the sun to shine indoors throughout the year. He commissioned the best artisans to create the iron for the locks and hardware and copper laminates and plaques that decorated the entrances.

And so the legend goes that Omar the Moor built the tower to keep watch for the arrival of his beloved. Who never returned. He aged and died disheartened in the old castle, which was later acquired by Juan's ancestors.

From the small tower, through the fading colored glass worn out by the ages and dust accumulated by forgetfulness, one could see the immense lines of olive trees in succession, their trunks excruciatingly twisted by the weight of time, overwhelmed by painful knots silently yearning for the soothing touch of their caretakers. Juan loved those fields that vanished at the foot of the mountainous range in the horizon, impregnated by the intoxicating scent of orange blossoms.

Facing any direction, one's gaze would get lost in the vastness, alighting occasionally upon the squares of multicolor strokes of greens and yellows, with orange and red touches; orchards, exclusively cultivated by the grandparents left behind in Alborde, boasted rows of different size and length in a capriciously harmonious march, north to south or east to west.

Traditionally, all Alborde families maintained private orchard for personal consumption, and each Saturday morning at dawn, families would gather in the main plaza to exchange vegetables and fruits; this was one of the main sources of delight and activity in town and one of the events Juan most celebrated and longed for.

For quite sometime, Juan had often noticed his grandfather silently crying, lamenting the passing of years, remembering events of the past, his adventures as an adolescent, and, above all, visibly anxious in the face of the ineludible departure of his life-long friends and his longing for those already deceased. Lately, the dark lady of death was visiting Alborde more often than usual, and the grandfather not only missed his departed friends, but he also sensed the coming of his own end.

Juan remembered most of his grandfather's friends and how they had been passing away one after the other in an interminable chain of funerals. Echoing in his head remained the long-ago tales, told by old men and women dressed in black, narratives that in the midst of rivers of tears and laments, enfolded in the smoke of burning candles, summoned new life and mysterious essence. Those were stories of exciting experiences and time spent with the departed, possibly adorned and amplified in the imagination of the mourners to ease their pain and the impact of death and separation. It was clear his grandfather's circle of friends was noticeably and rapidly shrinking.

Papa Fello, a term of endearment the grandchildren used for their grandfather, whose given name was Rafael, looked forward to and meticulously prepared the midafternoon *merienda* for Juan; the times Fello spent with his grandson were a palliative, providing him strength and something to look forward to. He had been living alone in the big house since Elena, his wife, had suddenly passed away after a heart attack seven years before, and he stubbornly refused to abandon his little castle that had been home to more than seven preceding generations for a period of about two centuries.

Fello's three children tried to convince him to move into town and live with one of them, but he would say that there was no difference between living alone in his own home and being alone in the home of one of his children, disrupting their family's routine or wandering in the streets of a town practically abandoned most of the year, for all intents and purposes.

Fello religiously prepared the afternoon nibble with superb care to have it ready at exactly four o'clock. After eating delicious crusty bread dipped in a spread typical of the zone made with crushed olives and sweet red peppers cured in olive oil and a selection of homemade peaches, nectarines, and red cherry preserves accompanied by a full pot of tea made with homegrown linden, mint, and lemon grass, Fello and Juan began to walk briskly across the three or four kilometers that separated the house from the plaza in the center of town where Fello usually met with other senior citizens to enjoy a little sun and play cards, checkers, and chess before dusk.

Although the sun went down early during the spring, that day Juan wanted to prolong their walk to be able the talk with his grandfather about the situation that aggrieved him so deeply; Juan was determined to find an ally to advocate for the cause that engaged his thoughts day and night.

"Grandpa, I want to tell you something," Juan started to say. "You know that my best friends have headed north."

"Yes," the grandfather said. "That's the way it has to be; it's been happening like that since before you were born. For a long time people have left town after the olive crop is finished. Otherwise they starve. Now, thank God, with the industrialization and massive production of agricultural products throughout the nation, there is work for all those who want to work in harvesting other products in other cities; they are able to continue supporting their families."

"But, Grandpa, you don't understand what I am trying to tell you. My friends leave every year and I am left alone, without anyone to play with, no one to share with."

"Don't think for a moment that I do not understand you. I, too, lost my friends for a few months every year when I was growing up, but they returned in the fall to harvest the olives, and I had to accept the reality of life just as you will, too. And besides, be thankful your parents don't have to leave Alborde to support your family. Look at your aunt Paloma. She stays now because her daughters are small, but her husband has to leave town to earn a living, and your aunt Maria has been fortunate to marry your uncle Ramon, who, being the only full-time state police officer in Alborde, can stay permanently here. Otherwise, your aunts would have to emigrate alongside their husbands in support of their work and to preserve their marriages, as commanded by God."

Juan lowered his head. His grandfather was right in pointing out what he had just said; what he did not agree with was that the situation had to continue unchanged for the sake of it, simply because it had been done that way for a long time. Juan was looking at events backward and forward in time and he became conscious of the need to reevaluate the state of affairs and prepare for a better future.

"Grandpa, why do you think things cannot change? Many years ago, you had all your friends; now many have died and nonetheless—"

"Hush, boy! Don't be insolent," the grandfather said. "One day, you will understand many things you cannot even begin to appreciate at this moment."

Juan did not argue; he was respectful. He had been taught to respect his elders and understood he could not start a quarrel with his grandfather. Nevertheless, he felt somewhat disappointed because he had been counting on his grandfather's support.

They walked the last few meters in complete silence. Juan, listening to the grandfather's difficult breathing, interrupted by a soft whistling, a poor impersonation of old melodies, distractedly followed the music rhythmically beating on the pavement with each step taken while thinking about how to resolve his dilemma. He had to find a strong ally to be able to seriously face the cause consuming him now.

They passed the old Roman aqueduct and he thought about the rich and long history of Alborde.

What would our ancestors think about Alborde's destiny and the problems oppressing our town today?

Juan was deeply hurt by the decadence he observed as well as the inaction of the local leaders regarding those issues. At thirteen years of age, he knew he only had about four years left in Alborde before having to confront a major decision regarding his future.

Will I stay in town perpetuating the traditions? Or will I go away forever, after finishing my studies at the university?

His father dreamed that Juan was going to be a lawyer like him, inheriting his practice and following his footsteps, but Juan knew that once he left town, the horizons would shift, and somehow he feared the moment when the road was inevitably going to split in front of him, forcing him to make a decisive choice.

They arrived at the plaza, and his grandfather's face lit up. A spark could be perceived in his smile, when after taking a quick inventory, he noted that all his friends were present. Everyone was alive and apparently healthy, save a few coughs or minor congestion.

Realizing this, Juan was deeply touched. He thought the time left with his grandfather was possibly very short; only God knew how long he had left, and he thought how much he wished to be able to stop the clock, to be able to enjoy his grandfather for the longest time possible.

"Grandpa, I have to go home to do homework, but we'll see each other later on when you come for dinner. Remember? Today is our turn to have you over for dinner."

His grandfather smiled. He was so proud of Juan! He had suddenly become a handsome young man easily reaching above his shoulders in height. Last year, he could almost carry Juan on his back on their way to town and now, suddenly, he was a teenager. His eyes filled with tears, thinking how proud Grandma Elena would be had she been alive, seeing her only grandson transformed into a young adult, responsible and capable.

Juan ran to the big house across the plaza, diagonally crossing the street. As he entered the house, he went to his father's office. Dr. Jorge Narváez occupied the main room with his legal office at the entrance of the dwelling on the left side of the atrium. Juan greeted his father with a kiss on both cheeks.

"Dad, remember Grandpa is coming for dinner tonight. You know, it seems like he's kind of sad."

"Son, you have turned into such an old man! There is nothing wrong with your grandfather. I'm really busy right now. Let's talk later when I finish organizing a few things here."

Juan noticed how little his father concerned himself with Grandpa Fello.

One day, when Grandpa Fello is already dead and it's too late, he is going to miss him a lot. Dad should do a little more for Grandpa, even if it is to avoid later feelings of guilt, Juan inwardly thought as he proceeded to cross the heavy door that separated the living quarters from the reception room and the law office and continued along the hallway, reaching the family room where his mother was. Susana was placidly sitting on a rocking chair, listening to music, while going through a basket full of freshly washed clothing, checking for missing buttons, and stitching whatever was in need of mending.

"Where have you been, Juan? I have been looking for you."

"I was at Grandpa's house having *merienda* with him."

"Oh I forgot you started your old routine with Fello again."

"Grandpa Fello is looking sad. Have you noticed? He is walking slowly, and his whistling does not even resemble the music he pretends to intone."

"Maybe he has the flu or something."

"Mom, I have been talking to grandpa about my friends...I want to do something to change things here in Alborde."

"And what is wrong with Alborde?"

"Mom, times have changed. People keep leaving town; soon there will be no one left. I "

"What are you saying, son? Are you implying that we have not done things right for you? Look, your father and I have worked long and hard to be able to provide for you and your sisters with the best education in town, the best clothing, and the best home. Arrogance has gone to your head. Do you really think you can do things better than your parents?"

Juan felt like crying; he realized his parents would never understand what he started to observe in Alborde. He could only bring himself to babble, "Mom, yesterday all my friends left town, the last ones left after the harvest, and I'm lonely!"

Frustrated, he broke into tears. Susana got up from the rocking chair, placing the shirt she was mending on top of the stool in front of her.

"Oh, my boy, you are so tall now. I forget you are still a child. Come to me."

And, holding Juan against her chest, she embraced him tightly, kissing his face and head repeatedly.

"Everything will be fine, my love; time goes by so fast. Soon you will be in the plaza, playing all day with your friends again."

Susana got flustered. Often, she was not as tender as she could have been with her boy; she was always too busy with housework, barely having time to finish her daily routines. Since Elena's death, the relationship between Juan and Grandpa Fello had grown stronger, and she now realized she had neglected Juan quite a bit. Perhaps because she knew the grandfather poured all his care and affection on Juan, forming a symbiotic and beautiful relationship, she pulled away. Nonetheless, during the last few months, she had observed a process of maturing in Juan and started longing for the little boy she sensed was left behind.

"Go tell your sisters to get ready for dinner; they are at your aunt Paloma's home."

"Forgive me, Mom. I can't go. I have to study for tomorrow's tests. If I go, my aunts will start talking to me, and I don't know how to tell them I can't talk and I have to return home right away without offending them."

"Ah, you are always so sweet with your aunts. That's why they love you so much! I didn't remember your exams. Don't worry. They will probably come home with Fello when he goes by the house to say hello to his daughters before coming for dinner. Go ahead; go study."

Juan went to his room and opened the algebra book. This was his first year studying the subject, and he was fascinated by it. As he took steps toward understanding the subject matter, he felt as if he were entering a labyrinth of long hallways with secret doors under lock and key; the more he studied, the greater his ability to open each door with its corresponding key, or even open the locks without even touching them, almost as if by magic.

As he practiced the equations, he thought about the algebraic meaning of the letters X and Y. He drew a few symbols on a white paper, deducing, "X equals jobs for all inhabitants in Alborde. Y equals academic opportunity for their children. X plus Y equals my friends will stay in Alborde."

That night while having dinner together, his grandfather said to Juan, "Would you like to spend the next weekend with me at my house? I need your help packing a few things."

"Dad, may I?"

WEEKEND WITH GRANDPA FELLO

The week went by unhurriedly, as if time had decided to stop and deliberate upon the bitterness that was invading Juan. He had passed his midterm exams with excellent grades, but all he could do was to think about his friends who, if by now were attending a school, were probably feeling lost in a crowd of strangers, young people who often were unnecessarily cruel to the migrants.

Antonio and Jose had described to Juan how in the towns they visited, the majority of children made fun of them, making condescending comments about the lack of appropriate clothes or for not having school supplies, books, and utensils, or about using outdated or used old books, or any other nonsense; issues about which Juan never had to worry, because his parents had always taken care of every single detail regarding their education and necessary provisions for him and his sisters.

It was common knowledge that migrants often got into fist-fights, provoked by the local youngsters in every community they went to and, as a result, if the incident did not end in the suspension of student rights for the migrant, these humble travelers would be left frustrated and humiliated by the blatant inequality of treatment and the open unfairness of some. Consequently, and because they were transient it was difficult for them to study, rarely, if ever, enjoying any type of incentive.

Friday afternoon, Juan crammed a couple of outfits in his backpack and left for the country home before three thirty to spend the entire weekend with his grandfather. When they finished their *merienda*, instead of going back to the plaza as usual, Juan and Fello went out for a walk in the orchard. Although it was too early in the year to pick any fruit at all, Fello said, "Let's inspect the fruit trees in the orchard and see how the peach and cherry crop is beginning to look like this year."

As they walked between the rows of trees, the grandfather delicately separated the branches, inhaling the sweet aroma released by the fresh buds as he touched them.

Fello was a man of strong principles. His wide hands, mistreated and roughened by hard field work, revealed an indisputable devotion to his responsibilities and commitments. When Fello spoke enthusiastically, his hands acquired a life of their own, fluttering like excited doves trying to escape through the forgotten open door of their cage.

During numerous long walks in those very same fields, ever since Juan could remember clinging to the now trembling hands of the grandfather, he had found security, inspiration, and hope.

Strong, straight as an arrow, and of unshakable will from his youth, Fello had been in charge of the family affairs since his father's sudden death. This event forced him to give up going to the university in the state capital, where he had been a law student for a few semesters, and dedicate himself entirely to managing the great expanse of olive fields belonging to the Narváez's family in Alborde.

When Fello turned twenty-one, he proposed matrimony to Elena, who was the daughter of a laborer working on his parents' farm. Fello and Elena had grown up together, playing children's games and running in the orchard during the long summer days and drinking hot chocolate under wool blankets in front of the fire under the watchful eye and tender care of Elena's mother in the winter.

As they grew older, they learned how to help around the house and with farm duties. When Fello returned to the farm for weekends and during vacation periods, they worked hand in hand with the adults during the planting and gathering seasons.

They knew each other intimately; they had shared hopes and childhood dreams, building castles in the air, devising quixotic adventures, fighting windmills since early in their adolescence.

One Sunday afternoon, a little after Fello began his studies in town, when he was getting ready to return to the boarding school he regularly attended during the week, Fello softly took Elena's hand and said: "I don't want to be away from you. I cannot bear to wait until next Friday, when I can return home to see you again. I miss you already. I want you to cut a piece of your hair, so I can have a little bit of you with me at all times."

Elena blushed; she could hear the beating of her heart as if it were in stereo. Bashfully, she reached for the knife that Fello carried on his belt and, with a quick movement, cut off the end of one of her braids tied to a blue ribbon. Fello tucked away the relic in his billfold—he still had that lock of hair wrapped in wax paper, carefully stored in the chest of drawers in his bedroom as one of his most priceless treasures.

That afternoon, they promised each other an unbreakable love, overcoming the social and economic differences that separated them.

"Fello, I'll die if I don't see you every weekend," said Elena between sobs, recovering her hand to wipe the flowing tears, while thinking of ways she could match Fello's show of affection. She thought of preparing a special gift, something tangible to demonstrate that love, seemingly capable of breaking her chest into pieces. She wanted the gift to be very special, yet within her financial means, and she came up with the idea of creating fine linen handkerchiefs, embroidering Fello's initials with her very own hair. This project became an intimate tradition between them, Elena secretly confectioning one handkerchief for every week they were apart.

They had loved each other secretly since elementary school; although due to the respect prevalent among the youth of that time, no one ever noticed the furtive and tender looks interchanged between them or the fresh flowers in Elena's bedroom every time Fello arrived at the farm.

No one ever paid attention to the handshake that overextended a little bit longer than ordinary. And if someone ever noticed, it would have not been taken seriously, given the social conditions of the adolescents.

The marriage proposal provoked a grave crisis in the Narváez family. Marola, Fello's mother, was adamantly opposed to the wedding, citing how inopportune the timing was, given Fello's new obligation and commitment to the family after his father's death.

In reality, the opposition was based in the marked social differences between the two. What would the other families of Alborde think about the Narvaez family if Fello ended up marrying the daughter of one of the laborers?

Fello's love for Elena was strengthened even more so when he realized how easily his feelings were invalidated at the capricious altar of the family and the social self-importance of his mother.

Marola did not realize that the love between two people was more important than the social remarks of a few socialites; moreover, she knew that those quick to criticize the marriage of her son to someone beneath his class would not be willing to do what she was asking of her son—to forsake his personal welfare or give up his career to help her raise the family and manage the farm. Usually, people who gossip do not care about humanity at all.

The discussions continued for a few days after Fello announced his intention to marry Elena. Between sobs, long silences, and reproaches from Marola, Fello remained resolute. He had made up his mind, and he married Elena shortly after, but not before swearing on his father's grave that he would never forsake his commitment to take care of his mother and siblings as provider of the family or his responsibility to maintain their fields.

Finally, the wedding took place with Marola's reluctant blessings. It was an unpretentious wedding, as simple as the bride and groom. Elena's parents insisted on a celebration within their economic means; but the wedding was better attended than any other in the history of the town. Those who graced the celebration with their presence declared for a long time that it was the best wedding party Alborde had seen in many years.

Curiously, the union turned out to be very positive for both families. Instead of losing a son, Marola gained an entire family of dedicated and loyal workers devoted to the common good. And to everyone's surprise in the village, even though Elena came from humble ancestry, she was self-taught and displayed the finest education, earning the respect and admiration of all those who dealt with her.

Since Marola only had three sons, Elena came to be her favorite daughter, living with the family in the small castle at the insistence of her mother-in-law, who persistently asked Elena to call her mother instead of Mrs. Narváez, as she had always called her since her arrival at the house as a child. As time went by, Elena turned into the cornerstone of a great family. In less than five years, Elena and Fello gave Marola three beautiful grandchildren: Jorge, Paloma, and Maria, who, from the moment they came into the family, captivated the heart of their grandmother for life.

"You think I don't understand you? Eh? Since we spoke last Monday, I have been thinking only about how we can best resolve your dilemma," the grandfather said after walking down the first row of peaches.

"Really? I have been so sad thinking you didn't understand me, but somehow deep in my heart I knew I could count on you, Grandpa."

Fello continued. "I want to tell you something about our town. When I was little, many prosperous families lived in Alborde, and we enjoyed a strong economy with a good number of workers always available to work in the fields. The citizens belonged to two groups: the rich and the workers

"The Narváez family was powerful. We had extensive fields with plantations of olives and other fruits, orchards, and animals; the town was bountiful.

"The church organ was imported from Italy, a gift from the matriarch of the old Gonzalez-Cuevas family. It was a sight to see, with its long, silvery tubes rising above in irregular rows more than forty feet high. The music from that fine instrument proudly echoed beyond the cathedral walls and across the countryside to the delight of a place of worship full of enthusiastic people, grateful to the divine, happy to live in Alborde.

"The municipal band offered concerts at the central plaza every Sunday and on holidays. Happiness was in the air; the love of life was palpable. The families went out for lazy walks the length of the cobblestone streets and to drink the afternoon coffee in prosperous local establishments. The theater, now closed, presented different *zarzuelas* and plays almost every week

"The train station was busy, open, and beautiful; the main building had an elegant restaurant and gift shop attracting visitors and locals alike at all hours. Women used to wear graceful dresses adorned with lace as they walked the boardwalk in the plaza. There were elegant cars and carriages pulled by spirited horses decorated with paper flowers during the festivities of patron saints. Long ago, we really lived a golden era.

"Later, little by little, people started to leave for other, more affluent towns, and following the train trail, they disappeared along with the engine steam on the horizon. As time went by, we were left without laborers to cultivate the land; everyone was working in the big factories in the industrial cities. We nearly lost everything for lack of hands during the harvests. Local banks disappeared. People started to tuck away whatever little money they had under their mattresses; the town lost its financial solvency."

The grandfather stopped, pointing at the sunset in complete silence; the red horizon beyond the silhouette of mountain tops was impressive. Contemplating the spectacular nightfall, he captured the moment and savored it, possibly comparing it to other sunsets stored in his extensive memory, filled with fading images draped in nostalgia; slipped the fingers of his right hand through his white hair while lifting his brown suede hat with the left, and, after a short pause, he continued, "The fruit of our land kept Alborde prosperous through many generations around the cultivation of the olive tree. Although each family has always had an orchard and other minor products for personal consumption, it has been always the olive that has maintained our people throughout centuries.

"Do you know how the olive trees are planted? I think you have never seen an olive nursery since our olive groves have centenarian trees."

"No, Grandpa, I have never seen olive trees being planted."

"The olive tree is first planted in containers of three to four gallons, and when they reach about a meter in height, they are planted straight into the ground. It is the only Oleaceae species with edible fruit, and it is a perennial tree and surprisingly, its leaves last two to three years. Do you realize this? They survive the winter cold two or three times!

"The olive tree does well here in Alborde because it is not too humid and there is plenty sun throughout the year.

"You know what? I would love to be like an olive tree; its best production starts after it is eighty years of age. Besides, it is adaptable; if you pack the roots well, you can move it anywhere regardless of its age. It would be beautiful to be like an olive tree. Don't you think so?"

"Grandpa, I love the olive trees, but I only want to be like you. Besides, I never want to leave Alborde! Tell me more about the olives."

"I also wanted to stay in Alborde, even when I had the opportunity to stay in the big city. The olive not only supported Alborde for hundreds of years; olive farming molded the culture of the Mediterranean peoples. The olive has always been an important part of the Mediterranean diet.

"Information about the existence and benefit of the olive dates back to Greek mythology; according to legend, the first olive tree was born in Greece. Greek mythology tells us that Athena struck the ground with a spear, giving birth to the tree and ordering it, 'Your fruit not only will be good to eat; a marvelous liquid will be extracted from your fruit, and this liquid will nourish humanity. It will be rich in flavor and energy; it will mitigate the injuries of those who eat it, giving strength to their bodies. That liquid will be capable of burning and illuminating the nights.' Since then, it has always been an important tree; the olive branches have been used as a symbol of peace, life, victory, and fertility throughout history."

The grandfather was always passionate when he spoke about the tree that had supported his ancestry generation after generation.

"Did you know that the olive wood is hard and strong?"

Emphasizing his statement, the grandfather extended his strong arms with the intention of shaking a leafy olive tree that stood dauntless, extending its green branches toward heaven, fully determined to reach it.

"The olive trees reach almost twenty-five meters in height and almost ten meters in diameter. Well, and you know that the olive harvest, depending on the final use of the fruit, be it destined to be turned into pickle or for the production of oil, takes place between November and February and—"

Fello noticed the change in expression in Juan's face when unintentionally he made reference to the departure of the families.

"Come on, don't get sad, son! We will find a solution to this problem."

Juan wiped his face with both hands, erasing the expression of sadness; he loved to speak with his grandfather, his straightforward ways of telling things plainly the way they are, not dancing around the issue or inventing false stories.

He walked next to Fello on the path marked between the lines of trees, sometimes advancing a few steps, turning to catch the expressions of his grandfather as he spoke. Juan played distractedly as he walked, softly touching the trunks of the trees with a peach branch he had picked up at the start of the walk and at other times throwing pebbles he had found on the trail, launching them with precision a few meters ahead.

"Well, as years went by, only the landowners who later turned into laborers stayed on the olive farms Those who didn't want to work in the fields moved away; those who could not cover farming expenses and support their families by harvesting their olive fields started to travel, following the rhythm of the crops in other towns. As you see today, everything happened exactly as I tell you. Little by little, almost without realizing it, we were left living in a ghost town. I confess you made me think. For a long time, I had been blind to the situation in our town; maybe because it is easier to hide our heads in the sand, like the ostrich, than to question our actions or the results of our inaction and what is even worse, to confront our own failures.

"You know you are right. Maybe we can do something to turn around the depopulation of Alborde. Tell me, Juan, how do you define the problem? What do you think we can do?"

They sat down on the foundation of some ruins that dated back over five hundred years; perhaps a dividing or retaining wall that extended for many meters in length, with a depth of more or less one meter. The structure, damaged by the hands of time and the scourge of farming implements, was made of stones and adobe, a building material that due to its easy elaboration, abundance, and solidity has historically been the construction material of choice in the region. Large squares revealed the location of different buildings, and even the distribution of rooms remained identifiable.

It was common to find this type of archaeological ruin throughout the region. The national government had many times halted all new construction, and even farming land improvements, given that upon removing the upper layers of soil, ancient structures of extraordinary archaeological value were often found. Generally, the residents concealed the discover of such ruins for fear of having to abandon work.

Recently, an entire Roman town was unearthed in one of the cities near Alborde. Building details were well-preserved below thick layers of stone and clay. Utensils and tools in perfect conditions were found. The recently discovered public baths were practically intact, with their floor tiles that, more often than not, preserved the vividness of their colors. The National Department of History and Culture organized the restoration of the beautiful fountains in the center of the old city, richly adorned with figures of Roman gods. After refurbishing the original pipes, these fountains were awoken from their long slumber bursting, as if by magic, in sonorous waterfalls audible at the most distant corners of the Roman town. The melodic sound of falling water nimbly trickled down the stoned-paved streets, resonating in every corner and portico of the ancient city, which were gradually filled with the visitors who came from all cardinal points to explore the extraordinary findings.

The houses of noble Romans and the governmental buildings were easily identified and elegantly restored, including meticulous structural details, even replicating the furniture of the era. Likewise, the existence of wine cellars, public spaces and what appeared to be the market were verified, resurrecting the town to its former splendor.

The discovery of the Roman city provided an opportunity to develop a tourism project, impelled by the local citizens and their regional representatives, that proved to be beneficial for the economic development of the entire region in general.

Visibly tired by the long walk, the grandfather pulled out a handkerchief and wiped his face.

"Grandpa, since the vacation in December, I have been thinking a lot and talking with José and Antonio. There are many problems to resolve in our community. We know that there is not enough money here to earn a living throughout the year. But when the families travel, looking for work, their kids have a lot of problems and trouble adjusting in school. The entire family has difficulties with accommodation; there is no lodging available to them, and when they find a place, many experience difficulties securing housing, because few landlords want to rent their properties to migrant workers.

"On the other hand, at times, the money they make is not even enough to pay rent. They try to save some money; they decide to remain in temporary facilities or live inside their small vehicles until they can find something cheaper or a less burdensome arrangement. And often they park right in front of their working posts in the fields until they are ordered to leave the grounds. That is not living!

"They remain stripped of the most elementary components of everyday civilized living, with not even a bed to rest, without a toilet, without a shower, without privacy, without hygiene. It is a true pity because all the while they have a good home in Alborde, although it might not be deluxe accommodations.

"Besides, Grandpa, these subhuman conditions sow discord and the seed of evil in the hearts of these families that little by little become resentful of society and disenchanted! I believe irrational hate arises at that level when innocent people live in that kind of injustice, and they start feeding the grudge against those who have a little bit more or those they think are somewhat better off than they. When Antonio and José returned to town last year, they already brought with them the distrust they cultivated on their travels; they were reserved and distant. When we became friends, we frequently spoke about this topic. Some kids automatically blame society for their situation and seek ways to take revenge; hence the gangs and young delinquents so commonly seen in the big cities."

"I understand you, Juan, but the antidote to the wrongs you mention is to become aware of what is happening; it is to be conscious that although bad things occur to each one of us, without necessarily deserving it, and although we might find ourselves in situations over which we have no control, we have the freedom to choose how we respond to adversity; recognizing that we have options sets us free. Many people remain stuck in the victim mentality, pointing their fingers outwardly toward others, blaming society for all their problems, doing nothing to resolve them, waiting for government to free them from evil. All this victimizes them more because they don't learn how to analyze the situation, taking responsibility to straighten their mess. In addition, we all need to understand forgiveness and to act with love and compassion. I believe that in one way or another, we receive exactly what we focus on."

"But, Grandpa the kids have no options; their parents take them from one place to the next without even asking how they feel about it. How can you say they are responsible for their situation?"

"No, Juan, neither the minors nor anyone else is responsible for what happens around them. What we are all responsible for is the way we react to what happens around us. I am talking about that many of us spend our lives thinking about what we don't have instead of been grateful for what we have already received. But we are deviating from our conversation. Tell me, son, what do you think we should do now under these circumstances?"

"I think the first problem we have to address is to get a place in Alborde where the youngsters can stay to continue their studies without interruption, under adult supervision, of course. Let's say a boarding school or a home where they can live while their parents work in other towns until the labor problem can be resolved here."

"You are talking about a huge project. I don't know of anyone willing to be responsible for a group of adolescents for a period of eight months every year."

"Well, Grandpa, if it were not challenging, it would not be a problem, would it? Besides, you said we have to concentrate on the possible solutions and to think positively."

"You are right, Juan, I like the way you think. Continue."

"In reality, the ideal solution would be if parents didn't have to leave Alborde to earn a living in other towns, but if we succeed in making it possible for the kids to stay, we would ensure the return of the families, or at least help teenagers finish school before being forced to earn their own living."

"Well, Juan, you should also consider that many people do not have the mental capacity for advanced studies, or they have lost too many years of studies, and for that reason they have difficulties getting through secondary school; for some, the best option would be vocational training to allow them to earn a decent living when they reach adulthood. What I mean is that a great number of people have real talent for different occupations, not necessarily the preparation to be able to continue on to college or a university. Perhaps it would be good to pursue the creation of a vocational school for Alborde by legislative decree where our kids can learn masonry, tile, floor installation, plumbing, mechanics, stained glass, carpentry, etcetera, a vocational and technical school!"

"Hey, Grandpa! I like the way you think! But before we get to the vocational school, we first have to reach an agreement with the parents, allowing their children to stay in town under adult supervision."

The grandfather swelled with pride listening to Juan's reasoning; he saw himself in the attitudes of the boy, observing in his grandson the same concerns he experienced so many years ago, when he was a young student in the city, when he believed he could change the world with his ideals.

Times keep changing, but the same social concerns arise in the spring of each successive generation, starting with each adolescent, engendering in them lofty and noble feelings that give them reasons to live and to fight.

"And we are going to achieve it. The most effective way to resolve any problem is analyzing the situation as we are doing now and without blaming anybody. Concentrate on identifying solutions. We are going to discuss this issue with the elders in town and thus, by common consent, define the process to follow.

When each person makes a commitment to fight against adversity as a group, all together and the agreed upon course is maintained, any objective set by the group can be achieved," declared the grandfather with his characteristic simplicity and wisdom.

Fello's thoughts returned to Elena, his inseparable companion for over four decades, who tirelessly fought by his side against each difficulty he ever had to face. With an infectious optimism, Elena knew how to multiply the loaves of bread during difficult economic situations, even a civil war. With her special ways of being, she was the glue that kept the family unified; she made Fello feel invincible against the gales of life. The worse the situation, the more Elena was impelled to alleviate things, stressing the positives of each moment.

Fello missed Elena desperately; since her death, he had neglected all aspects of his life. The house was in ruins, the fine furniture covered by layers of dust where any seed could have easily been able to grow. He properly maintained the fields only because he could give free reign to his memories in the open air. As for his health, he had carelessly fallen into an overwhelming current that irremissibly dragged him toward his grave.

But in that moment, listening to the concerns of his grandson, he felt resurgence in his gut, the birth of a powerful spring that was going to lead him to recover his lost strengths. The fire of enthusiasm began to burn once again, awaking the desire to live and the spirit to energetically push forward.

He glimpsed a growing light in the horizon of his life upon perceiving Elena's approval; he sensed she was encouraging him to embrace this apparently impossible project. He was touched by his grandson's ideals, and for the first time in seven years, he felt a strong desire for something.

"Let's talk a little more. Before discussing this with the others, we have to define what we want to achieve: home for the students, vocational school, diet subsidy, etc. Let's make a very concrete and specific list; then we concentrate on looking for and recruiting allies when we speak. Let's not put anyone on the defensive; let's avoid making enemies; let's not blame anyone. At this point, we are all guilty and thank God we are still on time to get a few flowers out of the pen, as Elena used to say.

"The more people agree on our proposal and join us, convinced that it is a good alternative, the greater the opportunity to achieve our objectives. Remember, better yet, write down on a sheet of paper what are the four pillars that support a good project and keep it on hand to read and reread: analysis, focus, team development, and designing a plan of execution."

The grandfather went on to point out to Juan the importance of establishing a decisions-making process in a team, constantly emphasizing learning how to build consensus, understanding without a doubt that if an agreement was not reached, there was no plausible way to advance in the journey.

"One can't continue saying that someone else made us do this or that; we all can say yes or no. When we recognize we are responsible for our decisions, it is only then that we initiate the process of solving our problems for good.

"Frequently, we continue on a specific course because we gradually become accustomed to the situation, regardless of how absurd our situation might be. You have seen how the abandonment of Alborde occurred; nobody stopped to analyze it and to think of ways to improve the status quo. Often it doesn't occur to us that perhaps we can stop the course of events, that we can alter the results. Upon confronting difficult situations, it is easier to blame others for what happens to us and to think everyone else is supposed to resolve the situation than to accept our level of responsibility. We seldom think each one is responsible for what takes place in our environment, even if only partially. The saddest thing is that when one reaches success, everyone tries to claim a leading role, demanding recognition, even people who had nothing to do with the victory, even when someone else did everything to make our success possible."

"You are right, Grandpa. Everyone says, 'I made an A,' but when the grade is F, we say, 'The teacher gave me an F.'"

"We have become accustomed to transferring our responsibilities while continuing to demand our rights without thinking that each right involves a commitment, each social liberty brings with it a civic duty.

"We all want freedom of speech and it is granted in our constitution; this means that when we make use of it, we are responsible for the result of what is said. Look, Juan, I am so tired of listening to politicians say that their statements have been taken out of context. Or that their speeches have been misinterpreted. Nobody wants to be held responsible for what they say, or they want to have different meanings for different groups. It is common knowledge that no one can shout, 'Fire!' in a theater full of people, unless it is true and that whoever sounds a false alarm is held responsible for damages caused, according to the law, and in case of death resulting from a false alarm, the perpetrator can be accused of manslaughter. Nevertheless, freedom of speech is constantly abused. Today, most people lie or distort the truth as if it for sport, not only at a personal level, but also in the mass media. No one wants to admit that, once a false statement is made, especially against the character or the integrity of a person, the resulting damages caused by such actions can never be completely restored or reversed. Neither can the confidence of the people be renewed."

"I know, Grandpa; my teachers at school say that once a person is defamed, what has been said cannot be reversed. Last year, someone started a very ugly rumor against Gustavo Lopez's dad; it was said that he had lost his job because he was caught stealing from his boss. It was all a lie, and Gustavo felt humiliated. The nuns started an investigation to find out who started the rumor. They asked us to identify the guilty party or everyone had to pay the consequences. That same week, Don López came to school to demand that his honor be restored with a public apology. Since no one identified the transgressor and he or she didn't come forward, the nuns made us write one thousand times the phrase: 'No one should ever be defamed because it is impossible to completely recover from the damage inflicted.' They required us to complete the task in perfect calligraphy; we were detained all afternoon, furious with the defamer, because we had all been punished for his irresponsibility, we all received the punishment that was rightfully his. When we had finished, the papers were sent to Don Lopez."

"I am happy you experienced this. It is a good way to build character in young people. It is important to guide people to obey the laws or to suffer the consequences."

Fello rose from the stones each time he wanted to emphasize some specific point, with the enthusiasm and confidence of a university professor in front of his students.

"On the other hand, we certainly have the right to vote, but the majority of citizens do not participate in the electoral processes, as is their civic duty; they do not vote or recognize the importance and responsibility their vote implies. The right to vote is the democratic process in action, and it bestows upon us the responsibility to investigate the character and qualifications of the candidates. Tell me, Juan, when was the last time you saw someone seriously analyze the speech of a politician without allowing the demagoguery of the political parties to sway them, even worse without being influenced by the propaganda of the political machinery?"

"Grandpa, I believe that many don't participate because they think that although they involve themselves in the political process and make every effort to vote, they don't see any changes, and they feel used by the political machinery; they see themselves as impotent, thinking that only the rich and the well-connected really exercise influence in the political processes."

"Juan, that is surrendering without even putting up a fight! If we want to continue living in a democracy, we should get thoroughly involved in the affairs of our community; it is at the core of the community where the results of our vote can be felt; the municipality is the essential cell of democracy, as declared in 1835 by the French scholar, historian, and political scientist, Alexis de Tocqueville, in his book *Democracy in America*. That is why I love your proposal; each citizen should understand the benefits and shortcomings of each proposed law introduced and hold their representatives accountable, even if it is only for the sake of holding them loyal to the promises made during their electoral campaigns. The right to vote makes us responsible to be up-to-date with the actions of the elected officials and to demand their integrity."

Fello's passion heightened by the minute. He carefully walked along the edge of the ruins, pointing at the foundations with marked curiosity; he thought about the fate of the families that occupied these buildings that stood tall so long ago. He remained quiet for a few moments, reflecting upon whether these inhabitants ever concerned themselves about their future, participating in municipal matters, and what had been their social and economic condition. Fello shook his head, interrupting his wandering thoughts, and continued.

"On the other hand, we have the right to live wherever we want, but also we have the obligation to take care of the place where we live. If we want to maintain our right to private property, we have the obligation to respect the property of others, to pay the corresponding property taxes, in order to continue enjoying the benefits of an organized society and so on. Each right commits us to accept a social responsibility. If we are conscious of this, we avoid conflict and many headaches."

Juan listened entranced, eagerly absorbing the knowledge and wisdom of his grandfather. He was delighted to confirm that his social concerns and feelings of compassion had strong roots. From birth, Juan had observed and assimilated the integrity of Fello, who firmly practiced what he preached. Fello used to say, "Always do what is correct, regardless of what others do," and, "Everything in life has a cost; either pay voluntarily what is just and correct at the start or be prepared to pay double by force on your way out."

"I understand your proposal and apologize for not having recognized long before now the gravity of the situation. If there are no laws taking into consideration the conditions in which these kids are found, we will have to propose the appropriate laws and demand immediate attention from the pertinent authorities. The laws are simply that—a common agreement for the well-being of all. Just as each responsible citizen, must comply with the laws, so does he have the responsibility to denounce the wrongs and the carelessness of legislators, elected officials, and others in power. We should take ownership of the place due to us as citizens and co-owners of our society."

"We propose standards and norms for the social welfare of all citizens in our community to attain a reasonable order, but each individual must be held responsible for his acts, and we cannot expect anyone to resolve our individual problems. Neither can one wait to look for solutions only when the situation directly affects us. When we see wrongdoing, unjust, or illegal acts, we have the duty to act, propelled by principles, because it is the just and correct thing to do as you are proposing now."

Juan felt somewhat self-conscious, since what had driven him to take the civic action Fello was so profusely praising was the absence of his friends. Fello seemed to have read his thoughts.

"Many times, it is precisely our personal experiences that cause us to clearly see the depth and breadth of a situation, but even so, the noble and correct thing to do is to seek a solution for all to permanently remove the obstacle that affects the community and to prevent others from stumbling upon the same stone.

"If there is something I want you to permanently record in your thoughts, it is that a truly free man is the one who sacrifices his own liberty of action for the common good, submitting himself to the laws of the land as responsible citizen. The maximum expression of freedom is voluntary submission to the order because, upon obeying these self-imposed restrictions, we are freely delivering what we truly possess.

"The disorder, confusion, and chaos we see in newspaper and in the news the events that occur in larger cities—delinquency, truancy, laziness, lack of discipline—only demonstrate the populace is slave to vice and contempt. Don't be deceived by those practicing anarchy calling it liberty; there is no slavery more corrosive than the lack of discipline and judgment."

Fello sat down on the wall again, this time more reflective and slowly reaching the seat, and, as if thinking out loud, continued.

"What you have seen in Alborde is not indolence; it has been suspension of exercise of good judgment by neglect at times. The blows paralyze us or worse. When the fall is gradual, we do not realize we have fallen until we have reached the bottom. Frequently, the citizen's silence does not indicate one is in agreement with the course of events or the actions taken by politicians. What can one make of this is ignorance, impotence, and perhaps feebleness?

"Even then, we, the citizens of Alborde, are responsible for what has happened, especially our provincial representatives because they are well informed of our problems and were chosen to represent us in the process of change and to find ways to resolve our issues as a city. Besides, they clearly see the contrast in progress between Alborde and other towns, including the capital where they reside in fulfillment of their jobs as representatives. For a long time, they have not done a thing, and we keep on re-electing them without holding them accountable. Definitely, we are guilty; it doesn't matter how you look at it.

"We have not concerned ourselves with promoting laws in favor of the economic development of our town, perhaps due to neglect and ignorance. We have not done our part as responsible citizens. Most people in Alborde only travel as migrant workers under precarious conditions; they have the carrot in front of the horse and blinders to keep on going. They either can't look around or are too exhausted to make observations and propose solutions to their problems."

Fello started to speak with righteous indignation; he seemed to remember some incident that personally affected him. His face reddened as he delivered his discourse. Juan started to observe him carefully, trying to discern if so much excitement could affect his grandfather's health in any way.

"When these demagogues take power, they get blinded by power. Their only concern is how to conveniently preserve their privileged positions; they go through their terms avoiding difficulties, looking for photo opportunities to appear important and effective, doing nothing on behalf of the citizens. They avoid taking actions that could highlight their inadequacies or cause any waves that could sink them. They effectively increase or preserve their benefits at all costs. Their only clear goal is to maintain their posts, again, at any cost. They proclaim themselves public servants, but in reality they only serve themselves from the bounty that belongs to the people. If you pay attention, you can see that politicians will go to any length to increase their privileges—privileges we, the citizens, would never be able to obtain in our regular jobs. They have unlimited insurance, lavish stipends, unlimited resources, and perks galore. An average citizen can only look forward to, at best, keeping a minimum-wage job."

Fello smiled and then couldn't contain a laughter that interrupted his dialogue. Again, he pulled his handkerchief out of his pocket and, wiping tears from his reddened face, continued with a grin. "Come to think of it, we should initiate a movement to pay congressmen and legislators only minimum wage, plus the expenses of running their offices in this way. Perhaps they'll be forced to start thinking about their constituency and the benefit of blue-collar workers. Well, this is another issue. I am going off on a tangent again."

While saying this, Fello got up from the seat, holding his back with both hands; they had stayed seated on the hard surface for a long time, and he began to feel pain in his hips and some stiffness in his legs. Fello stretched, straightening his shoulders and raising both arms. Then he extended his right arm over Juan's shoulders, pulling him close as they started to walk again.

"We will have a lot of work to do this week. I think that today and tomorrow we have to dedicate ourselves to dusting off a few manuals and studying the rules of the game. We are going to win this match."

By then, both were walking as if they had wings on their feet. Juan ran a few steps, and Fello followed with firm steps; he was a different person, or better said, the old Fello was reborn.

"You know, Juan, I really like your proposal, and I am going to make a commitment to you. Together, we are going to stop this derailment; we are going to change the course Alborde has taken by inertia. Starting on Monday, we will begin a campaign to gain consensus, first with my old friends in the park. We will succeed by forming a task force, and together we will define short- and long-term objectives and come up with the best course of action."

Juan's head was spinning; he felt like a top in the hands of a child. He hadn't seen his grandfather this excited about something for a long time and was anxious to start their campaign. Neither one knew they were at the verge of taking a spin that would change their lives forever.

That day, amid their olive groves, unbeknownst to both of them, Juan arrived at the point where the road forked, and without even realizing it, he made a decision that defined his entire life. On the other hand, the grandfather could not stop thinking and talking. Something had been turned loose deep within him, and he continued, saying, "Remember that when one manages to bring people together to make decisions in common agreement, each one is forced to take a specific position regarding the issues at hand, in the definition of the processes to follow, and concerning the expected results everyone becomes co-owner of the plan and its final result."

Seeing perplexity in Juan's face, Fello slowed down his walk and paused the dialogue for a few moments.

"You don't have to think you are going to do all this alone. God has planted a small seed in your heart for you to share with others and inspire them to act on behalf of the less fortunate. The burden that is shared among all is light. Similarly, when we learn to share the rewards of triumphs with others, the feelings of goodwill and desire to serve are heightened, and more people want to join your cause. When we share the glory, we all win. Everyone wants to work when his or her contribution is recognized."

They were so energized and absorbed in the conversation, they didn't realize it had darkened, and soft stars began to illuminate the sky. The nights in the countryside were especially beautiful under a mysterious sky crammed with shivering stars and surrounded by the feeble lights of the many rural communities spread out in the distance.

They walked quickly to refuge in the house. It was cold, and Fello decided to gather wood to light a fire in the stove. Juan recalled when he used to spend vacations with the grandparents, remembering the blazing fireplace, the whistling wind filtering through the windows, crickets and frogs singing their songs in the field, the image of his grandfather arranging the firewood and his grandmother preparing churros and chocolate. His mouth watered thinking about the flavors of cinnamon, nutmeg, and chocolate, dipping the recently made churros in the thick hot liquid, which he hadn't tasted again since Elena's death.

"Grandpa, I love you very much."

Juan held his grandfather in a strong embrace without letting go for a long time. Beside his grandfather, he felt security, protection, and intellectual excitement. Fello knew how to respect the adult in each child.

"Do you want churros and hot chocolate?" said the grandfather, clearing his throat while reaching for one of the handkerchiefs embroidered by Elena from his back pocket. He looked at the cloth with nostalgia and tenderness, privately containing his tears.

It was the first time in seven years he offered to make churros; the kitchen had always been one of Elena's areas, and churros with hot chocolate were something very special that only she prepared during the winter, reaffirming the warmth and maternal aspects of the home they had formed together, where their children and grandchildren had forged such pleasant and unforgettable memories.

"Grandpa, this is the best day of my life!"

BUILDING
CONSENSUS

When Juan returned home that Sunday afternoon, he was a young man, not the melancholy teenager of the previous week. He made a pact with his grandfather. They committed to begin a relentless struggle, taking it to the end, starting that very same Monday afternoon in the park, making a formal presentation to the grandfather's friends.

The first task on his list was to investigate the current laws pertaining custody and protection of minors. The grandfather suggested not involving Juan's father until they had secured the support of the elders in Alborde, but somehow Juan would have to enter into his father's library, and he needed his permission to do it.

If there was an outstanding quality in Jorge Narváez's children, it was their impeccable upbringing. Jorge and Susana had instilled in them a deep respect for others, especially their elders, stressing respect for personal space and private property. Since early in childhood, each child had been assigned to a room of his or her own, allowing each ample privacy and latitude in his or her own space. In the same manner, invading the space of others was strictly forbidden; this included entering and searching in other parts of the house without proper permission, which taught them respect for the property, space, and right to privacy of others. Although they lived comfortably in abundance, Jorge and Susana taught their children to take care of their property and never replaced the personal belongings their children lost or broke due to carelessness or negligence, making them responsible for facing the consequences of their own actions.

They learned not to touch other people's belongings without permission, preventing their children from having the attitude so prevalent in today's youth, when kids act as if the world owes them everything they could possibly want, thinking they deserve everything without having to lift a finger to obtain it. The entitlement attitude was never allowed in the Narváez family.

It was a pleasure to take Jorge and Susana's children anywhere; they knew how to behave with courtesy and respect toward their elders, understanding their corresponding place as children.

One of Jorge's pet peeves was when people barged into other people's conversations uninvited, and he was especially irritated when parents allowed their children to interrupt adult conversations without consequence. This was the basic reason why he made a crusade out of teaching his children good manners and to maintain an appropriate distance during conversations, especially not to intervene in matters beyond their boundaries, unless specifically invited to be part of the discussion. The three Narváez children had learned this lesson to the letter. In his passion for oratory, Jorge instilled in his children the art of carrying on a conversation.

"Good conversation is an art; to enjoy a good interaction with others, one first has to learn how to listen. Only one person should talk at a time while others listen, with the same respect they expect to be listened to when it is their turn to speak. When the speaker finishes expressing his thoughts and ideas, the interlocutor confirms that he has listened and understood the message and, if so inclined, starts expressing his ideas deferentially. And successively, whoever has the floor, expresses his thoughts while the others listen and wait for their turn to participate in the conversation without monopolizing it. Ah! It is so beautiful to be able to carry on a great discussion!"

When Juan arrived at his house, he did not hear any noises and for that reason believed everyone was out. Susana, Paloma, and Maria always took advantage of idle Sunday afternoons to get their little girls together with the objective of providing the appropriate context for play while building good memories and traditions among the cousins. He concluded that his mother and his sisters would be enjoying the afternoon *merienda* at one of his aunts' houses.

He was surprised not to find Jorge in his office, where he generally retreated when his brother in-laws were out of town and could not join him, during the girls' long Sunday visits.

He walked to the main room and found Jorge stretched out in a comfortable chair, reading the official gazette and chronicles of his profession. A few embers of yellow and reddish charcoals were still burning in the fireplace, emitting a soft lingering warmth that caressed each corner of the room; a red wineglass, almost empty, rested on top of the little mahogany table adjacent to the chair, courting an oval ceramic blue plate filled with succulent cherries and fresh peaches alongside a plate holding a recently nibbled peach and several cherry pits devoid of any pulp.

Juan was glad to find his father at home. He swiftly entered the living room and greeted him with a kiss on his forehead and a quick hug.

"Hi, Dad. It's great that you're home I thought no one was here."

"Hello, son. Your mother went to visit the aunts after lunch; she said they would return after nine o'clock."

Jorge returned to his reading immediately, and Juan remained standing next to him without uttering a word. Noting the persistent presence of his son, Jorge raised his head, still holding the papers in reading position, displaying some impatience in his demeanor. Juan was observing the scene from the outside, as if hovering at the ceiling; he noticed the coldness in his father, whom he hadn't seen since Friday, in sharp contrast with the tender devotion of his grandfather.

"What is happening, Juan? Have you lost something? Are you trying to tell me something?"

"Dad, may I use your library?

"What do you need from my library, son?

"It's just that I want to read about some laws."

"Let's see, which ones? It pleases me to see you interested in my profession and my work." He placed the papers and magazines on the center table, and, lowering his feet from the ottoman, planted them in front of the chair where he remained seated. His face softened visibly, eliminating the wrinkles created by the frown in full view a few moments before.

"I want to know a little more about the laws protecting the rights of minors."

"What? Are you in some sort of trouble you haven't discussed with us? Do we need to talk about anything? Have you done something wrong?" exclaimed Jorge, returning to the posture of prosecuting attorney, already ingrained in his personality. Jorge rose to say something, but let go, falling again back into the chair.

Then, Juan continued talking. "No, no, Dad. Don't worry. It is that I have been talking to Grandpa, and I would like to know a little more about the rights of minors, the rights of my friends when they leave town, that is if someone has ever thought about them."

"Juan, Juan, Juan. Let's see what bug has bitten you now."

Juan sat on the ottoman where Jorge had rested his feet a few moments before, his legs separated, the tips of his feet touching both sides of his father's chair, his elbows resting on his knees, his head perched on his open hands, reaching his ears with the tips of his fingers.

"It's the same thing, Dad. I don't know what can be done for them and as the responsible citizen I want to become one day, I need to know for certain what is stipulated in the laws, what is the level of responsibility of the municipality, the county, and the state. Who do we have to appeal to in order to claim some action on their behalf, so my friends can know their rights and the accountability owed to them?"

"Bravo! You are starting to sound like a young man. Let's see how many other chimeras that grandpa of yours planted in your head over the weekend."

Juan felt a blow to the stomach; acid burning his guts started to rise, slowly but surely reaching his throat. He thought something was going to explode inside of him; he was going to vomit any moment. Juan could not put up with Jorge's irreverence toward his grandfather, but he also could not forget he was talking to his own father, to whom he owed unconditional respect. He stood up rigidly, tightening his lips while rubbing his hands against his face, as if wiping the dust caused by the unjust remark about Fello.

"Dad, Grandpa Fello listens to me and takes me seriously. Maybe you see me as a child because you are always too busy, and, well, never mind. It is not important. Let's forget everything. I only want to know if you can let me look for some books in your library to read."

Jorge, dumbfounded, carefully watched his son. Juan had grown at least ten inches from the last time Jorge had paid attention to his stature; although he saw Juan every day, he hadn't realized his son was transforming into a man. Juan was entirely right; during the last two years he had been involved in an endless judicial process, presenting an endless number of appeals before the land courts to avoid the transfer of title in some of the lands around town.

Jorge was representing a powerful family that, although none of their members had lived in Alborde during the previous one hundred years, were the owners of property titles of about one thousand hectares of farming land.

The dispute was based on an old law that protected the right of occupation of land generally not in use or abandoned by the proprietors only if the occupant cultivated the ground for personal, not commercial, use, and had lived on the property in question uninterruptedly for more than twenty-five years.

According to the law, after the stipulated period of time, the land became property of the occupants if they could demonstrate compliance with the special conditions abovementioned. Once the requisites were fulfilled, the occupant could appear before the land court, requesting that the title be transferred to his name.

Sometimes the occupants had lived on the property in question for so long, they had even paid taxes on the property and, in such a case, their claim to ownership became indisputable.

During the process of title issuance, the original owners are notified about the request for transference of title, and they almost always allege having gone through strenuous circumstances as the excuse for their neglect of the land in an effort to retain the property title in question. Nevertheless, an occupant who can prove the letter and intent of the law in his favor ends up with property title in hand.

Jorge had taken the case representing the Mendoza family to the detriment of twenty local families who had lived and farmed the land for two or three generations.

After the civil war, during the national reconstruction phase, people lived in a period of mere survival. The country had been left in ruins, without order or regulation, incited by anarchy and hunger; misery prevailed. Many families lost everything and tried to settle in any place where they could cultivate a piece of land for their livelihood.

The Mendoza family was not a farming family. Before the civil war, in collusion with General Marquez, the dictator who remained in power for over forty years, they became owners of everything within their reach. Like many other families, by the power of their impunity, they became billionaires, enjoying every possible privilege just because they supported the government of the general and remained deaf to the needs and suffering of the population.

The government of General Marquez was ruthless and cruel; he ruled with an iron fist, unilaterally imposing his will and criteria. Wielding the grip of terror, he crushed the people while the intellectuals remained silent. The means of communication were limited and misinformation kept the population stagnant and suspended in time.

People wouldn't dare to move away from their villages or even move freely in their own communities for fear of retaliation, exercised by militants of the tyranny; they knew that, if they were confronted by the authorities in a place where they were virtually unknown, they could end up capriciously thrown into horrible prisons, tortured, and eventually executed. To corroborate the terror their totalitarianism exerted on the people was the most sublime pleasure of the dictator and his henchmen.

The dictator declared that possession and issuance of passports was a privilege, not a civil right. And when any citizen filed a passport application, he or she was secretly reported to the undercover police and was subsequently monitored and harassed. From the moment a passport application was presented, the applicant and his family fell into disgrace before the dictator, remaining at the mercy of bloodthirsty police, simply for expressing the intention to travel outside the country, no matter what reason was stated as the purpose of the intended trip.

By contrast, families who supported and openly adulated General Marquez lived as kings, enjoying economic bounty and absolute freedom of movement within and outside the country. These privileged ones had the benefit of wide-ranging favoritism bestowed by the general himself, who allowed them to freely take ownership of any property and state enterprises as if they were personal possessions of the tyrant ruler. They also occupied all diplomatic posts abroad and misappropriated the revenues derived from the transactions handled at their embassies and consulates, while legitimizing under diplomatic immunity their financial portfolio in a foreign country.

During many long years, several insurgent movements were born throughout the country, which were often crushed by the military until the outbreak of a civil war that eventually overthrew the dictator. But many years passed before the country could fully enjoy the fruits of democracy, given the mistrust that prevailed in the citizenry as a result of the dictatorship.

"Son, forgive my impatience; you know I am now involved in a difficult case that consumes my time. I have sacrificed a lot, but this client has brought plenty of economic benefit to our family. I have been paid very well."

Jorge stood up without displaying pride or signs of impatience, a somber and indelible shadow playing upon his elegant figure. He extended his right arm, pointing the way to his office to Juan, and they began the short walk without haste.

"Come, I will guide you to the gazettes containing material related to the issue. I don't want to let grass overgrow the path between us. Come on. Let's go to my office."

Again and again, Juan had heard slurs about his father related to his representation of the well-known case Jorge had just mentioned, but now he preferred not to think about it and keep himself focused on the topic of Alborde's youth; there'd be plenty time to discuss other matters in the future; today he was on a mission and did not want to stop for anything. Juan felt invincible, counting on the grandfather's wings to fly him as high as he wanted to go.

Jorge Narváez was a methodical man and very proud of his work; his office revealed self-imposed order and discipline. And although he counted on the services provided by Mercedes, Paloma's sister-in-law, whom he had personally trained as a legal secretary, working in his office three days a week, the cleanliness of the office was his own doing, from the impeccably organized documentation to the tidily catalogued books that rested on each of the black mahogany shelves. Jorge was the one who chose the olive green color on the walls and the dark wooden armchairs covered by bright emerald green leather, held to the wood by nails with black, flat heads, which snaked along the edge of the seats, armrest, and backs.

The office was a large room of about five meters wide by eight meters long, originally intended as the formal living room of the big house they lived in, opposite the central square. When Jorge decided to organize his office in that room, he didn't want to build permanent dividing walls, but instead wanted to create a reception and waiting area separate from his office to provide privacy to his customers. So instead of building a wall, he separated the space with huge mahogany shelves, solid bookcases about ten feet high, crowned with beautiful cornices almost touching the roof, with full access from the reception area and his private office.

On the reception side, the bottom section of the shelves was covered by wooden doors with solid mahogany square overlays while the top doors were made of glass framed by thin strips of dark wood to allow a complete view of the objects on display. Each shelf was illumined with a small interior lamp.

Protected behind the glass, one could see the old collections of pipes, swords, guns, and daggers that Jorge had accumulated over the years, organized in chronological order. It was especially interesting to note the evolution of the revolvers. In front of each collector's piece, Jorge had placed a linen card describing in fine calligraphy the origin and history of the object.

The collection of firearms was one of Jorge's passions that originated when he was a child. Right after the civil war, he found a wooden box buried in the middle of the olive groves containing very old artifacts, swords, ammunition, and a dozen different pistols and revolvers, perhaps buried there for fear of General Marquez, who had deprived the citizens of their right to possess weapons and firearms. The finding transported Jorge to an imaginary world of pirates and heroes of war, which led him to intensively study the military accomplishments of his ancestors in the country and inspired him to begin a collection that was undoubtedly unique in the entire region.

Jorge's knowledge of firearms and ballistics proved useful in advancing his career and in the execution of his responsibilities as state prosecutor. From youth, Jorge distinguished himself as an expert on the subject, establishing a reputation across the province and later throughout the country. He often served as an expert witness, establishing evidence during trials involving the use of firearms; he also contributed to publications on the subject matter in magazines and national newspapers.

The bookshelf facade facing the office was a series of adjustable dark mahogany shelves that held all legal volumes published since Jorge's college days, meticulously arranged in chronological order starting downward from the top. The bottom right shelves of the bookcase contained the most recent numbers from the official gazette, bound in hardcover for better handling and collection of the material. Each bookshelf was marked with a copper plate that framed changeable cards describing the material catalogued herein.

Jorge put on his eyeglasses and bent down to reach for a couple of the bounded gazettes, took a step backward, straightened up, and carefully looked for other publications in the upper bookshelves. He took a thick and heavy volume, adjusted his glasses again, and opened the book with a black, thick cover, with its title written in golden letters and large print, "Juris Leg, res," which Juan could not read since it was covered by the hand that held it.

"The laws for protection of minors have been in place for many years, but in recent decades, this issue has come to light with more intensity, addressing aspects of the issue that previously were not prevalent, commonly discussed, or openly acknowledged in society, such as physical abuse and neglect, provision of food and shelter outside the family, and all aspects of parenting, neglect, and abandonment.

"This volume, published more than two decades ago, is the platform that supports the laws for the protection of minors in the nation. These two binders of the official gazette contain adjustments and modifications introduced as recently as a year ago.

"The legislature proposes adjustments based on the law contained in these volumes I am giving you. Actually, aside from the bulletins I am lending you, the law has not been significantly modified in recent years. I do not want you to think I don't listen to you. I will let you read and research on your own terms. If you need me, I will be in the living room. You can interrupt me whenever you want; it would not bother me at all. "

"Thanks, Dad. I want to learn all I can about this issue. Maybe after I've read these books and when you have a free moment, we can speak more at length."

"You can stay reading in my office, but don't make any marks in the books. You know I don't like to stain or make any annotations on the pages. I think writing on a book is an affront and disregard for the material, the authors, and future readers. On my desk, you will find a paper pad and notebooks in which you may take notes and write the information you might need. Stay here in my office so you can read in total peace; your sisters will return soon, and, well if you want to take the books to your room, you can also do that."

"Thanks! Thank you very much, Dad."

Juan grabbed the books and quickly left the office. Jorge didn't know what to say; he was left standing in front of the bookshelves. He opened his mouth to say something but was unable to utter a single syllable.

Jorge's thoughts flew back to the day when Juan was born, the first grandchild to both families, and the tenderness this child inspired in him when he held Juan in his arms for the first time. Jorge felt again the profound emotion that invaded him as he gently held those wrinkled little feet. The anxiety persisted for a few interminable minutes as he accounted for each of the perfectly formed toes and fingers at each extremity. What had become of Juan? Somberly, Jorge reviewed the conversation he had had with Juan just a few moments before, and it seemed to have happened years ago.

"I am losing him. He is slipping away like water between my fingers," he said to himself. He thought of Juan's first day of school, with his dark blue outfit, jacket with gold buttons, white shirt and navy blue thin tie that he knotted a few moments before arriving at the school, his half length pants, white long socks reaching just below the knees with tassels on the sides, touching the edge of the pants at every step the child took. He carried his book bag hanging from one of his shoulders, almost reaching the ground. His blond hair was freshly cut, and he held with both hands the navy blue beret that was part of the uniform, nervously wriggling it. Gently prodding Juan's back with his fingers, Jorge had led the boy to the classroom where a small group of children surrounded Sister Maria, the old kindergarten teacher, who died just a few months ago at over seventy years of age. She had been the kindergarten teacher in Alborde her entire life, leaving a legacy of personal alphabetization methods for generations to come.

The people in town told that Sister Maria entered the Salesian Convent at only sixteen years of age, against her father's wishes. Born in a small coastal village as tiny as Alborde, the town priests had noticed a strong spirituality and religious fervor in the child when they helped her prepare for her first communion.

This sensitivity was evident in the interactions of the young girl with most people in town; her unpretentious life evidenced what the priests determined to be religious vocation. Maria Saviñón gravitated toward the mystical life of the cloister convents, but since she was educated by members of the Salesian Congregation, she made vows of poverty, chastity, and obedience within this religious order; starting from an early age, her service was in education. From the time she entered the convent as an aspirant, she showed love and dedication to children, asking to be assigned to teach elementary school, preferably nursery school and kindergarten.

When Sister Maria died, among her personal effects someone found a poem handwritten on a yellowish, worn-out paper, which mysteriously began to circulate among those who knew Sister Maria and were devotees of the late nun. Everyone began to speculate about the identity of the love-stricken suitor rejected by Sister Maria. The poem explained the nun's devotion to little children, and although she always wrote the nursery rhymes and composed the lyrics and music of the songs children sang in her class, no other piece of literary work had ever been attributed to her until the poem was found. To this day, the mysterious poem continues to provoke tenderness, tears and respect for the author among those who knew her:

VOICES IN MY HEAD

Far, far away, beyond infinity
his gaze stroked the waves
both arms fixed in the sand
like apprehensive columns,
his frail voice transforming into sadness,
repressive anguish invading my soul
"Despite the long-gone years,
I still feel your presence,
your innocence, your care,
And the warmth of your heart,
The freshness of your virtues,
Abundant love and graces
And your motherly hands
Calming my anxious tears
Stirring throbbing in my aching soul
Your tender touch, your words
Sensible flowing like the gentle wind
Wise, pure, and simple slyly
Escaping from your cherry lips,
Dreams united our lives with silver silken ribbons
You were a child, sweet and inexperienced
You wanted to be a mother in the depth of your soul
Tell me those dreams that long ago we shared
Will we lose them forever? Are you going to forget?
We wanted to have children grow up to build a fortress
We created a child of sweet voice and delight in her eyes
You were going to teach her how to become a woman
With serene dedication created in your likeness
In the eyes of my mind, her hair was like yours
And her hands soft as petals, mirror image of you
And we dreamt of a boy; often we spoke about him
We thought of him as sailor, the seven seas exploring
A brave soldier in conquest, a doctor, engineer

I am missing those children.
What will become of me?"
And I noticed his quivering voice spin to silence
Still, quiet forever never heard him once more
Hopelessly tried to smile, but I could only mourn,
And a river of tears was unleashed at that moment.
I briefly touched his hands. "It's late," a whisper
And sitting on the rocks, I saw him vanish
Walking away forever tearing apart my soul
A calling sound escaped from the bell tower
The melancholic bronze
Tinted ocean and shores
Confused, swayed by emotions, I started to walk
The short walk to my convent
Steps besieged by waves, winds and eternity
And searching for a refuge, I found myself in church,
Seeking God in my doubts, inconsolably crying
Then, I heard voices I've never heard before
Stirred deep in my being were the voices of children
The cries of little babies bemoaning in my heart
Echoes and sounds from a world of nothingness
A voice calling me mommy! Later turning to silence
The bitter realization I will never have children of my own

Closing his eyes, Jorge could still see the rows of desks with chairs too tall for those little children, whose feet dangled as they sat at their writing tables thus developing the habit of swinging their feet during class, which exasperated Sister Maria.

He thought of the great windows with large frames opening onto the central park, filtering in the wind during winter and the rains in May late spring. He had attended the same classroom when he was little, and the sounds still echoed in his ears.

The morning of Juan's first day of classes, Susana had to stay at home taking care of their little girls, who had just fallen ill with fever and the flu. When they approached the door, Juan didn't want to release Jorge's hand. He had just celebrated his sixth birthday, and his blue eyes were sailing in two enormous clinging teardrops.

"Dad, don't leave me. I am afraid. I don't want you to leave."

Sister Maria came to greet them, and she took Juan's hand in hers, pleasantly but firmly.

"Come with me, Juanjo. You know who I am. We will have a very nice day; you will make many friends here. You look so much like your father! Come, the other kids are waiting for us."

Sister Maria gently pulled the little boy by the hand as he looked back, trying not to lose sight of his father, and guided him to join the group of children sitting on the floor, forming a circle in the middle of the classroom, and proceeded to take her seat at the center of the circle. Juan sat down, dropping the book bag by his side, curiously watching his little classmates.

Sister Maria had been the kindergarten teacher since the school opened fifty-three years back. Everyone in town knew her and probably received from her the first correction and punishment outside their home.

In Alborde, nobody questioned the disciplinary acts of the teachers; parents understood that the teachers were their representatives during school hours. Teachers could educate, discipline, and inculcate respect, counting on the full support of parents, including on rare occasions even applying some corporal punishment if a child was out of control.

On the rare occasions that it occurred to Jorge to criticize the actions of any of his teachers, he found himself against an unwavering wall at home; both Fello and Elena defended the teacher's viewpoint, and it was not until Jorge became an adult when he realized that his parents had also met with the teachers, advocating on his behalf, when something seemed wrong or inappropriate to them. But they never disavowed the teachers; they remained the highest authority in school. Jorge continued with this tradition, following the same educational philosophy when he formed his own family.

Jorge had become rather saddened upon seeing how easily Juan joined the children's circle and he prudently stepped back, leaving before the child could become aware of his presence again. Upon leaving the building, he saw Fello and Elena in front of the entrance gate, both peeking through the classroom windows, trying to catch a glimpse of Juan.

"We wanted to see Juanjo on his first day of school," they said in unison, justifying their presence when they realized Jorge was scrutinizing them. They kissed their son, and the three of them crossed the main street to have coffee in the plaza. They extended their gathering more than two hours; none of them wanted go away from the school, although they made no allusion to this obvious fact. The grandparents asked Jorge to allow them to pick Juan up at the end of his first day of classes. Jorge agreed to it, thinking it would be a relief not to have to interrupt his work routine again.

That afternoon, Fello and Elena waited for Juan at entrance door with an attendance certificate made by them in beautiful calligraphy and a bag of imported chocolate coins in celebration of his first school day. Skirting the park, they walked the block and a half to the house where a proud Juan declared to the family how well deserved his certificate was and later asked Susana to frame it. That certificate still hung on a wall in Juan's bedroom.

Suddenly, Jorge realized he had never sat down to talk to Juan about his feelings in any aspect of their lives. He noticed that between them, they only talked about what was directly linked to obligations at home, work, or school projects. But Jorge immediately justified his behavior upon realizing this, inwardly asserting he had kept their conversations at an intellectual level because he wanted to instill character, masculinity, and wisdom in his son, rationalizing that the sentimentality, childishness, and tears were feminine behaviors.

He decided to give his son ample space to conduct the investigation on his own. That way he could learn something practical about research. However, he made a quick note in a block of paper he left it on his desk.

Subject: I must reconcile my relationship with Juan; he has become withdrawn, distant from me, and I don't want to lose him. I feel somewhat jealous of his relationship with Dad. Resolution: I have to systematically dedicate some time to reconnect with him, play a sport? I must find common ground, definitely.

Juan arrived in his room and placed the tomes on the night table beside the bed, adjusted the pillows to read, and lay on his back. He stared for a few moments at the ceiling, noting the harmonious symmetry of design in the cornices lining the ceiling and overlaid circles slightly intertwined, which right in the middle of the roof appeared to hold the old chandeliers that languidly illuminated the room with invisible hands. He looked around and decided to read at his desk, where he had a potent, mercury reading lamp. He opened the book that, according to his father, contained the basic principles of the country's child protection laws and grabbed a notebook he kept in the upper drawer so that he could write down points to use in his argument for his cause.

CHAPTER ONE

Scope and General Principles
In applying this law, the best interests of minors takes precedence over any other legitimate interest that might surface. Therefore, any measures taken under this act shall be of educational character. The limitations on the minor's ability to act will be interpreted in a restrictive manner.

Article 1: The public authorities shall ensure respect for the rights of minors and adjust their actions to this Act and corresponding international norms

Article 2: Right to honor, privacy and self-image.

Article 3: Right to access information

Article 4: Freedom of ideology

Article 5: Right of participation, association, and assembly
Article 6: Right to freedom of expression

Article 7: Right to be heard

He wrote down and underlined the points that seemed most relevant as evidence. He was fascinated, although he realized he did not understand all the details and particulars of the legal lexicon used. He thought it would be very important and beneficial to all citizens if the laws were written in clear, concise, and simple language, easily understood by all, without needing a lawyer for interpretation.

1. Minors are entitled to receive from public administration the appropriate assistance for the effective exercise of their rights and to ensure their respect.

2. In the defense and guarantee of their rights minors can:

   a. Request the protection and guardianship of the public entities responsible.

   b. Inform Public Prosecutor Ministry of situations considered to infringe on their rights, with the purpose of establishing and promoting appropriate actions.

   c. Bring their complaints before the Public Defendant for the purpose of obtaining the appointment of Deputies of appropriate institutions, to permanently take over all matters related to minors.

   d. Request the social resources available from public administrations.

He believed to have found key points to gain the support of the elders in town and he wrote down the page numbers where he found each item of interest. He read each chapter avidly, unable to stop.

He felt a soft tap on his left shoulder; it was Susana. She found him asleep with his head resting on the desk, arms crossed on top of the notepad and Jorge's books. She stroked Juan's back and shoulders tenderly, and giving him a kiss on the cheek, she said, "Juanjo, wake up."

Juanjo was the nickname the family affectionately called him, combining Juan and Jose, the two names he received at baptism. Juan liked the affective tone the nickname imbued in conversations, making him feel pampered and loved.

"Go to bed; it's already ten and you have school in the morning. How did it go with Fello? I see you are very tired. What were you two doing? Would you like a glass of warm milk before going to bed?"

"Forgive me, Mom. I didn't hear you come in. I've been reading some articles regarding laws that interest me. Do you know that Grandpa agrees with me? He thinks it is important to do something to keep the migrant kids in town."

Susana sighed; she loved the relationship between Fello and Juan, although she wanted to see the same type of relationship between Juan and his father. She wanted to see Jorge spending more time with their son, showing greater interest in him. It wasn't that she didn't appreciate the efforts of Fello—who always said it didn't take any effort to demonstrate the love he felt for his grandson—it was that she was starting to resent Jorge for his obvious detachment from family matters, especially when it came to Juan.

"I know Fello would do anything for you, including making a fool of himself."

Susana playfully rubbed Juan's head with both hands; he pulled away and looked at her straight.

"Mom, exercising our moral obligations as citizen is not acting ridiculously. Grandpa Fello has noticed that for a long time nothing has been done to resolve the situation affecting the minors in Alborde; the children suffer a lot with the lack of a stable home throughout the year."

"Aha! Now you want to lecture us. Eh?"

She interrupted him, somewhat impatient.

"No, Mom; I just want you to be open to listening to us."

"To listen? To whom?"

"To those who are going to defend the proposal Grandpa Fello and I are going to write and present to the corresponding authorities."

MEETING WITH ALBORDE'S ELDERS

Alborde never had a traditional public library; everyone used the book collection at the Catholic school, a private institution funded and managed by members of the Salesian Society. This library was nothing more than a medium-sized room surrounded by high, dark wood bookshelves reaching the ceiling, with long tables in two rows at the center of the room and heavy, dark wood chairs, too uncomfortable to sit on for lack of cushions.

During the day, ample light poured through the four windows facing north, interrupting the procession of bookshelves that appeared to hold up the roof. If it weren't for these windows, no one would have been able to read during the day; after dusk, the dim light timidly emitted by the old chandeliers barely broke the shadows, further discouraging readers.

The Salesians make vows of poverty, chastity, and obedience; consequently, based on those principles, they have never been a wealthy congregation. Therefore, for economic reasons, their library included few current publications and a limited number of classic books available to students on restricted schedules. Given the scarcity, nobody was allowed to check out books from the library, which somewhat discouraged research.

One of the reasons why the grandfather had appointed Juan to perform the research and to identify the laws in support of their proposal was precisely because he had access to his father's library. Jorge's library was the only source of legal information in town and the most appropriate path to follow for the purpose at hand. Besides, Fello wanted Juan to understand and experience every step of the process.

Fello was not surprised when Juan showed up that afternoon, armed with a manila legal folder filled with notes and comments. They had given up on their traditional *merienda* that afternoon and agreed to meet at the cafe on the main plaza around five thirty, just before Fello's friends and acquaintances arrived for their regular gathering to play tabletop games.

When Juan saw Fello, he embraced him, euphoric, as if he hadn't seen him in over a month.

"Grandpa, I have enough material to arm a brigade! I have spent hours reading the books Dad lent me, researching. The majority of the laws relevant to our project are already written; all we have to do is find ways to enforce them. What do you think?"

"Did you talk to your father about this issue?"

"I only told him I wanted to do something for Alborde's youth; he inquired about the purpose of the investigation when I asked for permission to use his books in the library."

"It is fine, son. When I told you not to involve your father, I didn't mean to imply you should keep secrets from him. However, I didn't want to force you to talk to him, not until you're ready to defend your proposal. Jorge has good intentions, but somehow he has lost the way to his heart in recent years. He was profoundly distressed by Elena's death and instead of expressing his sorrow, he became callous to all human suffering. He was Elena's favorite child; that is why Paloma and Maria always came to me when they wanted an accomplice to get away with small things; the girls always tried to find an ally in me."

Fello smiled; his thoughts wandered to long gone times when he was raising his children at their home in the country. Now things were different, but he knew the values he and Elena instilled in their offspring would never die; those were planted too deeply within each of them. Fello and Elena embraced the hope of seeing the fruit of these values in their children's children as a precious inheritance. And they were not disappointed; Fello saw this legacy in Juan.

It was only a matter of time before Jorge would join the noble cause proposed by his son, a proposal that gave Fello an irrevocable reason to keep living.

"We will present this project to Jorge once the task force is assembled and we have a work plan summarized. I know your father; he doesn't do anything halfway when issues are presented to him and he sees it clearly. Jorge either supports the proposal or sums up forces squarely opposing it until he exterminates it. If I am sure of something about Jorge, it is that he has passion in his gut, although at the moment it seems like the opposite. I know he will guide us and lead the project proposal directly to the provincial government.

"Do you know the reason why your father became a lawyer? It was because since he was small, when we spoke about issues and everyday matters of life, as you and I always do, I told him many times that my dreams were cut short by life itself. I told him I had wanted to be a good lawyer to defend the integrity of local processes and procedures. We used to have long talks about injustice and the lack of integrity of governing authorities at all levels, in local, county, and state government. I believe that due to the dishonesty and abuse of politicians, people are losing their faith in democracy; people feel powerless. Those in power perpetuate the abuse and the supremacy of social classes based on the economy, and they do this subtly, almost imperceptibly. Before, long ago, the difference was between nobles and commoners; now the supreme classes are politicians and senior executives who give themselves exorbitant salaries and grotesque benefits, alongside special interest groups that pay for political campaigns, conforming the politician's circle of influence; all other citizens stay outside the privileged circle; hence the apathy of the people.

"It is a vicious circle that is decaying democracy. I wonder how long it will take until changes are made. Perhaps the answer will be to constitute a direct democracy. Get rid of the vices of representative democracy, forcing candidates to campaign with a predetermined budget, establishing better rules to prevent peddling of influence."

"Grandpa, then democracy is not as good as it seems; it might be better to have kings than elected governing authorities; that way one knows who is to be blamed when things go wrong."

"Juan, don't speak nonsense! You have to study a little bit more about democracy; democracy is the people's voice in action! Representative democracy when done well allows the expression of the will of the people from all social strata in an orderly fashion. In addition, remember what we have discussed so many times. When there are problems, the most important thing is to find solutions and not stop until the objective is reached, to know once and for all what or who is the culprit. What is needed is to educate the people about the responsibilities of citizenship; we need more education and active participation in social and political processes."

"Grandpa, it seems absurd to me how political campaigns are carried out because there is not a process in place promoting the proper qualification of candidates, a simple way to guide the people to grade the candidates, matching job description with qualifications. Isn't it the same as when job openings are posted by a company? I have never seen the profile of qualifications for any political office; the taxpayers continuously pay to train unqualified candidates; meanwhile, no respectable organization would publish a vacancy without posting the required qualifications for the position, hoping that workers will vote for the new employee without any further review of qualification. What I see in a democracy is that we allow all political posts to be filled by the person with the biggest campaign budget, not with the best qualifications."

"You're right Juanjo. Electoral reform would be a nice project, but I think that the first issue at hand is to solve the dilemma of the migrant kids. From an early age, Jorge promised to work to address things that were within his power to resolve, and he has done so. He was devoted to his studies; he served in social causes when he reached high school; he joined civic action groups. During the weekends he spent most of his time visiting the sick at the public hospital, which today is nothing more than an unfortunate medical clinic. He was an altar boy; he never gave us headaches of any kind; he was of flawless integrity. Jorge was not drawn to triviality; he didn't waste his time going out with friends, doing the silly things young people do just to have a good time. He married Susana when he was very young, two years after college graduation; he met her in college and immediately after convinced her come to live in Alborde. She was delighted to move here, inspired by Jorge's relentless struggle for citizen's rights. That's why your father served in so many posts within the judicial system; he was prosecutor, attorney general, and trial judge. He has held many public positions and has never personally benefited from his service; no one can accuse him of impropriety. That is your father, although he now appears in short supply of sensitivity and lacking a heart; he will recover very soon, I promise you."

"Thanks, Grandpa! Last night, I avoided Dad, not because I didn't want to talk to him, but because he doesn't respect my ideas, my thoughts. He always sees me as a child. He doesn't listen to what I want to say; he only listens to what he wants to hear."

"Juan, all parents, we all do that, and you will also do it to your children when God sends them to you. I myself see your father as a child. No, don't laugh at this; it's true. For any parent, our children never grow old. The greatest challenge for every parent is to understand that during the period of raising and educating our children, we must remain parents, not friends. We are the authority in charge of educating our children, without leaving any room for doubts. We need to instill respect and obedience to social and civic laws, teach them spirituality, and all those values that, as parents, we have the moral obligation to infuse in our children.

"We also have to exert our role with conviction and confidence. If we question ourselves too much or at every step, we do not teach discipline. We are defeated first by insecurity and second by the tenderness a young child inspires. It's easier to say yes to everything and let anything happen than to discipline a child. Well, it's easier at the time when they are tiny, cute, funny, and friendly, and they do not have to deal with the rest of the world outside the family.

"If we don't discipline our children when they are tender and pliable, under our tutelage, we all have to live with the monsters we have created for the rest of our lives And, at the same time, spend the rest of our lives in agony, seeing our beloved children suffer as social misfits unable to adapt to social norms, knowing that the children we fail to discipline are incapable of submitting to the order and discipline that life within an organized society requires, which is imperative for their success. The pain we avoid inflicting on our small children with sound discipline will haunt them; society will make those children pay with interest for the rest of their lives."

They were seated in front of a table belonging to the cafe, facing the central square where the concerts took place during the holidays. It was a circular stone building with red roof tiles, contrasting with the white lime covering the columns that contentedly held the roof.

A twisted wooden railing surrounded the platform raised up to three different levels, interrupted only by four heavily built arches that framed the entry access, coinciding with each of the cobblestone walkways, leading to the gazebo at the very center of the square.

During the spring, climbing roses and honeysuckles hugged the arches in explosive fragrance; roses of red palette lined with orange and yellow strokes interrupted the whiteness of honeysuckles in bloom.

With very little effort, spring conjured the most beautiful flowers, planted throughout the years between moss-covered rocks rooted in bygone eras, leftovers, perhaps, from times of abundance and prosperity. At that time of year, the gardens of the central square in Alborde were spectacular in their spontaneous outpouring of color, delighting all who walked through the plaza.

The extensive garden triangles were exquisitely framed between the four walkways, which formed a diagonal cross on the surface of the square. These trails were paved with intricate designs made out of river pebbles of various sizes and colors, a legacy of the Moors and Romans who perfected the art of mosaic, creating designs with decorative stones and other materials on flat surfaces. The spacious gardens were originally covered with fine flowers, and, although the flowerbeds had never been completely eliminated, they had shared space with festival kiosks, chairs, and foodservice tables, as well as many other events held in the central plaza.

Fello saw one of his friends arriving at the plaza but decided to wait until the others came to avoid interrupting the engaging conversation he was having with Juan.

"When children are already grown, generally when they are in high school and sometimes even in college, they start a transitional period; it is the moment when each person begins to compare the values received from his parents with other values, contrasting those values with what he sees in others or what he finds out for himself in society in general, he begins to choose what he considers valuable and discards what he considers useless, and although it hurts, we must accept it; it is the beginning of emancipation.

"At that very moment, we have to gradually change our role of parents and start cultivating that of a friend in the lives of our children, hoping we didn't ruffle their feathers too much or hurt their egos during the years of development, confident that we were able to show love along with discipline. It is not easy; it's a continuous juggling. If we were able to communicate and express love, we will find a friend in our children."

"Grandpa what happens if we have been hurt so much that we don't want our parents as friends?"

"That is a good question. If as parents we do not find a friend in our sons, it hurts a lot, but we cannot surrender or hold a grudge against a child. We must continue trying to get closer until the day we die. Far and foremost anyway is a child's education; it is more important to give them the best education and training rather than wanting to be friends. We only have one opportunity to educate every child, only one opportunity to be a dad or mom to a human being. During childhood and adolescence the school is full of potential friends. I always thought it was more important to establish order and authority and obtain respect from the children when they are small, but certainly always with love.

"To sacrifice educating our children by wanting to be their friend is a crime. Many parents don't educate their children for fear of offending them, and in so doing they end up providing their children with a foundation made of gelatin, tin columns, and a straw roof, and those children have to spend their lives inside that unsafe and insecure structure. It is the duty of every parent to provide a solid moral and emotional foundation for their children, strong and secure against life's gales, one that can't be broken easily. We need to give our children a firm foundation over which to build their lives, to shelter them from the storms. There will be plenty time along their lives to reflect on the past, time to explain the reasons why we did what we were supposed to do, time to forgive.

"Children confuse the desire to be friends with weakness, and they take advantage of the situation; it is human nature. What is absolutely unforgivable is not to educate our children. When you see a person lacking dignity, without a sense of discipline, incapable of sacrificing anything, always ready for pleasure, looking for the loophole in every law, you can believe without a doubt, his or her parents tried to be friends, not educators, and weren't able to be good parents and establish any type of authority in their children's lives. They were unable to make their children understand the meaning of responsibility for their own behavior."

"I understand what you say. Sometimes discipline bothers me, but I have to admit I like when my parents are concerned about me. Sometimes I see kids at school that make me feel ashamed of their behavior; they have no honor. And you, Grandpa, did you also resent your parents?"

"Of course I did! My father's death affected me deeply. I felt anger against him for a long time for having died, leaving us without a father because my life changed completely after his death, and I had to give up my studies. What an indolence of mine! As if Dad had a choice; I rebelled against Mom and her social whims. Well, that's another story that one day I will share with you.

"Sometimes it takes a long time for a child to understand that the love of his parents is irreplaceable, insurmountable. Even the clumsiest of parents are always willing to give their lives for their children.

"When people find themselves on their deathbed, nobody thinks that they should have made more money or had written more professional publications or had built a better house or had bought newer cars or traveled more or collected more exotic objects. What we all think is that we would have liked to have more time and better relationships with our loved ones, with our parents, our siblings, our spouses, and our children; nobody thinks of the stupidities of high society when facing death."

"Grandpa, I love you. I don't want to lose you, and I know Dad loves you, too, in his own way."

"I know that, son. I know it. I also love you very much, and Jorge too. I have a feeling you will soon see a significant change in your father. I know I have contributed to his isolation, having sunk in my own pain, without thinking that Jorge was also suffering as well. I did not support him as I should have when Elena died. Do you know? I feel in my heart that Elena wants this project. Your interest in improving life in Alborde has given me courage and desire to live longer. It has propelled me back into the world of the living. Thank you, Juanjo! "

"Papa Fello, I learned from you that one should not live a life without purpose, that only human beings choose their own destiny; you have told me many times that even animals are born with the specific purpose of reproduction and each follows its inner call, perpetuating the species unquestionably. I don't want to lose the best years of my life spinning like a top, without defining where I want to go, without setting my goals."

Juan was intelligent and sensitive; he was open to learning new lessons every day, and he clearly understood the meaning of individual responsibility for every action that is taken. Lately, he had opened his eyes to cause and effect.

"I've seen how many people don't want to own their actions or the outcome of those actions, they blame others for their failures and remain paralyzed instead of analyzing the facts. I like to learn from the mistakes of others. You know, Grandpa? I want you to help me come up with a realistic agenda for achieving my personal goals, taking into consideration the conditions of our environment, but regardless of the actions of others, I want firm goals and objectives. Can you help me?"

"Of course! I am so proud of you! Besides, it will be good for me, too. I must confess that I have neglected everything lately. I have not practiced what I preach."

"When I managed to understand the concept of cause and effect, I felt in control of my life, even facing the limitations that pain us. I noticed that when we proclaim that things happen to us or that one cannot achieve this or that objective due to someone else's fault, we are surrendering control of our lives to others, evading our responsibilities, consenting to be victims."

Juan firmly promised himself to be responsible for all his actions, to be consciously aware of every decision and the possible corresponding results, and to persuade people around him to become masters of their actions, one action at a time.

"While I was waiting for my shots at the clinic, I read in a medical publication that human beings try to avoid pain at all costs, thus evading situations that make us feel uncomfortable. For this reason, we tend to postpone taking any action on the subject that afflicts us, without realizing that unresolved business is waiting to confront us along the way, until we have no choice but to address it head-on. With inaction, we only succeed in prolonging what torments us."

"It is amazing how much you have matured in the last few months. Tell me, what else did you learn?"

"I understood the importance of admitting the truth, independently of how bad the consequences might be. If it is true, sooner or later we will have to face the actions and their results."

"Yes, Juanjo, the recognition of truth sets man free in a practical and tangible way."

"Grandpa Fello, from now on, I promise you that I will search for the truth in every situation, to proclaim the truth and act according to the truth. And start doing this right now—the sooner, the better."

Fello was silenced as he listened to the innocent wisdom of his grandson. As he raised his head, his gaze remained fixed on the gazebo. Gradually, the square filled with people; his friends had already started a game of chess, and he thought it would be appropriate to approach them. He placed on the table the total amount of their consumption; he took a long look at Juan, swelling with pride and satisfaction and clearing his throat said, "My dear lawyer, are you ready for the best presentation of your life? Let's go. Everyone is already here. Remember what we discussed about building consensus? That's what this is all about' people fight for what they love and understand."

They approached the square and entered the gazebo, greeting everyone, Fello slightly raising the right wing of his felt hat as he strode strong and secure, without hesitating for a single moment. He stopped at the first step of the platform where their game tables were set up. He did not climb to the second level. He signaled Juan to step up; Juan had fallen behind greeting his grandfather's friends, who returned the greeting by tousling his hair or affectionately pulling his ears.

"Allow me a few moments of interruption," Fello said, raising his voice.

They all lifted their heads; it was unusual to address the entire group at once since their communication within the group was circumscribed to small groups of three to four people at a time. Nobody took the stand unless it concerned a serious matter.

Fello continued, "How many of you think that the situation in Alborde is optimal, that everything is going well? Last week, Juanjo proposed something to me that I want you to hear directly from his own mouth, something that caught my total attention and initiated a visible change of attitude in me with respect to Alborde, perhaps because I was ready to hear something new and honest. Come, Juanjo, get up on the platform to share your proposal with my friends."

Suddenly, Juan got nervous; he felt his stomach ache and his entire body tremble. The portfolio he firmly held a few moments before started to shake slightly. The town elders were there, the sum of over a thousand years of experience, lived by each of those present at the time. At that moment, inwardly, he reaffirmed that only a citizen who is involved in the governmental process can produce changes and that the phrase "Every people has the government it deserves" was a phrase with merit. He nervously cleared his throat a couple of times before starting to talk.

"Last week, Jose and Antonio, my best friends, left with their parents, following the harvests up north."

Looking straight into the eyes of one of the elders in attendance, Juan continued, "Don Domingo, I know you miss your grandson. Antonio misses you, too; he told me that often this year."

Everyone turned to see the face of Domingo García, one of the best farmers in the region, who was in the process of claiming title to his property title in a dispute with the Mendoza family, which was legally represented before the land court by Jorge Narváez.

"Yes, I miss my grandson. I miss the whole family. And above all I dread the vicissitudes and difficulties we have to endure. I also have to live in uncertainty because your father wants to deny us the right to title of the only home we ever had, the land that we have worked for three generations."

"That's right!" said a few.

Fello scanned the group and turn his head to directly look at Juan and possibly go out in his defense, but Juan straightened his torso with dignity, saying, "Today I am not here as the son of Jorge Narváez! I come before you to seek your support and collaboration as the sons of Alborde that we all are, albeit of different ages, concerns, responsibilities, and convictions." And without waiting for a response he continued. "For many years, Alborde has been stripped of our young people. I come to ask that we all join together to reclaim our right to a better education and stability in our own town."

He made a short pause, waiting for some interruption, but this time nobody spoke. Their eyes were fixed on Juan; some of them were smoking their pipes; others were leaning on their elbows, playing absentmindedly with the dominoes between their fingers. However, all sat in expectation of the next word out of Juan's mouth.

"I talked with Papa Fello about this issue because I had never before had friends as close as Jose and Antonio, and they have left not by choice but by necessity. Grandpa says that it is only when something powerful touches our heart that we are really ready to fight. My friends have touched my heart. I want a solution for them for all those wishing to be able to live all year in one place without having to travel like gypsies so they are able to establish roots here.

"Grandpa and I spent the weekend talking about the different problems in our town; everyone knows what those are, but everything points to the lack of work in Alborde, which has resulted in the instability of families, failure in education, and the lack of training that leads to more unemployment. We need to pool our thoughts to generate ideas and find a clear and simple solution to change the direction Alborde has taken, be it unwittingly or by neglect. We are not going to blame anyone; we need solutions.

In this portfolio I have gathered a summary of laws regarding the protection of minors."

Having said that, Juan gave the yellow folder he had in his hands to his grandfather, taking out a couple of sheets of paper in which he had written down some points to be discussed, and Fello circulated the folder and notes around the group. Juan no longer felt any insecurity about expressing his thoughts.

"I know many see me as a child, but soon I will be fourteen years old. Besides, this concerns all of us—the old, the young, and the children; we must all take responsibility for doing something. There is a law that dictates that it is the duty of the ministry to act in favor of children and their representatives without affecting the actions of parents and representatives of minors. Therefore, by law, the public authorities must act to resolve the problems affecting the young people of Alborde."

Domingo García was the first one to speak, but this time he did it with affection and respect.

"You are right, Juan. Forgive my previous outburst. What are you proposing? Do you have any specific idea?"

"Thanks, Don Domingo. I have taken no offense whatsoever! Yesterday, reading and researching in Dad's library, I found out that there is a law that defines the right to education and other benefits for minors, including a home under adverse circumstances. I think the first thing we need to do is facilitate a house; the optimal solution would be a boarding school so that all those who didn't want to fall behind in their studies could remain in Alborde under the care of tutors or mentors."

A murmur swept throughout the group, growing more audible as everyone started to talk at the same time.

"But who could do that? You are talking about a very big project; we do not have the necessary resources, not even to sustain ourselves, much less to support all the kids who might want to stay," said Domingo, raising his voice a little bit, and Fello immediately intervened.

"We know that, Domingo, but if we prepare and present a clear and specific request, we can get the attention of the ministry and corresponding authorities. Besides, I believe we have had enough inaction so far. We are dying of boredom in a retirement imposed before due time. We all can do something to contribute to ensure our grandchildren remain in Alborde to afford them the opportunity to grow, get educated, and fulfill their potential here with us. I am willing to fix my house and offer it as the first home for these kids," said Fello with a strong voice filled with conviction, leaving everyone astonished, without a word, for a few moments that seemed like hours. They could not believe what they heard from Fello's mouth. Silence erupted into a choir of comments.

"But what are you saying, Fello? You do not have a woman in the house to take care of the children and take care of the chores," said Domingo, and Fello interrupted him again.

"If we want to accomplish anything, we have to be willing to make sacrifices and do things we already forgot how to do. We can do very well. He who wants something can accomplish it any which way. Who is with me?"

Domingo was the first to raise his hand, followed by Manuel, José's grandfather. Both elders lived an austere life; their wives stayed home, and they cultivated the orchard as full-time jobs to keep bread on the table. They received a sad pension that barely covered the costs of living, including utilities, water, gas, electricity, and some groceries. The money earned by their migrant sons was barely enough to cover the primary expenses for the family on the move. The story of the rest of the attendees was similar with very small variations. The two old men looked around them to see who else was in agreement with the proposal, and more than half had raised their hands. Fello continued, pointing to those who did not respond.

"Tell me, what prevents some of you from joining this noble proposal? All we ask is your approval and whatever anyone can contribute, be it in material objects or physical effort at your will and personal discretion.

"The law states that minors have the right to seek, receive, and utilize information adequately for their own development.

Our children have been so busy trying to earn a living in hostile terrain that they don't even have access to the information that can save them from their own misery, and here we are, seeing life go by as spectators in the Roman circus, watching the battle that our children live from the outside, as if we had no other choice but to see life pass them by like a bad Hollywood movie. The law states that parents or guardians and the appropriate authorities will ensure that the information received by minors is truthful, pluralistic, and respectful of constitutional principles. Now, you tell me. Do you know something about this law so far? Have you seen the government act on behalf of our families? The laws serve no significant purpose if the recipients are unaware of it. Our children are working from dawn to dusk in order to survive. Let's make the decision to help them see a better way of living. Better yet, let's start paving the way for them.

"Our grandchildren don't have a steady residence or the opportunity to take root in a suitable place. They don't even have full knowledge of their rights, much less a chance to claim them. They don't spend enough time in one place to find out what those rights are. Perhaps our responsibility as parents ends when our children are grown up and leave, but the love and concern of parents never ends We have an opportunity to straighten their twisted roads. Let's take the control and demand our grand-children's rights before the public agencies. Our representatives haven't done their job, and we have allowed it. The municipality is duty-bound to facilitate the access of needed services to minors, and they haven't done so in Alborde. Let us join together to achieve the equality, solidarity, and respect that corresponds to our loved ones. Our children here in Alborde are as deserving of their rights as the kids in the big cities, who receive all the services they need, as prescribed by law. Let's fight for the rights of our children"

At that moment, they all raised their hands, and the air was filled with a whisper that took shape as comments, suggestions, and expressions of volunteerism. Juan and Fello ignited the fire of service and duty, almost extinct in the hearts of these elders, exhausted by work and hopelessness, renewing their strength to fight for a cause. Domingo intervened.

"I will talk to Isabel, and you, Manuel, talk to your wife to see if they will commit to help us in keeping up Fello's house. For a long time now, I have been thinking about the foolishness our children learn traveling from town to town while they are still malleable and innocent. Although everyone, including minors, has the right to all freedoms, including freedom of religion and ideas, I think our kids deserve refuge and must be protected to ensure they receive a single directive as minors. They must adhere to what their parents teach them and establish until they can be responsible for their own lives, until they learn how to support themselves under their own roof. Kids can decide what to believe and what to think when they know for sure what life really is. They have their entire lives ahead of them to experiment, but they should only be free to experiment when they are accountable for their own lives before the law, never when they are minors and the adults are still responsible for them. As long as they still live with their parents, they must respect and follow the rules of their parents or adults in charge. Some behaviors are not acceptable, allowing brats in your own home, contradicting their parents, opposing their own parents only because someone else on the streets convinced them that anything goes or not being able to pray at the dinner table because even as young children they boast being atheists and don't believe in anything; it makes me feel sick to my stomach."

"What? You mean to tell me Dominguin doesn't believe in God?" said Manuel.

"No, sir, I didn't say that! I saw this in a television program. They had a panel of experts saying that our children have the right to think whatever they want and I don't believe in that. They can think whatever they want to think when they are capable of supporting themselves, when they have no direct and practical use for the values and convictions of their parents. They can think whatever they want when they don't need their parents to rescue them from the problems they fall into precisely because they didn't follow the principles their parents taught them.

"To give you an example, we are responsible for the actions of our children until they become adults before the law at eighteen. This means that even the law was based on the assumption that our children obey our rules and mandates. If I taught my children not to steal, I expect them to believe honesty as a basic value; however, if I steal, my children learn it is fine to make use of what is not ours. But if the new school of thought is to disassociate my children from my values, I should not have to be responsible when they deviate from my principles. Am I making sense?

"Today's youth get in trouble with the law because they have not cemented their values and they are swayed by peer pressure and a sick media; they think they can do anything without facing responsibility. However, it is their parents who have to rescue them from the mess, guided by the same values their children refused to adopt, values that don't allow us to abandon our children, even if they are ungrateful. That's what I mean. I see the media and a free-floating liberalism indoctrinating our youth, turning them against us. Even when they are unclear about things stimulated by this 'invalidate the old man, he doesn't know anything' movement, kids look for answers in the wrong places and what they see in the media ends up confusing them, which is why there are so many problems today."

Trying to reach a consensus, Fello answered, "Gentlemen, the law dictates that minors have the right to freedom of ideology, conscience, and religion, but also that those rights are limited by the fundamental rights and freedoms of others. Parents and guardians have the right and duty to cooperate so that minors exercise their rights, contributing to their integral development. I think we all agree on this."

"And where are we going to raise the necessary money for all this?" someone in the group said. It was Silvano Mendez, the old accountant of the grocery warehouse, now employed part time due to staff reductions necessary to keep the doors open for business. He continued. "I don't know where young people get the idea they deserve everything without any effort on their part. The cause of many of our labor problems is that many, especially young people, think they deserve the salary without applying themselves only because they show up to work. If they were willing to do their part—"

"I understand what you say regarding work conditions," said Fello, "and we will get to that point once we settle the residence of our young people, but we can't face all the problems at the same time. We're trying to do our part to change the course of events here starting modestly, with a home and a way of supporting them. Later, we will deal with labor issues

"We will educate these children to the best of our ability and unprejudiced. Many teach their children to be responsible, and that is why they sacrifice so much, traveling under horrible circumstance to work and support their families. It is not fair to let good people pay for the sins of others.

"We very well know that the only thing every human being deserves without effort is the unconditional love of his parents; everything else has to be earned each and every day.

"I propose to convene a committee to formulate the plan and formally present it to the appropriate authorities. I offer to put in order my house as soon as possible to begin providing temporary housing for these youngsters. We will need the cooperation of everyone in this group and the support and collaboration of those who agree with our proposal in town."

"I nominate Juan as president of the committee!" said Domingo García, filled with excitement.

Everyone was in agreement except Juan, who said he wanted his grandfather at the helm, and he volunteered to be Fello's assistant during the course of action. He also added that his emotions were not blind to the reality of his limitations and lack of experience and that the only thing he wanted was the unification of the people to procure a definite change in their town.

Everybody stood up, giving Juan a standing ovation and enthusiastically showing respect for the kid. In just a few moments they had recruited a small army with its corresponding board of directors. Everyone wrote his name on a paper, committing to Alborde's Rehabilitation Project. Even the waiter serving in the café, plus a couple of patrons who happened to be there and overheard the discussion insisted on joining the group.

President: Fello Narváez
Assistant to the President: Juan Narváez
Vice president: Domingo García
Treasurer: Silvano Méndez
Board of Directors: Manuel Domínguez
Narciso Rodríguez
Toribio Martínez

Fello called upon the improvised order they had just established. "For the record, let's vote on the following issues. I ask for a show of hands from those in favor. Juan, make note of the total in favor and against each time after every question: (1) Who is in favor of proceeding with the proposed project for rehabilitation of Alborde? (2) Who is in favor of formally registering the new organization? (3) Who is in agreement to start procurement of a home where minors can stay for the purpose of continuing their education in Alborde without interruption? (4) Who is in agreement to start and collaborate with the refurbishing of my house to be able to immediately offer the house as youth shelter? (5) Who is in agreement to establish an account, managed by the treasurer of the organization, for the purpose of raising the necessary operational funds? (6) Who is in agreement to procure temporary custody of the minors to be able to act in their favor before the law?

"If anyone has any other issue to present to the group, this is the time to speak."

Each one of the actions discussed was unanimously voted in favor of, preceded by short discussions. Fello continued presenting the laws Juan had compiled for the purpose of disseminating some of the precedents and other relevant data among members of the group as a basis for the argument they were preparing to present.

"According to existing laws, children have the right of association, the freedom to belong to associations and youth organizations, political parties, and trade unions, and to become part of the governing bodies of these associations. The law also provides the right of minors to participate in public meetings and peaceful demonstrations. We have to appeal to these rights to provide a better future for our youth. "

"We will join together so our displaced children can express their needs before the courts, and we will find ways to make the needs of our youth an urgent regional matter. We need to capture the attention of the public throughout the province so we can motivate immediate action from our representatives; we will stop being a marginalized and anonymous group of peasants and everyone will have to listen to us," Silvano Méndez said.

"You are right, Don Silvano. The law clearly states minors are entitled to freedom of expression, including the publication and dissemination of their views, and the right to be heard, both within the family as well as in any administrative or legal proceeding in which they are directly involved," Juan replied.

Fello continued on reading. "It is clear in this law that minors can exercise their right to be heard either directly or through another person designated to represent them until they acquire sufficient capacity for judgment, and in the person of the new organization, we will be able to represent our youth."

Everyone agreed it was important to study and become familiar with these laws, especially the articles about representation, in preparation for the introduction of the project, and all agreed to read them.

One of the most significant points revealed by their research was the right of children to access the assistance provided by public agencies. They uncovered how the legislature had allocated funds for different causes and how politicians had later diverted these funds for their own personal projects or invented phony institutions to misuse the designated resources, hurting the truly disadvantaged in the process or perpetuating the problem for the purpose of maintaining the structure of their agencies and their position in government.

In order to optimize access to the funds established for the welfare of minors, they unanimously agreed to formally identify the existing social benefit programs, find out who administered them, and get familiar with the established processes so they could instate those services in Alborde.

In addition, they all agreed any kind of support system they might want to establish in Alborde would also include an exit strategy or plan for independence to preserve human dignity and to teach participants how to fend for themselves.

That afternoon the meeting at the park, which usually took two or three hours, lasted more than five. They no longer gave the impression of a group of old folks wasting their time in the park; there was a visible difference in the posture and gesture of each one of them. The sense of purpose that motivated them to act in the service of and on behalf of others could be clearly seen. They were no longer thinking about arthritis, coughing, the flu, or constipation. Simply looking outside of themselves had rejuvenated them. They managed to leave the maze in which they had been inexorably but inadvertently lost.

Silvano was the most aloof of the group, tall and lanky, his demeanor at times in slow motion, resembling the futile movement of a rusty clock. He now moved quickly from one group to another around the tables, speaking up a storm, recounting a variety of ways funds could be raised for a cause such as theirs and for the founding of a nonprofit organization. It was about ten in the evening, and no one made any move to leave the pergola.

Suddenly, the figure of Jorge Narváez appeared in one of the arches; his unfolded shadow licked the tiered platforms, pitifully extending across the floor and pavement like a wounded giant. Juan felt a blow in the pit of his stomach; both he and Fello had forgotten about the traditional Monday dinner with the grandfather at home.

"Good evening, good evening." Jorge kept repeating the salutation, passing in front of the old men, rapidly approaching Fello.

Jorge whispered in Fello's ear, "Dad, what are you doing? We have been waiting for you to serve dinner at home. Don't you think it is a little late in the evening to be here, wasting time in the park with Juan? This is not only irresponsible; it is downright inconsiderate to the rest of us. Juan hasn't even done his homework; Susana and the girls are waiting. Come, let's go and have dinner!"

"It is so nice of you to join our group! I knew we could count on your support," said Fello, raising his voice so everyone could hear.

Juan inhaled, a little bit more relaxed, but his stomach was still hurting. The state of impatience and intolerance that distressed him was evident in Jorge. With his lack of compassion, his father raised an insurmountable wall around himself that separated him from the rest.

"I know you are too busy and that's why you weren't able to come before now, but I will tell you everything over dinner. We'll get together again tomorrow, boys, at the usual time."

The group broke apart slowly as Fello, Jorge, and Juan silently walked toward the house—three generations with their unique views, dreams, and aspirations, so different and identical at once! The grandfather whistled happily, making an attempt to casually leap after every three or four steps. Juan stayed closer to his grandfather during the short stroll, following with his eyes the design in the mosaic of pebbles as they walked. They were small river stones worn out by the currents of various shades and colors artistically placed to create flowers and geometric shapes, constituting the pavement of the park and of many plazas and porticos throughout the city. This technique, a legacy of the Moors, was widely used in the pavements of the zone.

Dinner was already served, and the family was seated at the table waiting for the three men of the family. The grandfather entered the room with a smile on his face, giving Susana and his little granddaughters a kiss on both cheeks. Juan did the same and both sat in their designated places at the table.

"Juan, bless the table." said Jorge without uttering another word.

"Dear Lord, bless the food we are about to eat; bless the hands that cultivated the land, those who collected the fruit of your undeserved love for us humans. Give bread and the opportunity to work to every parent head of household and hunger and thirst for righteousness to those who of us who already have bread, work, and a home. Thanks for inspiring Alborde's elders to fight to keep their grandchildren in our town. Amen."

Everyone sat wide-eyed, staring at Juan and the grandfather. Jorge broke the silence saying, "Dad, we seriously have to have a talk."

"Yes, son, I think it is time we spoke at length."

UNIFICATION CAMPAIGN

The supper went on smoothly. Grandpa Fello spoke without taking a break, recounting humorous familiar stories evoking his youth, delighting Susana and his grandchildren, who worshipped their grandfather without a doubt. Jorge smiled a few times, returning immediately to his rehearsed I-am-annoyed performance each time he realized he was enjoying the moment and relating pleasantly.

Susana was delighted with her role as matron of the family. She enjoyed the household chores, especially getting creative in the kitchen, frequently preparing extra special dishes for the family, unrelated to any special occasion or reason. She also loved to place fresh flowers and candles at the center of the table and to bring out the fine dishes, glasses, and silverware to serve their meals, and when Jorge or the kids asked her if they expected some important guest, she would say, "Yes, I am expecting you! Today we are celebrating our family, the fact that we are all together, healthy, and happy to be alive; we are celebrating togetherness. What good does it do to have fine silver and china if we don't use it with those who really matter in our lives? Let's make a toast to love, health, and the time we now share. There will be times in our lives when we will miss these moments, unable to be together again, for whatever reason there may be."

Each time the grandfather went to have dinner with them Susana went out of her way to prepare his favorite dishes. She felt sad seeing Fello living by himself in the farmhouse without a person to take care of him. Susana had tried to convince him to move in with them each time the issue of his life without help on the farm was discussed. But he insisted in having his own personal space without bothering anyone.

That evening, Susana had prepared a succulent *cocido,* a typical chickpea stew made with ham hocks, potatoes, and greens— one of Fello's favorite dishes—and he couldn't stop praising her cooking while cleaning off what was left of the second portion of *cocido* on his plate with a piece of crusty bread.

"You are an exceptional cook, way ahead of the competition. If we had more people in Alborde, I would advise you to open a restaurant, Alborde's Delicacies, and it would be filled to capacity all the time."

"You exaggerate, Fello, but that is why we love you so much."

The girls giggled in complicity, listening to the conversation. A warm and cozy fire burned in the hearth, keeping the dining and living room at a reasonable temperature, comfortable through dinner. Susana suggested Fello and Jorge go sit in the family room to have their coffee in front of the fire while she and the kids finished clearing and organizing the dining room.

"Thank you, Susana, but instead of coffee, could I trouble you for a little mint and chamomile tea? Lately, if I have too much coffee, I can't fall asleep, and today, in particular, I am a little wired."

"Good idea. I would also like to have tea instead of coffee, darling," Jorge added while walking toward the living room.

They sat in front of the fireplace, Jorge in his favorite chair and the grandfather in a reclining one, generally designated to him when he visited them. Susana and the children cleared the table and washed the dishes like a team of veterans.

In Jorge and Susana's family, the household chores were shared; only Jorge was exempted from this duty because he really worked tirelessly twenty-four hours a day. Susana had established with their kids that Jorge was the head of the family, and that his job consisted of providing financial stability and sustenance for the family, not the execution of household chores. Nevertheless, Jorge was always ready to help Susana in any task around the house when he wasn't busy with important matters related to work.

Susana sent the kids to retire for the night and get ready for bed, arguing it was very late and they had school the following day. Juan made clear he had done all his homework before going with his grandfather. The three children said good night to Jorge and Fello with kisses and hugs. Juan embraced Fello, holding on to him.

"Thank you, Grandpa. Good night. We will meet again at the park tomorrow, won't we?"

Fello gave a reassuring pat on his grandson's back, winking at the same time. "We will meet there again."

The freshly brewed tea slightly burned their lips, and the fragrance of mint and chamomile swiftly penetrated Fello's nostrils, causing a tingling sensation that made his eyes water. The two, in unison, inhaled the swirling vapor pirouettes rising from the hot cups and unconsciously closed their eyes in a meditative manner while breathing in the smells, each searching his innermost thoughts, looking for the appropriate way to initiate the impending conversation.

Fello recalled long ago times when he so easily spoke with his son, wondering at what moment it was that each began to take distance from the other. Fello cleared his throat a couple of times, the way he always did when he was about to engage in a conversation about which he didn't feel confident.

"Jorge, son, do you remember that morning when Elena passed away? We were at the sanatorium. I had taken her there early in the morning. She had experienced chest pain for several days but didn't tell me about it because she didn't want me to worry, but that day before dawn, I heard she was having breathing difficulties and immediately jumped out of bed and rushed her to the hospital. I felt helpless like a child. When she was ushered into treatment and I was alone in the waiting room, the only thing I could think of besides your mother was talking to you. I wanted to send someone to find you. I needed your presence, but she asked me not to tell you; she wanted to wait a little longer so you didn't have to wake so early in the morning. She always worried about you because of how much you worked; she told me her symptoms were nothing serious, that it was going to be fine, but then the doctors diagnosed a massive heart attack. I felt the walls closing on top of me. I begged the doctors to do everything possible to save her. I saw her so vulnerable; I sensed I was losing her.

"After their diagnosis, they quickly placed some medication under her tongue, immediately conducting an electrocardiogram and other tests. Everyone was rushing; they placed tubes through her nose and an IV in one of her arms. I was afraid they were going to hurt her; she looked so fragile! They continued to conduct a number of tests until they were able to stabilize her. She even started to feel better. When your mother thought she was well, she asked me to phone you; she wanted to see you; you were her favorite son."

"Dad I want—"

Fello didn't let him finish.

"When you arrived it was eight forty-five in the morning. Elena had already died—she went straight to heaven like the angel she was—silently without calling attention to herself. We didn't even notice; we all thought she was asleep. It was a sad surprise for the doctors, who believed they had stabilized her and positioned her on the way of recovery.

"Jorge, don't blame yourself anymore for not having been present; it was not your fault. You didn't know the severity of the case. I didn't communicate that to you; that's why you went to your office before heading for the hospital. You were doing what you considered necessary in the optimal exercise of your functions as judge. I know you wanted to set the day in order before leaving your office to be able to dedicate your full attention to your mother for as long as necessary.

"Unfortunately, time is served to us without a container; it is placed directly on our hands, and like water, it cannot be retained between the fingers, inevitably escaping from us. Today, I ask your forgiveness for having been offended by your absence during that crucial moment of my life, no, that crucial moment of our life. For a long time I felt rage against everyone and an excruciating pain deep inside my soul. I forgot my duty to you as your father. I know you suffered a lot. I was selfish. Forgive me, my son."

Fello turned to look at Jorge; Jorge was silent, immobilized by the spell of that moment, engrossed in the words of his father, staring at the burning embers of undulating bright red waves in motion. A river of tears traced Jorge's face. Feeling the compassionate gaze of his father, Jorge burst into sobs like a child. However, he didn't move or break his silence.

"That day, instead of being the father you needed, I turned into a hopeless orphan. I was supposed to be the emotional support of my children, but Elena took all my strength with her; her death tore my world apart a world she had built for me, for our family. I truly feel I failed all my children and grandchildren, especially you Jorge, because I didn't offer you the shoulder of a father to cry on, the way it was supposed to be, to give you the opportunity to let go and express your feelings of loss. I think you were never able to articulate your pain and openly deal with the loss of your mother; you did what I was unable to do—you became the support for everyone; you mustered all the strength you could to allow the family to cry on your shoulder. You supported all of us emotionally; you gave us strength to continue on. You are a great man, and I am very proud of you. On the other hand, I was a coward. Please forgive me."

"Dad…Dad." Getting up from his seat, Jorge knelt down next to the chair where Fello was sitting and, like a small child, placed his head on his father's lap, sobbing unstoppably. For the first time in many years, Fello caressed his son's head, and he did it, pouring all the tenderness he was capable of. His thoughts went to the paternal home where he had also raised his own children, recalling similar moments sitting in front of the shimmering blaze, inhaling the intense herbal aromas that permeated the early morning air.

That day, while drinking tea with his father made of ginger, cinnamon, allspice, and fresh orange leaves, they awaited the arrival of newly hired farmhands to start the olive-picking season.

Many winters had gone by, but that particular one was unforgettable. It was the first workday of a family his parents had contracted with a double purpose: the father was hired to work as labor on the farm and the wife to help his mother with housework. The new family was provided with a comfortable home within the farmstead, part of a series of edifices built to shelter the workers. Fello and his father leisurely awaited the arrival of the new workers; the first sunrays were breaking through the fading winter night when they finally arrived at the main house.

Holding tight to the hand of a young, energetic woman was Elena with her blond braids escaping from under the dark wool blanket covering her head and resting on her small shoulders. She was six years old, but in her delicate frailty she looked even younger.

"Go ahead, my son; let go of your feelings. You have kept your pain inside for too long. I want you to heal. It is time for me to step up and give you all the support I should have given you all these years—a shoulder to cry on—if that is what you need. It's time I be a better father to you and stop feeling sorry for myself. I recognize that the pain of losing your mother was not mine alone; it was and continues to be our loss, our pain. I want to rebuild our relationship.

"I think it is time to remember and celebrate Elena's life, all she gave me since she was a child. Did you know, Jorge, that I lived more time with Elena than with my parents? When I met her, she was six years old and I was eight. We played on the farm all day long until I started going to elementary school. When she arrived at the house with her parents in the mornings, her mother prepared churros and hot chocolate for us, the same way she did for all of you. Those churros dipped in thick hot chocolate warmed our bodies during the winter and calmed our restlessness in the summer mornings. It was comforting, it was our soul food. Elena continued her mother's tradition. With her, I learned sensibility. I believe that it was from her that I learned all that has been useful throughout my life. That is why I lost everything the day she died, but I don't have the right to make all of you lose it as well."

"Dad, I'm the one who needs to ask for forgiveness. When mom died, I felt responsible for her death. I felt I failed both of you; I wasn't there when you needed me the most, and when I finally got there, I couldn't do a thing. When you called me, I was getting ready for a hearing in court. In retrospect, I could have postponed it; this tortures me every day of my life. But I made the decision to go to the office and give instructions on how to proceed, so I could dedicate the rest of the day to Mom and you. I never thought I was exchanging the last moments of my mother's life for a pat on my back, to look good at my job, to please everyone else instead of attending to those who really mattered in my life."

"Jorge, stop blaming yourself; you could not see the future. Besides, if there was one thing that made Elena proud of you, it was the strong sense of responsibility you have shown since you were a child. We often talked about that gift of yours, showing off and celebrating it every time we could. The only thing we can do is deal with the present; the best we can do is love our dear ones incessantly, to focus on building good memories with our children so those loving images accompany them when we are no longer here. Jorge, I love you; you are a good son, a magnificent husband, and terrific father. I want to rekindle our friendship, start afresh, building good memories for the future."

"Yes, Dad, I also want that."

Hiding in the kitchen, Susana wept silently; she had listened to the entire conversation without making any noises, not to disrupt the dialogue and the process of reconnection between Fello and his son. She remained there, sitting on the floor behind the kitchen door, embracing her legs, holding the kitchen towel in her hands, her forehead resting on her knees.

Since Elena's death, she had noticed the gradual toughening and aloofness in Jorge's character, even reaching a certain level of hostility against members of the family. Jorge had visibly isolated himself from all—from his father, his sisters, his children, and even from Susana herself. She loved her husband immensely, but the intimidating disposition he had adopted during past few years was affecting their relationship and damaging their marriage. She sensed if something positive didn't happened soon, the breakage would be irreversible.

She fondly remembered her arrival in Alborde after getting married, when her heart burned with passion and certainty; she admired Jorge and was convinced that his commitment to help the poor and the dispossessed in Alborde was going to make a remarkable difference. He exuded commitment to principles and devotion to social work and civic service. Everything that made Jorge so passionate, exceptionally special, and different from other men had vanished. Jorge had certainly achieved financial success; they were one of the wealthiest families in town; nonetheless, she felt they had lost their way during the haggle many kilometers ago.

Susana had recently written a note in her old journal:

Dear, God,

I am writing you this letter because I know you love me and you care, and I have no one else to talk to and help me find peace in my soul. Lately, I am full of anger and don't even know why. It is a vague feeling that taints all my activities.

I try to understand the true reasons why I am angry, and my thoughts are as scattered as my feelings. I don't remember when was the last time I felt so lost and without a clear purpose in life.

I love my children and the people around me, but even when I turn to them for a reason to be happy and peaceful, I can only see the weight of the burden they represent, and even though I know it is not fair, I feel used by them. I feel overburdened. I experience similar feelings at work; that's how I know the problem must be in me.

Please, Lord, I know that you created and own wisdom, peace, happiness, and love, and no one can find these without you. I need you to help me decipher the problem so I can start working toward a solution with your divine guidance.

As I try to enumerate my problems, it all begins with lack of discipline and self-control. I get emotional, too easily bothered by the actions of others. I get upset at my kids instead of addressing the issue and correcting whatever they did wrong.

I stay angry with my sisters-in-law because they are not as careful and thoughtful as I think they should be, and they overstep their boundaries, infringing in my family's disciplinary actions. I know it is my fault for not knowing how to establish the necessary limits and lines of authority.

I also feel abused when they continuously ask Jorge for financial help; they spend money carelessly, and when they really need the money they pilfered, Jorge has to bail them out. I think it is abusing our family's finances. It seems like we can never do what we feel like doing in our intimate circle, always having to carry along some relative with us, hindering our finances; we will never be able to get ahead. Dear, God, am I being stingy?

I confess my concerns about the girls; I want them to be close to their relatives and wouldn't want them to know about these feelings and thoughts; sometimes I can't hide my feelings and those seem so miserable! Juan gives the impression of been distracted and forgetful, but he has advanced considerably since Elena's death. I am afraid he might notice these things. The darkest of my thoughts have to do with Jorge's behavior, although I try to keep it out of my mind to avoid feeling tormented, but it is always there, hiding in the depths of my mind.

Dear God, I am confused, disoriented, and angry. I need you, Lord; I believe in you; please don't fail me! I know I haven't been the best I could be, but I haven't been the worst, either. I love you, and I want to please you. Send your Holy Spirit to fill my empty life; let him renew my mind, my soul, my spirit. But let it be now!

If I continue on feeling this way, I will lose everything, starting with my sanity. I need you, Lord; come to me.

Recalling the entry in her journal, Susana felt embarrassed and promised herself she would tear out that page. This conversation between Fello and Jorge was a direct answer to her prayers; she had asked God to intervene in the renovation of her husband's heart. Although Jorge was very similar to Fello, they were dissimilar in their willingness to be spontaneous and sentimental. Jorge frequently disapproved of the generosity and openhandedness of his father. Since a couple of years back, he had started to label his father as gullible and accused him behind his back of acting irresponsibly and without thinking about the consequences of his actions.

Susana opened the kitchen door carefully and quietly, slipping to the bedroom wing unnoticed. Before reaching her room, she made sure all windows were tightly closed and heavy blankets covered the children. A very cold night had been forecasted; a freeze was expected to last well into the following day. She went to bed thinking things were about to take a very positive turn for her family.

She placed both hand on her womb, considering whether to tell Jorge they were expecting a child. Perhaps it was better to wait after seeing the doctor again. She had thought about sharing the news with her family that evening, but with the mounting tension generated by Jorge with Fello's delay for dinner, she preferred to wait for another more pleasant moment. The announcement of a new child should be a special occasion, a source of joy. With the anxiety she had experienced during the last few months, she hadn't recognized the pregnancy symptoms, and when the doctor told her she was expecting that afternoon, instead of welcoming the news, she simply broke into tears.

"I am going to wait until next Monday to announce the good news to the family when Fello is with us; it will be very significant to him."

Jorge cried next to Fello until he spent the last of the bitter tears he had kept inside for so long and different tears began to flow, tears sweetened by Fello's paternal love and the eminent forgiveness between father and son.

Jorge sat again in his chair with his legs rolled up, almost in a meditative yoga position. He wanted to continue conversing with his father. To get back the last seven years in a couple of hours was impossible, but suddenly he had realized how wrong he had been in distancing himself from his father and he wanted to repair the situation even though he didn't know quite how to begin.

The most intellectual native of Alborde could not find the appropriate words to address his father and to demonstrate the openness of his heart.

"Dad, thank you for understanding me. I haven't realized how much I needed you as my father, how much I missed our conversations, how much I need your approval in everything I do. Please, stay here tonight; don't leave. I want to continue talking to you as much as possible. Tell me more about ... about anything you can think of. Talk to me about your youth, your childhood, about when you met Mom. I want to take advantage of every minute I can spend with you."

"Jorge, my son I've missed you so much!"

Fello started to cry. Both father and son needed this encounter; it was a healing ointment on their aching souls. Fello always said that forgiveness not fully expressed got corroded inside the spirit, like water kept in an iron pot: no matter how pure it was, it gradually turned into rust.

He got up and stoked the fire, moving the burning coals with a long poker, and added a couple pieces of firewood to the hot embers.

"I think your mother told you our story more often than she told you the tale of Ali Baba and the forty thieves."

Fello and Jorge burst in laugher like a couple of adolescents.

"Elena and I grew up together. From the moment we saw each other for the first time, we knew we were going to share our lives together. We were inseparable. When I started school, the moment I got home, I shared everything I learned with Elena. We did homework together; she was much smarter than me. Without realizing it, I became her elementary school teacher, and she learned how to read and write with me. And although she never formally studied beyond secondary school, she was wiser than any doctor, more courageous than the beasts of the jungle, and more generous than the saints.

"She worked with her parents in the fields from dawn to dusk, and in the evening, she did embroidering, sewing, and weaving. When each of you was born, she prepared the entire collection of outfits, embroidering beautiful baby clothes, complete with little boots and hats. She was so proud to declare she did it herself, down to the last stitch. However, do you know what Elena's most transcendental quality was? It was her inexhaustible generosity. She gave herself completely to others; she could not hear that someone needed something without acting upon it. She would run to assist, insisting on helping to solve everyone's needs, regardless of whether they were friends, acquaintances, or strangers. Each time, Elena proclaimed that one should not wait to be asked for help when the need is evident and in plain view. I don't know how she managed to do so much each day with only twenty-four hours!

"With Elena, I learned how to give, not from my pocket, but from within my soul. Any person can give a few coins or any article in his possession, but very few people give from their hearts or from their personal time without making the receiver feel that along with the gift, he also contracted a heavy obligation to the giver, turning the act of giving into an unsolicited exchange.

"Your mother was exceptional. Remember how she always set extra plates at the dinner table? Her philosophy was simple: the door was always open for whoever wanted to join us for dinner, especially in an effort to share from the abundant gifts God had always bestowed upon our family. Juan inherited Elena's heart."

"Dad, I want to thank you for filling the gap I unintentionally allowed to open between Juan and me. I promise to remedy this situation. I love him immensely and recognize I have gradually neglected him, perhaps because I saw him getting so close to you, almost taking my place in his life. Tell me, Dad; what can I do to reach Juan's heart?"

During this conversation, Jorge kept using the word *Dad* every time he could, like a litany or healing mantra. He was in a hurry to recuperate the time he had wasted, reclaiming his place as Fello's firstborn and only son.

"My grandson, your son, has awakened to his adolescence; he has stopped being a child and started to worry about the well-being of others. He can no longer derive joy from what he has without having earned it one way or another; that is a sign of maturity. Do you know that Juan has changed my life forever during the course of this week? I feel that Elena wants me to join Juan in his quest for positive changes in the lives of Alborde's youth, to help them find a better future, but we cannot do it without you. We need you; I need you."

"Dad, I promise to help you; you can count on me. Furthermore, I am going to take on this issue from my office with the same seriousness and commitment I deal with issues pertaining to my clients."

"No, son, I want you to invest your heart in it, your passion your enthusiasm, the traits that characterize you, the most beautiful qualities of Jorge Narvaez, my son, my friend, my attorney."

They spoke all through the night until dawn. Fello told Jorge about Juan's concerns, and shared how he swelled with pride listening to his dissertation at the park. Fello had forced Juan to do the research and to make the presentation on his own in order to measure the extent of his commitment to his ideas. The boy had demonstrated commitment, dedication, and humility beyond his tender years. Many adults would have given up, unable to assemble the information Juan had taken to the park. They would have surrendered before having to carefully write down all the information by hand in only one evening without making a scratch in his father's books.

In the seventies, things were not as easy as they are today; there were no computers readily available, and very few people had electric typewriters, much less in a little town like Alborde. Computers were something from the space era, used only by big corporations.

The majority of professionals, like Jorge, employed secretary stenographers who would take dictation and expertly transcribe the information using mechanical typewriters, now obsolete. During that decade, the electric typewriter was introduced, followed by the word processors, but computers did not become a common office tool in markets until the eighties.

Nonetheless, Juan had spent the night reading and taking notes to deliver the clearest and most concise information to Fello, and Fello underscored the merits in Juan's actions, bringing special attention to his dedication to ideals and clarity of thought.

He also told Jorge about the reaction of the old folks in the plaza, how at first they were somewhat reluctant but later poured themselves into a show of solidarity, recognizing that everyone in Alborde had one thing in common: the pain caused by the absence of their loved ones.

Fello shared the initial response from Domingo Garcia and the courage and integrity Juan displayed in his answer. And when Jorge tried to interrupt Fello to explain his actions regarding the property titles, Fello did not allow him to proceed; he reassured Jorge that an explanation wasn't needed; he trusted Jorge's personal integrity and professional judgment completely.

With utmost detail, Fello recounted the events over the past two weeks, culminating in that evening meeting at the square, revealing to Jorge the unencumbered proposed work plan and the names comprising the emergent board of directors. With particular pride, Fello described the moment during which his friends proposed Juan as president of the new organization and how his grandson, instead of basking in the apparent adulation and glory, opted for relinquishing the presidency, proposing his grandfather as the best person for the job, placing the helm in his hands. With that gesture Juan showed that the success of the project was the most important thing for him, not the adulation and praises he could personally gain.

Jorge was moved by the account of events. Fello was introducing him to a son he had never seen before, observing from a different perspective, perhaps under a different light. Jorge couldn't stop asking for forgiveness for his aloofness, his lack of consideration, and his disaffection so belligerently manifested toward both his father and his son over the last few years.

"Son, I promised Juan to allow the use of my house for this project to accelerate the returning process of these youngsters."

"But, Dad, you can't do that. Who is going to help you take care of these kids and with the house chores? It is not easy."

"I feel as if Elena had placed that idea in my heart. From the moment this thought entered my head, I experienced an enormous fortitude of spirit. Even the arthritis pain disappeared. If there is anything available in this town, it is capable hands to do something, anything. Look around us. I am not that old; I am only sixty-three years young. The majority in Alborde has retired for lack of work and inspiration. Domingo and Manuel already volunteered to help clean the house and prepare it for the kids; they even proposed to ask their wives to volunteer and maintain the house when the children arrive."

"I see you are serious about this, Dad."

They rose from their seats, and Fello extended his right arm over Jorge's shoulders. They stood in front of the warm hearth, ready to walk toward the bedrooms. Fello turned his head to face his son.

"I love to hear you call me dad, the way you did when you were young. I have thought about this well and long. In the beginning I want to offer my house so those who want to return to Alborde can do so immediately. I know things can be as simple or as complicated as we want them to be. I want to simplify the process. I want Juan to see the result of his undertakings as soon as possible, in a tangible way. If the positive results take too long, he is going to be disillusioned, and he has invested too much in this proposal. I don't want him to sink into negativism. This is my way of investing in Juan."

"You move me deeply, Dad. Someday I would like to be like you."

Jorge insisted on taking up the case in a professional manner, reiterating promises of perseverance and commitment to success of the proposal.

"Dad, when we get up in the morning, I am going to ask Mercedes to prepare a draft with the articles of incorporation of the new association. To create a nonprofit corporation in accordance with federal laws is the first step; next it is to open a bank account in the name of the association. I am going to contribute by making the first deposit in the name of Alborde Rehabilitation Project into the new account. Is this what you want to call it?"

"Yes, Jorge. I knew we could count on you, and you don't disappoint me ever!"

"Dad, I am going to abundantly restore the seven years we have wasted."

ALBORDE'S REHABILITATION PROJECT

The blissful ruckus of the children when they awoke and found Fello drinking coffee at the kitchen table was beyond description. Juan ran to him, embracing him tightly, and Fello kissed him on the forehead. Alicia hung on Fello's neck, kissing him on the cheeks; and Sofia, the youngest of the three, jumped over, making an attempt to sit on Fello's lap, using an arm of the chair as leverage, spilling coffee over Fello's shirt, the table, and his chair. The little girl started to whimper. Fello promptly rose from the seat and tried to clean up the mess with a kitchen towel he found on the counter while Susana rushed to relocate the coffee cup left too close to the edge of the table, impatiently saying, "Look what you have done, silly."

"It wasn't intentional," answered Sofia as Fello lifted her up in his arms, resting her head on his shoulders, softly caressing her coffee-colored curls in a protective gesture.

"I know, dear. It is fine. I bet you can find one of your dad's shirts and lend it to me, and I bet you it is going to be newer and nicer than mine. Hey! Don't tell anyone I deliberately spilled the coffee so I could wear one of Jorge's shirts today."

"Grandpa Fello, are you going to stay to live with us?" asked Sofia, drying tears and snot on Fello's shoulders.

"Right now I am here with you; that's what counts now. Perhaps one day."

"Fello, it would be such a pleasure to have you living here with us; you know it well. You are so sweet and understanding with the children. Go, Sofia; go get a shirt for Fello in our bedroom; they are on the right-hand door in your father's armoire."

And Sofia left the kitchen in a hurry, repeating, "Right-hand door, Dad's armoire right-hand door, Dad's armoire, right-hand door, Dad's armoire."

A few moments later, she yelled at the top of her lungs from her parent's bedroom, "Which shirt do I take?"

Sofia returned to the kitchen holding on to Jorge's hand, dragging the shirt on the floor.

"Good morning, Dad! I hear Sofia tried to give you a coffee bath."

Everyone burst out laughing. Jorge bent down to kiss his father on the forehead and then squeezed Juan's shoulders, kissing both of his cheeks, repeating the same gesture with Alicia; then he took Susana by the waist, pulled her toward him, and embraced her, softly touching her lips with his in a kiss.

"Good morning, my love."

Susana blushed and her eyes swelled with tears of joy. Jorge woke up a new man. She sensed she was facing the start of a different chapter in her life. She had just finished cleaning the mess Sofia made, and she could not believe Jorge wasn't exasperated by the small incident. She dried her wet hands with her apron, thinking miracles were still possible.

"I am going to serve breakfast here in the kitchen; it is warmer than the dining room. Juan, go and finish dressing for school; you too, Alicia. Sofia, go change your pajamas. Look, they are getting stained with the coffee. Leave the pajamas in the sink with a little water so the stain doesn't set in. Hurry up; breakfast is almost ready."

They sat at the kitchen table; it was made of solid rustic wood, same as the chairs of high wooden back and crossed bolster with dark green fabric pads, cushioned seat and back, tied to the frame with bows made of the same material.

It was a big kitchen with high ceilings and splendid windows almost reaching the roof. The kitchen cabinets, made of the same rustic washed wood as kitchen table and chairs, formed an inverted U, open to the space that constituted the informal dining area; the upper cabinets were taller than a meter in height, making the use of a three-foot stepladder to reach objects placed on the top shelves indispensable; this ladder also served as extra seat when more than six people were sitting at the kitchen table.

The space between the counter and the cabinets was covered by white ceramic tiles with navy blue borders; the cabinet doors on either side of the U were made out of glass through which one could see the ceramic plates and other objects carefully arranged on display.

A copper smoke extractor hung directly on top of the stove, with hooks holding decorative kitchen artifacts. The cupboards were close to the table and held beautiful ceramic serving dishes Susana used when they ate in the formal dining room; when they dined in the kitchen, she simply placed the same cooking containers straight from the stove onto the table, protecting the table with ceramic mosaics she had made for this purpose.

The kitchen windows faced east, beckoning the magnificence of the morning sun. That day in particular, the kitchen vapors fogged the windows, producing a mysterious and balmy effect. And in the spots where the humidity accumulated, the incoming rays unfolded into multicolor rainbows, projecting over the different surfaces, as through a prism. In full view through the windows was the orchard with blooming cherries and apple trees. And the spicy smells of herbs recently picked—oregano, thyme, basil, and mint—roamed the kitchen, seducing the senses. The kitchen ambience was simply cozy; all visitors ended up in the kitchen, eventually turning it into the main gathering place of the house.

That day, breakfast time became a display of harmonious peace; it had been so long since they lived as pleasant a moment that Susana was unable to recall when the last time was they all felt as happy. Her family with Jorge was all she had in life, and seeing her children interacting with their father without tension was like reaching the heavens with her hands.

Susana was an only child in a completely dysfunctional family; her father never exercised his full duties as provider and caregiver, and her mother subconsciously blamed her for the horrible relationship they sustained as a couple. Although the relationship between her parents was never harmonious or acceptable, except during the short time of courtship, the distance between them widened after Susana's birth, and she was continuously reminded of it to the point she felt responsible for the disintegration of her parents' marriage.

Before Susana turned ten years old, her father enlisted in the army, and her mother classified this action as the final rejection and affront she was going to tolerate—the proverbial straw on the camel's back. A few months later, her father was transferred to a military post overseas and they never heard from Sergeant Leonardo Martinez Rivas again. The mother often said with reproach, that her husband was engaged in polygamy when he married a Moroccan national in his military post, a rumor no one ever corroborated, nor was Susana able to confirm.

Susana's mom fell to alcoholism, neglecting her completely; she grew up on her own, practically an orphan, receiving sporadic care from neighbors, good Samaritans, and rarely from distant relatives because when her parents got married, they had immediately moved to the state capital, unintentionally breaking family ties. Although her mother had been negligent in her education, during her adolescence—a time during which youngsters either gain or lose confidence and self-assurance—Susana found solace in learning, turning into a model student at a Catholic school she attended thanks to a scholarship the Salesian Society granted to disadvantaged families.

She remembered the disagreements and arguments between her parents that frequently escalated into fights, often left feeling responsible for the disputes. Susana's mom sublet her room to transient people of little income and education to help with the rental payments. So this poor child miraculously survived like a flower in a pigsty thanks to the charity of the Salesians and the compassion of a few neighbors who often gave her the opportunity to raise her nose above water to take fresh air when she was able to break away from the maternal home to do the small jobs they offered her—babysitting, attending kiosks, and other unskilled tasks—that, although modest, allowed Susana to save some money and assimilate other behavioral models.

And so it was that Susana finished secondary school and, unintentionally emancipating herself, was able to attend the university where she met Jorge. Fello knew the whole story of Susana's life, and it was perhaps one of the reasons why he had taken her under his wing with so much devotion, indulging her as much as he could. He felt like a guardian of the girl who had given all her love and all she could ever be for his son.

After breakfast, Jorge excused himself, explaining he wanted to initiate the process of forming the new corporation immediately and that after concluding a couple of previously contracted obligations in court he would be available the rest of the day in his home office.

The kids left the table to finish preparing for school. Sofia had already started first grade. Jorge said he would take the children on his way to court. Susana and Fello were left alone in the kitchen, her washing the dishes and him helping pick up the leftovers and plates from the table and placing the clean silverware and dishes in their respective places.

"I notice something different in you, Susana. I see you sad. Is there something wrong? What is happening to you?"

"Fello, today is the first day of harmony in this house in a long, long time," she said while dabbing her eyes with a handkerchief.

"Thank you for talking to Jorge last night, for starting to crack the wall he has built around him. He had detached himself from all of us for so long. You don't know how many times I have thought he doesn't even want the family responsibility any longer, that he feels trapped at home, or, even worse, that he is in love with someone else. I don't know what to think anymore. I feel so insecure!"

"Woman, woman, don't be silly! Jorge adores you; you are the only woman in his life. I know it for a fact. Aside from loving you in marriage, he contracted a lifelong commitment with you, and Jorge is a man of integrity; he would not abandon his family for anything or anyone else. We men often feel lost, and we take distance from everyone in an effort to find ourselves; it also happens to women. What is important is that the affected partner keeps his kindness toward the other and strengthen his love and commitment, not caving into disheartenment or disrupting the intimacy and integrity of the home.

"Couples that truly love each other have to store a great amount of understanding, patience, and forgiveness. That way, when one is weakening, the other has the strength to sustain the family and the sense of home. One always returns to a home where love and forgiveness abound.

"When I was an adolescent, my father told me the story of a young man who was going through a confusing period in his life. It made me think a great deal about the human heart. Let me share the story with you.

"According to my father's story, this young man was lost in his own town; he could not understand how he had lost the notion of the roads he was supposed to follow and the streets and city blocks he had walked since childhood looked like giant labyrinths, dark and hostile.

"He followed his daily routine, not even knowing why, but he would follow it to the last detail; that's why no one really noticed that the man was totally lost. The young man observed everything sunk in despair, unable to identify who he was as a son, a friend, or even as a fiancé; he already had a girlfriend. But he was required to fulfill these roles and he did so to the best of his ability. He was so overwhelmed that he started to feel alienated from the people he served and recognized as important in his life as well.

"He was a good man—hardworking, intelligent, and devoted—and he loved his family, but he felt detached, living outside of himself, and he started to think he was not really loved as an individual, that he was only valued for what he contributed in his different roles, not for his own qualities as a human being in and of himself.

"And it so happened that one day he found a young woman who was also feeling antsy and lonely, perhaps even more so than him, and they started to share their thoughts. The woman recognized the spiritual and human qualities in the young man, who, in turn, found what he was looking for in the woman: someone to value his emotions, his thoughts, his ideas, and to treasure him as a person, not tied to a deed or specific societal functions.

"The young man told this woman about his experiences, how he cultivated the land since he was a child, and since she didn't know about agriculture, she was fascinated by the stories, and a flame started to burn in their souls, giving birth to a great love. Together, they started to share the seeds they carried in their hearts, seeds that no one else valued, chunks of their souls.

"And their hearts became intertwined. And when it was sowing time, they decided to unite their seeds and plant it as one. And they did it with the hope of producing a new type of tree, one that could shelter their loved ones to provide food and refuge to their families and friends.

"And the tree grew really fast, strong, and powerful in the midst of the plain. The birds in the sky found shelter in its branches and their loved ones relief in the shade below it. It was a tree that extended its branches, offering protection and refuge. And both feverishly dedicated their life to take care of the tree.

"The young man reconnected with his emotions and was able to love unquestionably, and the woman was happy simply by being a part of his life. Under the blossoming tree they lived very happy moments for a time.

"One day, the woman started to see yellow leaves under the tree, and she thought it needed more water or perhaps fertilizer. She was terrified with the possibility of losing it; she had given her best efforts to this tree.

"The decline was almost imperceptible. Something was poisoning the tree, and although it continued giving fruits to all those who wanted it, yellow leaves kept falling to the ground, debilitating it further. The woman sensed her own death with each one of the fallen leaves.

"Then, one dark and somber morning, the young man told the woman he wanted to cultivate other trees with other women, perhaps a tree not intended to shelter others, just for fun, but he made it clear he didn't want to lose her love and affection. He simply said he wanted to plant other trees close to her wonderful tree.

"And she responded by saying that if he dedicated himself to other trees, their generous tree born out of unselfishness would die. 'Only time could tell which trees would survive,' said the resolute young man.

"The woman didn't know what to do; she didn't have any more seeds to plant. She had given it all to the young man for the creation of their tree. She knew all trees needed space to grow, and if the young man insisted on planting a tree next to hers, one would surely die.

"She wondered what to do; she needed to convince the young man that abandoning their mission was a mistake. She could not understand why the man was neglecting their creation, the tree he professed to love.

"After listening to him, she understood why the leaves started to fall; the tree needed both of them to survive, but instead of fighting and crying, she kept silent, letting the man go free. Although she wanted to die at the foot of the tree to nourish it with her own body in the depth of her soul, she knew the young man loved their tree, and one day he would return to find shelter under its branches.

"And so it was that mistreated by life itself, the man returned to the woman, asking for forgiveness a million times over, vowing to dedicate the rest of his life taking care of their generous tree, finding refuge in the woman forever without ever questioning again the value of his loved ones and the commitment he owed them."

"Fello, I don't understand the meaning of the story. The woman gave everything, and the man used her without facing the consequences."

"Precisely. We don't always receive what we deserve; nonetheless, at the end, the one who does what is right is a winner. That little story taught me many different lessons. In fact, I always find new lessons every time I recall it. Right now, I see the need to recognize the intrinsic value in each person, the importance of what we have, and how we shouldn't take it for granted and risk it by thinking we can easily get something better somewhere else. It is about identifying and rejecting the thoughts born out of selfishness. It is about giving without hesitation to those we love. It is about forgiveness, a forgiveness that forgets if we want to protect the relationship with our loved ones. It means to be willing to grow, to sacrifice, to wait patiently, and to forgive. The woman in the story valued what they had built together; that is why she was willing to protect it with her very own life and to forgive. We men are lost most of the time until we find a great woman to bring us to our senses. You women are stronger; you are the ones keeping the home intact. You are stronger, wiser, and perseverant. You know how to close an eye to our blemishes to preserve our self-esteem. When you really love, you know how to wait and forgive, although most women need to learn how to forget."

Susana kept quiet, pensive; she and Jorge had cultivated a splendid tree under which the entire Narvaez family was sheltered. They were the protectors of sisters, in-laws, and cousins. Knowing they were the protectors gave them both great satisfaction. It was better to give than to receive.

"Fello, is it true you want to offer your own house to shelter the kids now traveling with their parents? I certainly don't want you to make such a commitment only to please Juan."

"On the contrary, Susana; this project has resurrected my spirit. Juan has inspired me to come out of my self-imposed exile form society. Since I made the decision to act in favor of these kids, I feel stronger and healthier. I am sure my friends in town will feel the same revivifying effect as we advance. Besides, God opened this window so we can work together with Jorge. What else could I ask for? Life is smiling at me."

At that moment, they heard the front door open; it was Jorge, who was returning from court and going into his office but decided to show his head in the kitchen, saying, "I'm glad both of you are still here! I would love to have a meeting with the three of us, I mean, the four of us, counting Juan, to work on creating the strategic plan of the organization so you can take a draft to the park this very afternoon. Have you told Susana already?"

Jorge entered the kitchen to reach Susana, embracing her close to him as he spoke. "Dad, if you like, please stay to have lunch with us and we can have a formal meeting immediately after Juan returns from school. Is it okay with the two of you?"

He let go of Susana for a few seconds to read the expression on her face following his question, soon returning to his tender embrace, as if it were the first time he had done it in a long time.

Fello was in heaven; he never thought the situation would take such a quick shift of direction. He was thinking about the changes he needed to make to allow children to adequately live in his house again. It was a big project, but he was totally convinced he could face it victoriously. He made a mental note to speak with Caridad, the woman who used to do the housecleaning at his house when Elena was alive. Perhaps he could contract her again to help with some of the household chores, even if it was only a couple of days each week, as money permitted.

There was something very caring in Jorge's look now; he caressed Susana's back softly, moving his hand from her neck to her waist. He thought about how much he cared for her, how much he loved her, and how little he had verbalized it lately. He made a mental note and whispered into her ear, "I love you. Forgive me for failing to be all you wanted during the last few months."

And as he walked toward the kitchen door, he said, "Dad, come and sit with Mercedes; she already started drafting the articles of incorporation, and it would be helpful if you could communicate to her what you want to include in the corporation."

Fello stood up and followed Jorge along the hallway leading to his office where Mercedes was waiting for them with a thick bundle of papers in her hands that she immediately handed to them.

They worked all morning until about two o'clock in the afternoon when the kids returned from school. Since before one o'clock, the grandfather could barely hold his hunger. The smell from Susana's kitchen invaded the entire house, making his stomach growl. Fello was mortified with embarrassment each time his intestines produced any noise in front of Mercedes.

Mercedes was bashful, of little conversation, but extremely efficient in her work. They finished the draft barely before lunch, and Jorge asked her to stay over to eat with them; she could also take shorthand notes of the meeting they were preparing to have in order to prepare a work summary plan for that late afternoon gathering at the park.

Susana peeked through the office door with Sofia, who again jumped on Fello's lap, repeating in a musical tone, "Grandpa lives with us. La, la, la, la, la. Grandpa lives with us. La, la, la, la, la. Grandpa lives with us. La, la, la, la, la."

When the family sat at the kitchen table, everyone wore smiles in an atmosphere charged with goodwill, peace, and harmony. Sofia sat on the step-up ladder next to Fello, constantly leaning to hug and kiss him. Juan simply smiled without making any comments about the project. Although he was not fully aware of the details, he knew something good was happening there; he sensed it and didn't want to even open his mouth to preserve the enchantment of the moment.

Susana started to bring food to the table; she placed a big salad bowl overflowing with fresh lettuce and tomatoes from their orchard and fat olives seasoned with olive oil, basil, onions, and vinegar. She pulled a loaf of crusty bread from the oven, placing it next to a big ceramic container filled with a stew made out of red beans and blood sausage, whose swirling vapors had already fogged the kitchen windows.

Jorge blessed their meal. "Lord, we ask you to bless the food we are about to receive; blessed are the hands that prepared it. We are grateful for the undeserved blessings you bestow upon us, for Dad's perseverance, and the love you pour through each member of this family, and for inspiring my son to serve his fellow man. Amen."

That afternoon, they worked nonstop; they didn't take a nap, nor did they permit Mercedes sleep the customary siesta. And Jorge formally volunteered to serve as technical director in the signature collection campaign to prepare and deliver a formal petition to the appropriate representatives, requesting the institution of a local home shelter for elementary school children since Fello's house would only be appropriate for a few middle and high school teenagers. Jorge considered it important to separate the residents according to sex and age to simplify matters.

When Jorge, Fello, and Juan arrived together, Fello's friends were fascinated, perceiving that, with Jorge's participation, the project gained credibility. Everyone knew Jorge was one of the busiest men in town, but that he was nevertheless choosing to volunteer his valuable time to a beneficial cause, which, although not designed to produce money, was going to affect all the residents of Alborde.

With the authoritative energy that the execution of his profession had embedded in his character, Jorge started to appoint work and function to each one of the members of the incipient board of directors, asking all those in attendance to congregate and sign up under one of the directors according to their desired function, with the purpose of organizing the different working committees. Jorge gave each group the task of developing a list of obligations, self assigned duties as each saw fit, according to their personal understanding of the organization.

"I offer to volunteer handling presentation of this case in front of the state representatives. Dad, as president, is in charge of the administrative processes; I recommend to all those inclined to administrative and office duties to register with Dad. I also ask everyone to be flexible as now we must work together developing different functions and jobs within the group; therefore, I ask the executive board members, Manuel Dominguez, Narciso Rodriguez, and Toribio Martinez, to take the lead according to their assignment and abilities to manage and sign up volunteers for the following projects: (1) Physical work in preparation of Fello's house; (2) Forming a committee and teams for repair and maintenance of the house; (3) A committee in charge of obtaining the necessary food supplies for the kids; (4) An education committee to ensure the development of an ethical and civic culture in these children and to develop an enforceable manual of conduct under the president of the committee; (5) A committee to raise funds for all aspects of the project under Silvano Mendez; and (6) A committee for health and social security under Domingo Garcia.

"At this moment, I request to separate into the different groups of interest and openly discuss your concerns for a while, what each sees as the functions of his committee, and if during the conversation you find out the group you are in is not what you prefer, go ahead and change to another and so forth. I am not trying to be your boss; this is your project, and I will only take the role of advisor. I am here to clarify any organizational issues and to answer any legal questions."

After saying this, Jorge approached Domingo Garcia, asking him to step aside from the group to discuss something in private.

"Don Domingo, I congratulate you for the decision you made along with my father and my son to engage in activities to change the course of events in Alborde. Foremost, I request your forgiveness for the difficulties my professional engagements have caused you and your family; I want you to know that today I have made the decision to resign as representative of the Mendoza family."

Up to that moment, Domingo had kept silent, looking at Jorge with skeptical eyes. He suddenly started to cry, speaking unintelligibly.

"Although I wish I could repair all the damage I have caused and reverse the course of events, for ethical reasons I cannot defend you professionally, turning against the family I have represented, but I assure you I will not take any further actions in favor of this case. I believe that by default you will receive the property title you have awaited for such a long time."

Domingo tried to say something, but he was only able to give Jorge a grateful embrace. Still, he could only see him as one of the town kids, which is why he had taken Jorge's acceptance of the Mendoza case as a personal affront.

"Thank you, Jorge! Thank you!"

That night, upon returning home, Jorge went directly to his office and drafted the following letter:

Distinguished Gentlemen,

Upon conclusion of the third anniversary of my services representing the case in defense of the property titles of the lands belonging to the Mendoza family situated in the proximity of Alborde, with legal description of said properties contained in an enclosed document, dispute by abandonment of property that continues valid in the corresponding court of first instance, I have had a feeling of revelation that obligates me to present my resignation as representing attorney to your distinguished family.

Since three years ago, I have been tirelessly working in preparation of the different aspects of this case in irrefutable compliance of my functions as defender. With this objective, without even trying to do so, I have betrayed my social and Christian commitment toward the people of my town, advocating zealously against compliance with a law, which is not the final authority on the just and fair use of the land that

God has given humanity for its sustenance, the land that during millennia has engendered the fruit that feeds us, and that the man created to govern over her cultivates, modifies, and improves with his hands, obedient to the divine and natural laws of earning his bread with the fruit of his labor; but the aforementioned law also watches over the general interest of the communities and the preservation of those willing to toil in the honorable and devoted work that is farming the land.

What is the land good for if it is allowed to sleep like a giant; lazily lying down in the intoxication of her abundance, while the hands of farmers remain constrained by property titles, restraining them from awakening the land from her involuntary slumber, even as before her, starving workers stand motionless, eager and anxious to make her bountiful

That light that today knocks me off my horse like Paul on his way to Damascus, has made me see that the productive use of the land, the land no one can replace, move, or take with him after death, is an intrinsic right of men, in force throughout history, for it is appropriate and fair to secure the sustenance of the people, and that is explicitly expressed in the laws of right to property by fruitful occupation.

Conscious of the consequences implicit in my decision, I declare my deepest and sincere remorse for having fought against the democratic rights of the people eliminating them from consideration and hindering that wise law, a supreme act of social justice that secures the productivity of the land that, if not in farming hands, would be nothing more than impenetrable silos, doors blocked by ruthless lords, guarding them from starving people of innumerable misfortunes who would immediately disappear should the silo doors be broken.

Consequently, effectively immediately, I hereby tender my resignation as defense attorney for the Mendoza family in the abovementioned property title dispute.

Sincerely,
Jorge Narváez

ALBORDE RECLAIMS THE RIGHTS OF ITS YOUTH

The following weeks slipped by like vanilla ice cream in the hands of children on a hot August afternoon. Events were happening so quickly and smoothly, the members of the rehabilitation group were hardly able to keep up with the distribution of information, and even so, the executive committee and the most dedicated members would meet almost daily. Little by little, the park gatherings had moved into Fello's home, turning into productive and efficient sessions that further united the participants.

During the first week, under Toribio's directive, a group was dedicated to visiting every home in town, collecting signatures and distributing letters describing each detail pertaining to the project, instructing families to inform their traveling relatives as soon as possible about the events unfolding in Alborde. The letter presented different options to the parents and also informed them that Fello's house would be available by the holy week to serve as temporary residence to middle and high school kids wishing to reintegrate themselves to their classes in Alborde. One of the main goals of the letter was to communicate the project's distinct phases, given the scope of the undertakings. The letter outlined (1) the nature of project, (2) a list of supporters of the organization; (3) the finance model; (4) the purpose of each phase of project: to stop the migration of youth, to create a home for children, to provide special education for youngsters and workers, to improve existing social assistance programs; (5) the support from pertinent agencies; (6) the budget; and (7) the success markers: number of participants, functional social agencies in town, building of essential structures, etc.

After gathering the signatures of most of the residents in town, Jorge helped draft a project proposal that made every member of the committee proud. They immediately decided to present the project to the mayor and municipal council members.

These politicians, although informed of what was happening with the new rehabilitation movement in town, had shown little enthusiasm, staying away from the meetings, claiming conflicts of interest, alleging they had already tried to do all that was humanly possible to help Alborde's citizenry, although unable to show any positive results.

But after reading the document, realizing the potential impact this project could have on Alborde's future—aside from perceiving that staying removed from such a popular movement could mean political suicide—they eagerly incorporated themselves into the enthusiastic ranks of the group, offering to accompany the group when ready to take the project to the appropriate state authorities.

The board of directors of the Committee for Alborde Rehabilitation Project drafted a heartfelt letter requesting to be on the agenda for the next session of the house of representatives. The answer was prompt and affirmative.

Jorge and Fello circulated a pamphlet explaining step by step how an idea became a law, trying to explain that not all proposals were taken in consideration and became law.

An idea is born and is presented to the legislative session through its corresponding representative who formulates the bill.

The corresponding senator agrees to introduce the bill

The bill enters the drafting process

A bill number is assigned

First reading of the bill in chambers

President of the Legislative Chambers takes the bill to the appropriate Legislative Committee

Hearings take place at the legislative committee level and votes are counted in favor or against the bill

A date is set for consideration of the bill among its sponsors

A date is established for reading and debate of the bill in legislative chambers

The bill then goes to the Senate for discussion and same process from step one to eight starts in the Senate

Senate accepts the bill for consideration

Vote in the Senate

Legislative Chamber and Senate approve the bill that, in turn, becomes law

Governor signs the new law

New law becomes effective sixty days after it is signed by the Governor

The trip to the state capital was a heartwarming event. With his own resources, Jorge rented two comfortable tour buses to transport every one of Alborde's citizens wanting to go and attend the general audience at the state capital. The group was comprised of grandparents, retirees, and a few women with small children.

Each family had prepared a variety of snacks and fruit to share during the trip. The air was filled with a sentiment of unity and harmony engendered by that group of citizens, whom taking into their hands the competencies conferred by law, within a democratic system, demanded rightful execution of same, inspired by a young man who had not yet been trodden and hardened by the disappointments we often allow life to impose on us.

The trip would last at least three hours, and they stopped at the rest area because one of the children vomited, and the mother needed a bathroom to clean him up. As they waited for the mother and her little one, many decided to take advantage of the sanitary services and others stepped down the bus to stretch their legs, approaching the handrail to look at the scenery.

They were crossing the chain of mountains surrounding Alborde, and the landscapes were truly impressive, reminiscent of a bucolic utopia portrayed by some Renaissance artists. From the top of the mountain range one could see the valley where Alborde was carved in—placid and serene, surrounded by rivers and sprinkled by small ponds bordering the olive gathering stations. One's gaze got lost in the horizon blurred by the morning fog that gently rested on a land plagued by asymmetric pieces, a giant quilt of different plantations of all sizes and colors.

Many years had passed since the last time a group of citizens was mobilized in this manner. Jorge recalled a similar trip with their parents after the fall of the dictator when, in an effort to reinstate democracy, many citizens' assemblies were celebrated in the capital of the state; then it was imperative to establish consensus for the institution of democratic processes that today were solid and constant, often taken for granted.

Fello remained speechless, overwhelmed by emotions, meditatively practicing the words for his presentation. He felt more than gratified by the events of the past few weeks: he had recovered his son and his sense of social and civic duty, recuperating his love for life; moreover, now they were in the threshold of an event that was going to alter forever the destiny of their town and all thanks to his grandson, Juan!

Jorge approached Fello, openly showing his affection toward the old man, and moments later Juan joined in, taking the spot between his father and grandfather, placing his arms around them. There, fascinated by the landscape, absorbed in the emotions of this historic trip, three generations tightly held a tender yet symbolic embrace.

"Who would have thought I would reach heaven before dying?" said Fello as he held the embrace even tighter against his chest. "Juan, I am so proud of you! This trip is very significant in our lives. It is going to change the way of seeing things and thinking of all the participants, especially yours."

"I know, Grandpa, and I want to say to both of you how much I appreciate from the bottom of my heart all you have done to make this project a reality. I have a powerful premonition; I feel it right here in my heart. Alborde has already started the road to recovery, even before the kids are back in town."

"It is true. From the moment we initiated these activities, no one has gone back to the hospital, not even for consultation."

The trio started to laugh.

"The digestive problems, respiratory problems, the cholesterol count, arthritis, high blood pressure are no longer the main topic of conversation; those maladies have been left behind in the medical offices, out of our lives since we started our group's meetings."

"It is great to be able to give of ourselves completely and without expecting something in return. Let's go. I see people boarding the busses; we need to hurry to ensure our timely arrival to the capital," said Jorge with a smile, softly patting his son's shoulder while keeping the other arm wrapped around his father's shoulders.

During the rest of the trip, the travelers sang old songs, recited inspirational poems, and shared funny jokes and stories about local characters familiar to the group; and time went by quickly, and they found themselves quite suddenly in front of the parliamentary building.

The group was notably anxious. Only Jorge maintained complete composure, accustomed to all sort of legislative processes. The nervousness was evident in Domingo, who, against his usual communicativeness, would not even open his mouth. Toribio and Narciso did nothing more than read and reread the proposal, trying to memorize the arguments exposed on the many pages, without even making any comments among themselves. Everyone was anxious.

Before getting off the buses, Jorge addressed both groups separately. "Once again, I want to thank you for your courage and tenacity in starting the process of recovery for our town. It does not matter how many difficulties we might encounter. We have made a commitment and we will follow through until it is completed.

"I want to remind you that every people has the government they deserve because they elect it on their own accord within the democratic principles of their land. Only those citizens who exercise their democratic rights and fully follow the processes in place achieve fulfillment of their democracy.

"In a democracy, the elected officials are at the service of the electorate. They work for us, and we are here today to demand our rights and to question the representatives that have not done a good job representing Alborde's citizenry; we are here to give them their performance evaluation the same way it is done in the private sector, accompanied by a proposal to guide them in rectifying their actions and abandonment of Alborde's sons and daughters.

"We are here exercising our rights as citizens. We are going to propose policies and demand the fulfillment of the civil rights of our minors. Each and every one of you is the boss of those people representing us, the members of the house of representatives we are about to address. Don't be intimidated; they are simply our representatives, not divine entities or monarchs. Each one of you is as important as any of them. Do not let their grandiose attitude, appearance, or the glitter of these offices influence you. With respect toward each human, including ourselves, we can claim and demand anything, especially our rights."

Saying this, Jorge asked everyone to get off the busses and to enter the legislative chambers, adhering to the instructions of the officers in charge, taking their seats in the designated space. He encouraged them to stay poised and sure of themselves, remembering that each one was a citizen with absolute rights and power according to the laws.

During the weeks prior to the presentation, the committee had prepared a strong fight, sending hundreds of informative bulletins and press releases to the media, consistently detailing without a doubt each aspect of the situation and the particulars that impelled them to action, the inaction of the pertinent institutions, and the obvious consequences of maintaining the situation. To the surprise of all attendees, the local and state media, including a couple of international outfits advocating the rights of minors, were in attendance. The politicians were livid, unsuccessfully trying to control damage before the events in Alborde turned out to be national news, ruining their political ambitions.

Alborde Rehabilitation Project executive committee members stood up one by one, doing their part in the presentation. Fello explained how they reached the conclusion that they would have to take matters into their own hands to stop the deterioration of their town. Narciso Rodriguez and Toribio Martinez spoke about the different problems damaging Alborde as direct result of their citizens' exodus during more than eight months each year. Manuel Dominguez eloquently exposed how their youth had to drop out before reaching middle school, sentencing themselves to be day laborers in the fields for the rest of their lives. Domingo Garcia talked about the health issues of these children who did not receive the appropriate immunization, much less medical assistance when facing sickness, given the financial conditions of the migrants. Silvano Méndez spoke about the economic impact of emigration, surprising the attendees with his intrinsic knowledge of the issue and socioeconomic policies. Each one of the aspects of the presentation was discussed, inciting impassioned debates, especially regarding the urgency of the request for a boarding home and special school for Alborde's youth. The presentations were frequently interrupted by waves of applause from the audience. Finally, Jorge took the podium.

"Honorable President of the House, with deepest respect I bring to the attention of this assembly that according to our National Laws for Rights of Minors, the second article of the general principle states that: 'In the application of the present Law, the supreme interest of the minors will take precedence over any other legitimate interest that could concur. Likewise, as many measures as may be adopted under the present Law, it should be of an educational nature'. For many years, Alborde's minors have been condemned to transitory labor work, relinquishing the opportunity for a formal education enjoyed by the majority of the children of this nation, what constitutes massive discrimination of this group of forgotten citizens.'"

Jorge kept defending each argument, one by one, advocating the laws that covered the citizens of this nation and that, due to lack of knowledge about their rights and to some extent carelessness, Alborde's citizens hadn't claimed before.

"The moment to compensate the innocent who unjustly suffered from our carelessness and negligence has come. The future of our youth is in your hands, and this organization has the civic and moral right to make effective the existing laws, making use of all valid and pertinent means of retribution and compensation. From now on, not even a single youngster in Alborde remains condemned to be left behind or to live in ignorance. We have paid too high a price for our inertia. We want our children to achieve the academic level that is owed to them so that they may have the means in our town to develop their vocation, no matter what field they aspire to be proficient in, so when they reach adulthood they may be capable of enjoying with dignity the fruit of their labor, bestowing it upon their children and their children's children.

"And consequently, to make this feasible, we need to institute a boarding home for young children, a vocational school, and sources of work so that their parents don't have to leave Alborde to earn their family's sustenance, wandering from town to town. Our laws clearly establish the principles governing administrative actions. Article two of the law also states, 'The public administrations will facilitate to the minors adequate assistance in the exercise of their rights. Policies will be established to rectify social inequalities. In every case, the essential content of the rights of minors will not be able to remain affected for lack of basic social resources. In the scope of its jurisdiction, integral politics directed to the development of the minors will be articulated through the appropriate means, especially as it concerns the rights enumerated in this law. Public administrations will maintain the adequate regulation and supervision of spaces, locations, and services, in which children habitually stay, and to their sanitary and physical environmental conditions, the related human resources, and educational projects, the participation of minors, and other conditions that contribute to assure their rights. The minors have the right to receive from public administrations the adequate assistance for the effective exercise of their rights and the guarantee of respect of said rights.'

"Finally, to consolidate our request, I summon the principles that govern the action of the public powers: (1) The supremacy entailed in the interests of minors. (2) The importance of maintaining the minors in the familiar environment of origin, unless it is not in his or her best interest. (3) The social and family integration of the minor. (4) Prevention of all those situations that can damage personal development of the minor. (5) Sensitize the population to confront situations of defenselessness in minors. (6) Promote social participation and solidarity. (7) Impartial objectivity and judicial security of protective actions, guaranteeing the collegiate and interdisciplinary character in the implementation of measures.

"The measures upon which minors are counting to facilitate the exercise of their rights are well defined and protected under the same legislation: (1) To request the protection and guardianship from the appropriate public authorities. (2) To call the attorney general office's attention to situations considered threatening to their rights in order to promote the appropriate actions. (3) To present its complaints to the public defender, to such end, an adjunct of said institution will be permanently assigned to resolve matters related to the well-being of minors. (4) To request the available social resources from the public administrations.

"Ladies and gentlemen, under the protection of our national laws for the protection of minors we, the citizens of Alborde, have come before you to demand the rights of our minors, shamefully neglected for such a long time."

At that moment, the house was filled with thunderous expressions of support and applauses.

After Jorge's colossal defense, citing the multiple legal provisions that protected their petition and that obligated the legislative body to listen and to act immediately in order to stop the detrimental path the welfare of those children had taken for such a long time, each one of the items was unanimously accepted and finally officially recorded.

It was not known if their success came about by the sheer record number of citizens that attended the session to expose the problem and to pressure their representatives to action or if the politicians finally saw the situation under the magnifying glass of the mass media present during the entire process; what was known for certain was that the delegates' visit initiated a series of positive events for Alborde's youth and later for the youth of the entire country.

Once the session ended, television cameras and reporters besieged the members of Alborde Rehabilitation Project, wanting to ask a thousand questions, asking for formal statements, specific information about the members, and inquiring about special interests. The international media was looking for human interest stories, and they had surely found one! The war against bureaucracy and complacency had started, and the citizens of Alborde were leading the pack.

Since they traveled most of the afternoon, they did not see the evening news in the capital or the local stories in Alborde; however, they heard that Alborde occupied a prominent place in that evening's national radio and television news, reading the front pages in newspapers and magazines the following day.

Filled with anticipation and excitement, Susana and the girls were waiting for the busses in the park, dying to know every detail of the presentation. Susana had prepared a very special dinner to welcome the men of the Narvaez family with honors. They were with a group of people that gathered in the plaza to wait for the presenters. They kept on making speculative comments among themselves, especially questioning the effectiveness of the presentation and whether the efforts had been in vain, as was expected of the political process based on their past local experiences. The afternoon sun was beginning to set when they saw the busses rapidly advancing on Main Street. Sofia started to leap joyfully.

"Here they come; they are here, Mom! What is the surprise you have for them??"

"You are going to find out during dinner like everyone else."

"That's not fair. Why can't you tell me a little bit? Come on, Mom, come on."

"Come, let's say hello to your dad, Grandpa Fello, and your brother."

The travelers started to step off the bus, bearing smiling faces, like champions from a national tournament. They moved unhurriedly, prolonging the emotions of their short trip. A new sense of community was noticeable among the members of that group of people that now had a glimpse of some sort of light in a future completely uncertain only a few weeks ago, when instead of activists they had been a group of citizens forgotten by their representatives, a group of citizens living mediocre lives oblivious to their environment.

In no uncertain terms, the group now understood the meaning of the expression "to take matters in your own hands" and started to implement it practically and effectively. They were called to action and bravely responded to the call, initiating a life transformation that infiltrated every aspect of their lives, affecting their beliefs, thoughts, and emotions.

A miracle had gradually transformed the core of Susana's family during the past few months as a direct answer to her prayers, constant prayers that had turned into litany while she completed her daily house chores and each day after lunch and when she stayed at home by herself while the children participated in extracurricular activities late in the day. She was now enjoying the family she had dreamed of building with Jorge when they first met, and she was profoundly grateful. Susana wanted to gather Jorge's three children that evening to let them enjoy the new Fello and the transformed Jorge. She invited her in-laws, Paloma and Maria, to have dinner at their house to celebrate the wonderful events surrounding the family.

Paloma, Jorge's second sister, was going with her daughters, Lorena and Luisa, because Bernardo, her husband, was out of town that week; although he visited them each time he could, he was temporarily living in a city some six hours away. Like the majority of the Alborde's citizens, Bernardo had to look for employment out of town, but unlike the migrant workers, he had a high-paying job as manager of an agricultural food processing plant that allowed him a great deal of mobility and schedule flexibility, making it possible for him to visit Paloma and the girls on weekends a couple of times a month. Although Bernardo had ample agricultural land in Alborde, for economic reasons, they had decided it was convenient to accept the job offer in the processing plant, something that aside from being a great line in his resume, gave them a good salary with opportunity to save some money to finish the reconstruction of the old house they occupied in the heart of downtown. Even though Paloma and Bernardo didn't want to live separately, they had reached the conclusion that temporary separation was worth the try; it was convenient and logical for several reasons: staying with the girls in Alborde, Paloma had the company of Mercedes, Bernardo's sister, who lived with them since they moved to Alborde. They also could count on the support of Paloma's immediate family, but what they considered most important was that their little girls could enjoy the interaction with their extended family, sharing their daily lives with their uncles and aunts, their cousins, and the grandfather, and maintain continuity in their education. But if they moved their family to the city to accompany Bernardo, they would be obligated to abandon remodeling their house and commit to the financial burden of an expensive rental agreement for five people. Above all, they would have to uproot the girls to live in an industrial city of tumultuous environment, away from the warmth of the extended family, and this was not acceptable for the couple. They had concluded that if they committed to sacrifice themselves and lived separated for two years at most, they would be able to finish their home construction project and pay for all the debts contracted since their marriage, including the modest vehicles they used for transportation. With a little planning, once they had paid off all their debts, they would be able to live without worries from the fruit of their own land. Although Paloma and Bernardo were married two years after Jorge, they postponed having children until after they had finished their respective postgraduate education, which was the reason why Lorena was only Sofia's age and Luisa was short of two years of age. They had met in college, and besides husband and wife, they were classmates and best friends. Bernardo received his degree in industrial engineering, and Paloma, even though her true vocation was teaching, opted for a degree in marketing and public relations to form a power couple of complementary professions.

Maria, Fello's youngest child, was married to Ramón Gutiérrez; they had been classmates since kindergarten and made a charming couple. Ramón was compassionate and committed, perhaps because he had been raised by his maternal grandparents, who instilled in the little boy an immeasurable sense of responsibility. His mother died bringing him into the world due to complications during labor. His father, Hernán Gutiérrez, was significantly affected by the death of his young wife, and after a year of bereavement and clinical depression, he left Alborde, looking for healing and the chance to rebuild his broken life in some other town, away from the bittersweet memories that tortured him, leaving Ramón under the care of the maternal family. Even though Hernán loved his little son, he could not get emotionally close to him; from the day he was born, his grandparents were the only parents Ramón ever knew. He saw Hernán as a nice and caring rich uncle who supported the family and appeared in his life once or twice per year, bringing lots of presents. Hernán took care of all of Ramón's needs until he turned eighteen years old. On the day of his eighteenth birthday, Hernán went to Alborde to celebrate the occasion as he had done every year and to introduce Ramón to a beautiful woman who was accompanying him, asking his son for his blessing of the relationship.

"Son, I know I haven't been the best of fathers, but since the day you were born, I did not want to dedicate myself to anyone in the world in honor of the memory of your mother. I only wanted to live for her and for you. Today you become an adult before the laws of men. With a mixture of sadness and joy, I started to wait for this day to start my life anew. I want you to meet Mariela and rejoice with me as I try to rebuild my life with a woman. In my heart no one can replace your mother; I am not looking for a replacement. I need a partner, and I want you to support me as a friend. Perhaps I can be a better friend than what I have been as a father."

Hernán's eyes swelled with tears, and he quickly embraced his son, waiting for some sign of approval; Ramón returned the embrace, holding on to his father tightly and prolonging the moment while saying, "Dad, you did the best you could and knew how. Although I often wished you had lived here, I always felt responsible for your absence and for Mom's death. My grandparents tirelessly took care of all my needs, and thanks to you we were never short of anything in our home. Thanks to you, there was overabundance at our table.

"Dad, today I want to thank you for all you did for us, the grandparents respect you and appreciate you, and they always say the best things about you. I want you to be happy; it's time for you to find happiness. Mariela, you have found a great man, a human being with a huge heart and superior sense of duty, who has been known to give and provide for us beyond all expectations, above and beyond the call of duty, with priceless generosity."

Ramón spent his entire eighteenth birthday with Hernán and Mariela; they left before nightfall under a torrential rain that prevented visibility beyond one meter.

Although they kept in touch via mail, through letters interchanged between Alborde and many parts of the world, Ramón didn't see Hernán again for a period of over four years. They met again when Ramón received the news that he had a half brother, and Ramón decided to go and meet him during one of Hernán's family trips to the country.

Hernán told Ramón that the arrival of Pablo, his second son, had made him understand even more so his reprehensible and unjustifiable behavior during his childhood, having allowed him to grow up without the warmth of a father, and although he appreciated all the efforts his maternal grandparents made, he remained remorseful and heartbroken. Although it was somewhat late, he still wanted to be influential in the life of his firstborn.

In turn, seeing a child so physically similar to him was stunning and captivating for Ramón, leaving him with the urge to form his own family as soon as he was able to.

Ramón proposed to María immediately after returning to Alborde. It was a Sunday afternoon when Fello and Elena traditionally gathered their family for Sunday meals at their home in the country after attending the eleven thirty mass. Ramón entered the house holding María's hand, both wearing a smile from ear to ear.

Ramon had softly whispered to María during the service that after Sunday mass he wanted to ask her parents for permission to marry her. María had turned apple red and could hardly control the impulse to shout her happiness in the middle of liturgy. When they left the church in a hurry, running like children, they embraced and kissed right in front of the congregation.

They were very young, only twenty-two, both without a profession, savings, or a house.

Fello and Elena were touched when the young couple told them about their wedding plans, reminiscing about their own marriage proposal, and they both kissed Ramón on his forehead with tenderness. They knew this boy well and welcomed the news with delight; they couldn't ask for a better candidate for their daughter. Ramón and María made a beautiful couple; they were magnificent human beings—innocent and overflowing with dreams. They were both straightforward and transparent, longing to pour their love each into the other, to form a home to shelter their new family, just like Fello and Elena's family, who always served as role model to Ramón.

Ramón and María never even considered the possibility of leaving their town, and when Fello asked him how he planned to support his new family, Ramón answered optimistically that he would find a good job in town. To everyone's surprise, Ramón applied to the police academy and was accepted, receiving his certificate with honors in record time: less than six months. It was exactly a year after that Sunday when he received the permanent job offer in Alborde's municipal government police department, and then they decided to celebrate their marriage as soon as possible.

Ramón conveyed the news of his marriage to Hernán, asking him to be the best man in the ceremony. Hernán was euphoric and arrived for the wedding preparations with ample time to spend with his son; after the wedding, he gave Ramón a thick white envelope as his wedding gift that, to the couple's amazement, contained the property title for the house Hernán had shared with Rosa before she gave birth to Ramón.

The house had been closed for over twenty years. It was a beautiful house, completely furnished and newly refurbished just for the newlyweds; this allowed the couple to get a head start on their new life together.

Hernán became benefactor of the couple, loyal friend, and confidant, and little Pablo found in Ramón a mixture between brother, authority, and role model. Since he joined the police academy, Ramón embodied the symbol of local authority, the only paid policeman in Alborde for a long time, loved and respected by all, receiving innumerable citations for his impeccable service to the citizens and his city.

They wanted to have children immediately, and their two girls, Isabel and Cristina, were contemporaneous with Alicia, Sofia, and Lorena. The five little cousins grew up more like sisters, very close to one another. Together, they attended school and all extracurricular activities; everyone in town regarded them as fingers of the same hand. And since they were so well educated and respectful toward their elders, they were invited to all social activities in town, according to their ages. The little girls sang, danced, and recited poems like angels; the quintet had turned into a joyful bunch, amusing attendees of the get-togethers of friends and family.

That evening, the entire Narváez family was fully assembled; Susana had prepared a special dinner and the favorite appetizers of each one of the members of the family, including prunes wrapped in bacon slices, Serrano ham, deviled eggs, salmon cocktail sandwiches, and meat turnovers.

The girls sat on the floor, near the coffee table displaying the appetizers, playing checkers and building towers with the dominoes, every so often asking politely for permission to serve themselves from the trays of goodies displayed on the table.

Paloma, María, and Susana were passing little Luisa from one set of arms to another while laughing at the gestures the little one made as the aunts sang nursery rhymes, teaching her how to identify the different parts of the body to the rhythm of the songs. Luisa's favorite song was the flight of Tom Thumb, erupting in a contagious laughter as she listened to the cacophonous sounds made by the adults upon singing the chorus of the rhyme.

Jorge was sitting in the living room surrounded by Fello, Juan, and Ramón, who were entranced, listening to the stories of collisions with politicians and bureaucrats he had experienced during his career in the capital. The adults drank happily, raising the wine glasses, serially toasting to the health of this or that person and in celebration of anything worth mentioning.

Before concluding the evening, Ramón had reiterated his devotion to the group more than a dozen times, contributing fresh ideas while at the same time asking for guidance on how to be of service to the organization in the most effective manner, but not before repeatedly expressing his point of view, indicating what he considered to be the best way to carry out the activities of the new committee. He couldn't stop praising Juan, asking Jorge to illustrate in detail the course of events, recounting the contribution of his nephew.

After listening thoughtfully, Ramón expressed how much he would like to have his brother Pablo exposed to these types of activities, adding that what was lacking in Alborde was more adolescents with the same service vocation and aptitudes as Juan. He raised his wine glass again, this time to the health of his nephew. Susana stood up, taking advantage of the moment and offered a toast, saying, "Thanks, Ramón. I know your words are sincere, straight from your heart; Jorge and I, the entire family, is very proud of Juan and all of our children, proud of the integrity of this group, Fello's children and spouses, product of Fello and Elena's love and efforts. That is why I want to share with this beautiful family that generously welcomed me with open arms so long ago that Jorge and I are expecting a new child."

Jorge was speechless; he leaped from one end of the room to the other to embrace and kiss Susana, who gently pulled a little from him to say that she was four months into the pregnancy and that she had the feeling it was going to be another boy who was going to bear the name of his grandfather. Everyone started to speak at the same time, and the room was filled with delight.

The next morning, the front page of the newspaper, *The Nation*, ran two pictures of Alborde's delegation taken during the presentation at the house of representatives, with the accompanying article detailing each step of the journey taken by Alborde's citizens, praising the initiative and publicly supporting the project as a national model.

THE FIRST YOUTH
HOME IN ALBORDE

The members of the executive committee felt somewhat let down by the reaction of the majority of migrant parents as many of them received the letter about the project unenthusiastically and, surprisingly, insinuated that the venture was not altruistic, that there were political interests behind the proposal for reform and even behind the creation a committee for Alborde's rehabilitation.

The members of the group, who by then operated with the warmth and solidarity of a brotherhood, decided not to be discouraged in their efforts, allowing to the end of the migrating season when migrant parents could observe firsthand upon return what they had planned and done as a committee.

Initially, only Antonio and José returned to Alborde to stay after the Holy Week; they were the first youngsters living in Alborde's Youth Home under the care of their grandparents, following the steps prescribed in the program. This small event brought great joy to the elders in town, seeing the first sign of success for their efforts in the decisions of these adolescents and the vote of confidence of their parents.

Antonio and José were the ones who conveyed to the group the comments made by many parents and the worries and concerns a few expressed about alleged political implications of the project. The thought was absurd. How could anyone smear the intentions of a young man who valiantly went out of his way to recruit volunteers to improve the conditions of the youth in his town?

Grandpa Fello spoke with Jorge about this issue. Jorge assured him everything was going to take a positive turn when the laborers were able to observe with their own eyes how well they had planned and conceived every aspect of the project; after all, they were doing exactly what any concerned parents should, and once they were able to corroborate that local and state authorities were directly involved in the project, they would be ready to participate, putting to rest any suspicion of ill faith, extricating the committee from any negative political implications.

They had agreed to start working according to the outlined plan, be it with one child or with fifty. Each group leader had been working with perseverance to create the rules of their respective committee following the overall development plan.

One of the most impacting projects, due to its ample reach and influence, was the creation of a manual for successful relations designed by the Committee for Educational Development and Social Well-being under the directive of Narciso Rodriguez. This committee attracted and united a group of people of great education and impeccable manners, who after carefully analyzing the situation of the youngsters, realized that given the social and economic circumstances of the migrants, no one had taken the time to provide these children with the elementary tools for their moral, social, and civic development.

Hence the idea was born to create the prototype of a manual to institute a uniform code of conduct for the Youth Homes in Alborde. That manual was intended to prevent embarrassing situations for the participants, their parents, and volunteer tutors. They attempted to cover different aspects of life based on the personal experiences of the members of the committee, and unanimously agreed on contracting a professional expert from the big city to edit their work and develop a perfect manual when they raised sufficient funds.

The last page of the manual was a form containing the basic elements of a formal contract between the adolescent and the Committee for Rehabilitation of Alborde, delineating line by line the obligations contracted and the rights of each participant, with ample space to make notations specific to each individual.

The form had to be signed by each participant resident, the parents, and the tutor, clarifying each applicable point. With the individual's signature, each youngster made a commitment to accept the stated rules of the home and to live in Alborde under the auspices of the committee, represented by the tutor.

It was clear that each youngster was obligated to obey the rules established by the manual and accepted the penalties imposed for lack of adherence to his or her duties.

The manual encompassed what was identified as "rules for good living" based in three areas of responsibility for each child: personal, home community, and civil society.

CONTENT

Personal integrity
Good manners
Responsibility: Obey the norms
Face the consequences of our actions
Nurture the spirit of cooperation
Commitment to truth and its consequences
Definition of reward and punishment
List of duties and daily responsibilities:
Personal
Home
School
The chart and how it works
Personal Behavior Agreement signed by minor and tutor

I Rules for good living: A guide to achieving success based on personal integrity, good manners, and respect for others.

While staying in someone else's home, be it your parents, tutors, or any hosts (visiting or temporary living), you have to know how to respect and obey the rules and norms of said home.

Practicing respect is the simplest way of getting along with others.

No one has the right to impose norms and rules in someone else's place. You must be in control of your emotions and be mindful of the following areas of your life:

Personal:
Personal cleanliness and tidiness
Disciplined study and intellectual enrichment
Norms of conduction and interpersonal relationships
Important qualities in interpersonal relationships:
Respect above all
Obedience to established authority
Compliance with laws and duties
Gratitude
Adherence to moral rules
Adherence civic rules
Community at home:
Self-respect
Respect for family members
Respect for the personal space and property of others
Gratefulness; show appreciation for what is given to you, demonstrate through your actions your appreciation to parents, protectors, tutors, and others
Obey the rules established at home
Comply with your individual obligations at home and in the community
Trust: gain it and guard it like a valuable gift.

Civil Society:
Study and understand your moral and civic duties
Respect the laws and social norms that govern the citizenry;
they have been instituted to establish order in society
Develop a sense of community

THE IMPORTANCE OF TIME

Each person has a personal account that makes us equal, independent of social status, personal wealth, religion, or sex. That account is renewed every day with a unique and irreplaceable treasure: twenty-four hours.

Some squander their time without appreciation; others use it to elevate their spirit and cultivate their intellect, which is wealth that no one can take away.

PRACTICAL DISTRIBUTION OF TIME

Eight hours to sleep
Eight hours to study
Eight hours for everything else

PERSONAL INTEGRITY

- Live with honor and honor the truth; it is the policy of this organization. Everyone must commit to always tell the truth.

- To lie is a major offense, and it is not permitted in Alborde's Youth Homes. Lies will be subject to punishment, as determined by consensus inside the group family nucleus under the direction of each tutor.

- An honor system will be maintained; each person is expected to accept the responsibility of following the rules.

- When an inadequate behavior or disobedience to the rules is observed, each person is expected to demand reparation from the transgressor. If the situation is not resolved, the case must be brought to the tutor in charge.

- All residents are subject to a fixed schedule of activities and are fully responsible for their adherence.

- Everyone is expected to treat others as courteously as one would want to be treated, using please and thank you in his or her interactions.

- Respect the privacy of others, including their personal space.

- Do not interrupt or eavesdrop on private conversations.

- Do not pry, snoop, or rummage around the private property or space of others, much less take advantage of their absence.

- Respect the order established in the home, including the placement of furniture and other objects of common use.

- Do not change the placement of anything without consulting the person or tutor in charge.

- Adhere to the schedules established for eating, study, recreation, and collaboration.

PERSONAL HYGIENE

- The effects of personal hygiene such as toothbrushes, combs, deodorants, and other products used directly on the body should not be shared.

- Try not to yawn in public, and if you must, discretely cover your mouth.

- Cover your mouth to sneeze.

- Do not pick your nose in public. If you need to clean your nose, use a handkerchief.

- Do not put your fingers in your mouth while in public view. Saliva transmits bacteria. Besides, it is unpleasant to see.

- We live in a close community. Each resident must maintain personal hygiene, take daily showers, and use deodorant so as not to become the source of offensive odors.

- Brush your teeth upon rising and after each meal.

- As a courtesy to others, be mindful of your breath; maintain good oral hygiene.

- Dress according to the occasion without provocation or aimlessly trying to get attention.

- Wear clean clothes. When you reuse clothing, you will smell bad.

- Change and wash your underwear every day; you can do it as you take your bath. In our homes, each one is responsible for maintaining his or her underwear clean; it does not go to the communal laundry.

- Each home will establish their common laundry policy as a collective chore.

- Be modest; do not appear without a shirt or in underwear.

- Do not get undressed in front of others; it is impolite and disrespectful.

- Wear appropriate clothing in the correct size. Oversized clothing and falling pants that reveal the underwear and behind only makes you look like a convict.

- It is distasteful to show your underwear; make sure your underwear remains under your regular clothing.

- Do not write on your skin or make notes on your hands or other parts of your body.

INTERACTIONS WITH OTHERS

1. Treat others with the same courtesy with which you want to be treated.

2. Be gentle and kind; do not use abrupt or angry gestures unnecessarily.

3. Speak the appropriate greetings when arriving at any place, and say good-bye before leaving, especially to the adults in charge.

4. Men should not wear hats inside a home; it is not appropriate.

5. Do not push your friends or use violent interactions, much less when you are upset. Remember that rough games lead to brawls.

6. Do not make up gossip or speak ill of others; learn how to reject inappropriate comments and stop gossipers. Once something is said, it cannot be taken back.

7. Be responsible for what you say; adherence to the truth is the best policy in life.

8. If you have said something incorrectly, responsibly admit you said it, ask for forgiveness, and move on.

9. Do not use pejoratives or offend your housemates unnecessarily.

10. Do not poke fun at others or stare at those with physical impairments or visible imperfections.

11. Identify yourself when calling on the telephone before asking for the person you want to speak with. For example: "Good evening, this is so-and-so. May I speak with so-and-so?"

12. Always address your elders as mister or miss; never call them by their first names; it is disrespectful.

13. When arriving at any place, especially to a private home, speak your greetings and introduce yourself with your name so they will remember you.

14. Be pleasant when you are introduced to others, saying, "It's a pleasure meeting you. My name is so-and-so" or "How are you? My name is so-and-so."

15. Never arrive to any place, especially a home, while chewing gum or eating.

16. Never chew gum inside (home, school, church, office) or talk while chewing.

17. Always act tactfully and politely; use diplomacy even in disagreeable situations. You never know when you might have to take back your words.

18. Learn to ask for forgiveness when you make a mistake or as soon as you notice your offense.

19. Be courteous in public places.

20. Respect the queue; never try to cut in front of others.

21. Do not praise yourself; it is unpleasant and inappropriate.

22. Never brag about your possessions, much less in front of those who have less.

23. Do not spit or blow your nose in front of others. If you must, separate yourself from the group and do it using your handkerchief or disposable napkins.

24. Do not put trash outside the proper container, especially candy wrappers and food.

25. Do not eat while walking, much less inside a home or establishment.

26. Do not raise your voice in public; keep your conversations privately without bothering or invading the space of others.

TABLE MANNERS

1. Wash your hands before eating.

2. Wait until everyone is sitting at the table before serving yourself, and if it is a buffet, wait until all

those sitting at your table arrive before beginning to eat your food.

3. Use your silverware appropriately. Do not lick them, wave them, like a wand, or use them to point at other people or things.

4. At the table, do not reach over, placing your arms over other people's plate. Politely ask someone to pass the dish to you.

5. Place the napkin on your lap before starting to eat.

6. Serve yourself small portions in consideration of your mealtime companions.

7. Place in your mouth small amounts of food so that you are able to chew with your mouth closed.

8. Do not serve yourself more than what you are going to eat; do not waste food. Always think about others.

9. Never use the fork with which you are eating to serve yourself from the serving dish or help yourself from someone else's plate.

10. Never use your fingers to serve food; use the appropriate serving tools.

11. Eat with your mouth closed; do not show what you are chewing or stick out your tongue.

12. Do not make unnecessary chewing and slurping noises, especially when having soup and hot portions.

13. Do not eat from someone else's plate unless specifically offered.

14. Do not speak with a mouth full of food.

15. Do not burp at the table.

16. Do not pick or blow your nose at the table.

17. Do not eat with your hands.

18. Use your napkin only to wipe your mouth, not to blow your nose or wipe other parts of your face.

19. Eat carefully; do not spill food on the table and surrounding areas.

20. Do not lick your fingers or place them in your mouth while eating.

21. If you have food trapped between your teeth, get a toothpick and discretely cover your mouth with one hand while using the other to extract the food with the toothpick. If you are not successful, excuse yourself from the table to do it privately.

22. When you ask for something at the table, always remember to say please and thank you.

23. When eating in a public place, keep your conversation to a low voice to avoid bothering other guests.

24. When you are invited to eat at a restaurant, never order the most expensive or largest dish; it is not polite, unless you are going to pick up the tab.

25. When finished, be gracious and thank the hosts who invited you and whoever paid the bill.

INVITATIONS

1. A polite person always waits to be invited to any event, including birthdays, weddings, meals, celebrations, etc.; never invite yourself to any private event.

2. Always consult with the adult in charge before inviting anyone to the house. Each tutor designates and plans for visiting times.

3. When receiving an invitation, always consult with your tutor before accepting, so he/she can coordinate all details with the inviting adults.

4. After attending an event, do not forget to thank the hosts for kindly inviting you.

5. If the gathering had been held in your honor, you must send a written thank-you note to the organizers and hosts.

6. When you are a visitor, respect the specific norms and rules of each place.

7. Respect the adults and their personal space.

8. When visiting someone else's home, do not change anything around, especially what is not yours.

9. When you leave the location of your hosts, you must leave things exactly as you found them, if not in better condition.

RESPONSIBILITY: OBEY THE RULES

According to Webster's Dictionary, responsibility is a noun defined as: The quality or state of being responsible. A moral, legal, or mental accountability. Reliability, trustworthiness. Something for which one is responsible: burden. A capacity existent in every person, the right to recognize and accept the consequences of an act freely executed.

Responsibility is the capacity of each individual to make himself responsible for his actions, and to know how to gracefully face the consequences of his actions.

If there is anything truly magnificent about a human being, it is his capacity to give up his own individual freedom to obey the norms established to rule and benefit the society in which he lives.

Only a free man is capable of submitting to the laws because we can only give what we truly possess, and only those of us who own our freedom can agree to suppress our individual actions for the good of society.

We consider Alborde's youth individuals capable of obeying the rules prescribed for the most advantageous operations of their homes because these youngsters have made a commitment to personal success, understanding the sacrifices made by their parents in order to achieve a sustainable situation for their own personal benefit and their social, intellectual, and physical growth.

This manual has been compiled as a living and evolving document to help in the order, discipline, and success of these homes. The enhancement and enforcement of these rules is left to the discretion of each tutor, in hopes that they will be useful tools in the development of each one of the participants, starting foremost with the sense of responsibility of Alborde's youth.

FACING THE CONSEQUENCES OF OUR ACTIONS

Each decision made catapults us to a definite result, be it by executing a well-studied strategy or by abstaining from taking action.

With the intention of nourishing democratic values in each home, structured family reunions will take place every week to encourage the participation of its members in the continual edification and integration of each family.

Everyone will have the opportunity to freely express his or her thoughts and opinions without fear of repercussion, stimulating constructive criticism and identifying any changes necessary within the group.

The goal is to cultivate the spirit of cooperation with active and sincere participation of all members, aspiring to achieve a small democratic society in each home where the values and ambitions of the group are reflected and expressed: respect, individual rights, commitment to society, to truth, to justice, to cooperation, to peace, to harmony, and to the right of each person to the opportunity for well-being and prosperity.

Every home will keep a board with the names of each member of the family in the first column; the following columns will have a heading with the weekly responsibilities of each member of the family. The tutor in charge will note in the corresponding boxes the completion of each task, using a system of colored dots: Green equals completion; yellow equals unsatisfactory completion; red equals failure. These dots translate into a system of rewards and punishments. The tutor will keep an account of the system score, making each youngster responsible for his or her actions.

The green dots are a sign of optimal completion of tasks and adherence to the norms of the group. There is an opportunity to accumulate extra points for initiatives above and beyond the call of duty. The yellow dots are used to reveal unsatisfactory completion of a task and conflicting or disagreeable behavior that is not completely contrary to the norms, and the red dots reflect an unfinished designated task and failure to comply with the rules and regulations of the group.

The tutor will administer the distribution of points at his discretion, using additional points to reflect behavior as each situation merits.

Each Friday night, during the family get-together, each person will receive the final tally with its corresponding rewards or punishments according to his or her actions during the week.

Examples of punishments at the tutor's discretion: community work inside or outside the home, limits on leisure time, grounding, and other measures according to the severity of each case.

Example of rewards at the tutor's discretion: tickets to movies and other events, outings, and gifts.

These points are cumulative; each person can invalidate a red dot with five green dots or erase five yellow dots with one a green dot.

The point system is an honor system with the intention of nurturing a sense of responsibility without the need for tutors to be constantly vigilant.

A human being without honor is deficient in every aspect of his or her life; honesty, straightforwardness, loyalty, morality, and soundness of character are virtues that develop the conscience and define the character quality of the individual, not wealth or fame.

When a person takes a critical look at himself in the mirror, confronting flaws and virtues, only those who have lived with honor and integrity can peacefully accept what they see.

NOURISH THE SPIRIT OF COOPERATION

To live in an organized society is a privilege, not a right. No one has the right to boycott the order democratically established by the majority.

Although we continually witness transgressions against public order, especially in bigger cities, the violation to the right of others and the propensity toward disorderly conduct are not acceptable.

Unfortunately, in today's society we see a tendency toward abandon and lack of integrity, pernicious to the human spirit. Values are in decline and out of fashion, but if we don't act now in favor of cooperation and respect, there are going to be repercussions for generations to come. Our children's children will have to live with a mediocrity born out of permissiveness, total lack of discipline, disorder, and a self-centered vision of life.

Everyone should contribute toward having the right to enjoy the common benefits within reach, be it in our family nucleus, at school, at work, or in society in general.

Only a small child who has not developed the ability to contribute has the right to enjoy benefits and care without the obligation to give back and collaborate toward the common good, but even that child must be disciplined for order to prevail.

If we start from this foundation, we can practically ensure we will live in peace and harmony and we will attain the success we yearn for.

Hence, we exhort our youth to become an integral part of the nucleus that serves them as family in the absence of their parents; to become productive members of society, collaborating in the optimal functioning of the homes in the performance of daily chores, in the revision and elaboration of the code of conduct, in the implementation of those rules for high-quality living; overall, to feel responsible and useful in the core of their nucleus and in society; to be willing to ask oneself, "How can I serve others?" instead of, "How can I serve myself from others?"

COMMITMENT TO TRUTH
AND ITS CONSEQUENCES

The commitment to truth is liberating. If we reflect on the waste of time and energy spent on covering up a lie, we would understand how easy it is to deal with the truth from the onset of events, confronting the consequences we must rightfully face.

Truth is expected in each youth home in Alborde. It does not matter how embarrassing the consequences might appear; each tutor expects to deal with the truth and only the truth. Each resident can count on the unconditional support of the nucleus as long as he or she is telling the truth.

The person who lies or helps others lie will be severely punished. Sanctions will be imposed according to each individual case. At the third failure to comply, the young person will be ordered to appear before the Committee for Social Wellness, which will then dictate the corresponding punishment for the actions. The maximum penalty is loss of the right to residency in the youth home.

DEFINITION OF REWARD
AND PUNISHMENT

The norms outlined in the manual are subject to revision and modification in a democratic fashion. Disobedience to each of these norms has a corresponding punishment.

Both punishments and rewards for good behavior are based on common sense and the customs of each institution.

The severity of the punishment is directly related to the significance of the offense. The exact nature of the reward or penalty will depend on each tutor.

Any disagreement not resolved within the home can be submitted to the Arbitration Committee.

LIST OF CHORES AND DAILY RESPONSIBILITIES

Each youth will be responsible for completing his personal obligations and assigned home chores. The home chores are rotating household tasks to be assigned to each participant each week.

- Personal
- Personal hygiene
- Maintenance of personal space
- Cleaning and organize clothing and shoes
- Observance of designated schedules
- Home
- General cleanliness
- Order
- Dusting
- Floor cleaning
- Window and door cleaning
- Communal laundry
- Yard cleaning and maintenance
- Kitchen duties
- Dining room duties
- Dish washing
- Bathroom cleaning
- School

- Punctual attendance

- Maintenance of school uniforms

- Homework

- Extracurricular activities

List of Personal Objects and Provisions
- Toothpaste and brush

- Bath soap

- Shower cap

- Shampoo and conditioner

- Comb and brush

- Shaving implement

- Storage case for toiletries

- Disposable sanitary napkins

- First aid kit, including gauze, cotton, bandages, alcohol, hydrogen peroxide, aspirin, and prescription medicine as per house physician, if needed.

- Seven pairs of underwear

- A set of towels

- Two pairs of uniform pants

- Two dress pants (one black, another light color)

- Two pairs of shorts

- Two belts (one black, one brown)

- Five shirts

- Five t-shirts

- One black jacket

- One uniform jacket

- One winter coat

- One gym uniform
- Seven pairs of dark socks
- Two pairs of sports socks
- One pair of sandals
- One pair of uniform shoes
- One pair of black dress shoes
- One pair of tennis shoes
- Shoe cleaning kit
- One trunk with lock
- One laundry bag
- One umbrella and raincoat
- Permanent cloth marker
- School supplies

Tracking the scoreboard:
Each student has a designated scoreboard with his/her own personal activities. The Tutor keeps track of daily activities and applies the dots earned in each box (green, yellow, red). The final tally is delivered to students on Friday afternoon.

Name: **Date:**

Chore:	Mon	Tue	Wed	Thu	Fri	Sat	Sun	Comments
Personal:	Y/N	Y/N	Y/N	Y/N	Y/N	Y/N	Y/N	
Personal Hygiene								Completed
Maintenance of personal space								
Organization and cleaning of clothing and shoes								
Attention to designated schedules								
Home:								
General maintenance								
Keeping order								
Dusting								
Floor cleaning								
Windows and doors								
General/shared laundry								
Yard maintenance								
Kitchen duties								
Dining room duties								
Dish washing								
Bathrooms and dressing room cleaning								
School								
Punctual Attendance								
Uniform maintenance								
Homework completion								
Extracurricular activities								

CODE OF CONDUCT AGREEMENT

Formal agreement between the _____
family and Alborde's Rehabilitation Committee.

The minor child, _____,
legally authorized by_____,

signing parents, makes a formal commitment to obey the rules established by the youth residence located at _____ _____. And hereby attests to having carefully read this Code of Conduct Manual certifying via the signatures below complete agreement to adhere to the norms described in said document.

By means of this document, the minor will remain under the tutelage of:

_____

_____

Name and signature of the tutor

_____

Name and signature of the minor

_____

_____

Name and signature of the parents

_____

Name and signature of public notary:

_____

Executed in Alborde on the day: _____ of month:_____ year:_____

CC: Parents, Minor, Youth Home Files

Since they had started working as a coherently organized group, life in Alborde had completely changed for everyone. Although they always thought of themselves as inhabitants of a very small town where everyone knew each other, the newly found common goal had turned Alborde's citizens into a functional family.

Fello's home had been completely remodeled; he had used most of his savings for this project, and although no youth was living at the residence so far, he was satisfied with the efforts invested by the group in transforming his house into a home for these children in need. The leaders of the group had agreed that, when the migrant families returned home for the harvest that year, they would take the opportunity to host a series of events to showcase the newly renovated house and to gain the support and agreement of the parents to let their children stay in Alborde to continue their studies uninterrupted.

The Committee for Collection of Food was successfully working to capacity; little by little, they had accumulated a great inventory that had been stored at Silvano's home, next to the grocery warehouse where he worked, taking advantage of their refrigeration system as needed. They had stipulated that each family would need to allocate a small portion of their food budget to slowly build what would later become the pantry for the youth homes until they were able to secure the funding for a designated budget from the state agencies for the protection of minors and others.

The Committee for Educational Development recruited the support of the Salesian Society, well-known for their ability to manage youth, and they became totally responsible for the work of the committee and the academic curriculum of the children. They enjoyed the undivided support of the citizens and full cooperation in the procurement of support and subsidies.

Fundraising efforts expanded; contributions arrived from people of all levels of society, and their financial situation was strengthened with donations flowing from all over the country and the funding commitment of a significant amount of money from an anonymous source with the specific stipulation that the funds be administered by the Salesian Society.

On the other hand, the Committee for Health and Social Services, under the direction of Domingo García, managed to recruit the commitment of a famous retired physician and owner of a chain of health clinics who offered to open a primary health clinic in Alborde, all expenses donated, entirely altruistically for the purpose of providing medical assistance to Alborde's youth three times per week.

The Committee for Educational Development and Social Well-being became one of the most active. They counted on the collaboration of Rita Mendoza, one of the first benefactors of the movement, who, on the condition of anonymity, started to cover the operational expenses of the group and many aspects of the overall care of the returning young men and women.

Rita joined Alborde's Rehabilitation Group two weeks after having heard the details of their project on the radio, the day when the board of directors and the general assembly had made their presentation before the house of representatives. It happened fortuitously. That day, she was engulfed in a terrible depression, at the threshold of letting everything go to pieces. The house-keeper had forgotten the radio tuned to the local news, and Rita listened to it distractedly as background noise, without paying attention at all. Nevertheless, something managed to pique her curiosity when voices started to speak on behalf of the young men and women of Alborde. The precarious situation of these youngsters enthralled her, perhaps recalling her own son and the difficult relationship they had always maintained; the situation had noticeably worsened with the years, especially when he stepped into adolescence. Reflective, she thought that her prob-lems could have been much worse if she hadn't had the financial resources to confront them.

Many hours had passed after she heard the radio broadcast and before she gathered enough strength to find more information about that peculiar group from Alborde. She tuned in to the late afternoon news bulletins on the radio. She wanted to learn more details regarding the situation, but the news stories concentrated on the presentation itself and the responses from politicians. The tenacity of those citizens triumphantly meeting adversity head-on enchanted her, especially because a young man had inspired them. This event made Rita reflect about the course of her own life and the vacuity of her social activities.

That day in particular, she felt a pervasive coldness throughout the house, and it was not a physical coldness—she had a perfectly functioning heating system and appropriate provisions. This was a coldness that penetrated her soul, permeating the perfectly painted walls that exhibited elegant images and exquisite works of art in soft pastels and water colors—her favorite medium—and lovely silver-framed family pictures that beckoned a trip through time.

Rita had spent most of the afternoon sitting in the living room, practically immobile, under several layers of clothing and a thick wool blanket in front of the enormous three-pane window facing the anterior gardens. Ever since her children had moved away to college, she had been living alone, and that day the only sound she wanted to hear was the voices and laughter of her children, yearning for great times long gone and the tender embrace of the innocent babies that inhabited her memories. She missed the children she nurtured with love, giving them all she had. They, in turn, had given meaning to her life; but now as adults they appeared to have abandoned her, absorbed in their own lives, oblivious to the loneliness of their mother. At that moment, under the influence of prescription antidepressants, she was assessing the dimensions of her solitude.

"How had this happened? How can it be possible that someone like me, one who had loved so much, one who had given it all for her children like me, could end up being so lonely and emptyhanded?" she incessantly asked herself in her despondence, and what hurt her the most was that, even though she lived in the same city as her son, he did not care for her more, often completely ignoring her pleas for closeness.

"I would have never abandoned my parents like this. I was always with them, taking care of their needs and wants until they died. Although I don't expect any material things from my children, I cannot live without their affection and emotional support."

Almost a month had passed since her last conversation with Rogelio, and that dialogue had not been a pleasant exchange. Rita had promised herself not to call him again. This time it was Rogelio who had to come asking for forgiveness, as any civilized human would, recognizing his mistakes, his lack of tactfulness, and his indifference toward her.

Rita could not stop wondering where she went wrong in educating Rogelio, and she blamed herself for his character flaws and inability to deal with others in a harmonious way. In spite of all the money spent on psychologists and special treatments, Rogelio didn't exhibit the expected signs of improvement she desperately wanted to see.

"There must be a way to teach this son of mine to value and respect his family. Rogelio treats me with such disrespect! I am tired. I am not willing to continue allowing my son to get away with his unpleasant behavior, treating me like an old rag, even if I have to be alone for the rest of my life."

Torrential rains usually fell in the capital region in the spring. A rhythmic, persistent rain started beating the ground, casting spells on old memories that hurriedly ascended into Rita's consciousness, invading her emotions, frantically infringing on every corner of her life.

Fighting against the narcotic lethargy, she was transported to the instant when her son was born, twenty-five years before. She felt the scent of the birthing room clenched to her nose, reliving the tremble in her hands as she tried to reach her newborn, unable to touch him, hold him, and rock him in her arms. After his birth, he was placed on a cold, sterile table covered by white disposable paper and he cried heartbreakingly. She smiled ironically, thinking that Rogelio had been doing the same since birth: screaming until he got whatever he wanted.

Gonzalo Mendoza was not present for the birth of his son; he was busy, involved with other women. The events of the Mendoza family were public gossip, and although Gonzalo's indiscretions were obvious to everyone else, Rita, in defense of her marriage. was adamant in not inquiring after or openly giving credit to speculations. Gonzalo's absences were humiliating to Rita, especially since she knew he was unfaithful to her, destroying her self-esteem. To mitigate her pain and to forget her own needs, she concentrated on accomplishing her role as a mother, and for a long time she made believe she was happy in the relationship.

Rita came from a Catholic family, where divorce was not a viable option, and that very same religiosity drove Gonzalo to treat her with disdain. Nevertheless, she clung to the conviction that all was possible to those who had faith, and she prayed to God for the stability of her marriage. For many years, Rita thought she could hide the evidence of her failed marriage and that, fulfilling the promises she made at the altar, every disagreement would be resolved.

Perhaps by having sacrificed so much, she was overly sensitive about the conflicts with Rogelio, who never occupied a prominent place in the life of his father. Gonzalo was cold and distant with the child, although he knew how to be very affectionate whenever he wanted to. His rejection was evident from the moment Rita announced they were expecting another child.

"What were you thinking? How can it be possible! This is going to complicate everything!"

Gonzalo's reaction wrapped Rita in a shameful veil, feeling guilty of something she could not quite identify. She felt the world crumbling beneath her feet. She started living in a state of continuous anguish, with the premonition of an imminent tragedy, and a dark, ominous cloud looming over her at all times.

Rita could not find solace; she resigned to carry on her shoulders the complete weight and responsibility of her family and began to depend on antidepressants and sedatives.

That man to whom she had entrusted her life in marriage didn't know how to be responsible for anything or anyone, not even for his own paternity, and Rita went on to be the sole protector and provider of her family nucleus.

A few weeks after Rogelio's birth, Gonzalo announced, "I am in love. I have found someone who completely satisfies me. I don't love you anymore."

Rita felt herself die. She had married Gonzalo thinking the marriage would last forever, until death separated them. The prospect of turning into a divorced woman with two small children under her care in a society where divorced women were second-class citizens annihilated her.

Again, Rita found consolation in her faith. She begged God to keep her marriage in one piece. She was willing to do anything to keep Gonzalo. Rita didn't value herself; she didn't see her potential or the opportunities that were often presented to her. She clung to a marriage in which only she appreciated the commitment. She allowed traditions to imprison her, without taking into account other options for her life; she couldn't see any other alternatives. And, perhaps reluctantly, God granted her wish.

Even after the newscast, Rita remained sitting in front of the windows, absorbing the endless sequence of impeccable gardens and lawns in the residential community where she lived. The rain furiously assailed the windows, turning them into magnifying glasses that incited her recollections, digging into details long ago forgotten. Gonzalo's emotional abuse and neglect, endured for so many years, had been barbarous, and even worse was her willingness to allow it, irrationally holding on to a dysfunctional relationship. She started to realize she had to take ownership of her actions, recognize her responsibility in having facilitated the mistreatment; she had to stop her dependency on chemicals and sedatives. Only after doing so could she leave behind, once and for all, the memories of that rotten marriage and the self-destructive feelings that permeated all aspects of her life.

She had never completely trusted Gonzalo since discovering his vulgar tendencies and addiction to pornographic magazines. She had only been an object for him; he forced her to dress in provocative clothing he purchased to fulfill his fantasies, fully knowing the garments and styles were contrary to her taste and moral convictions. She still recoiled in repulsion remembering those times, resurrecting feelings of violation and hopelessness. She knew she had to learn to identify the lessons and learn them once and for all; she needed to be assertive and learn to openly express her opinions and desires. No more hiding behind some-one else's faults.

"It is so easy to blame others for what happens to us and so difficult to make the decision to be responsible for our own actions! Is this Jorge Narvaez in the news the same lawyer that represents Gonzalo's family? I am going to call his office in the morning."

Rita had a solid conscience; she was educated to fight on behalf of the poor and the needy; she was convinced that those who hungered and thirsted for justice were blessed because God himself would ensure their satisfaction, and she made the deci-sion to work with the youth group from Alborde.

Although Rita was very capable of working on behalf of oth-ers, her sense of justice betrayed her when it came to herself and her own good. For many years she wrote letters to her parents telling them exactly what they wanted to hear: "I am the happiest person on earth. Everything is going great. Gonzalo makes me so happy; he loves me." They were letters written with the purpose of reassuring her parents, to make them feel good about her mar-riage. She preserved them along with dozens of beautiful cards dutifully exchanged on anniversaries, birthdays, and Valentine's days—bittersweet memories, reminders of what had been her life, imaginary happiness carefully wrapped in tissues, stacked in a cardboard box next to handmade baby clothing embroidered by aunts and grandmothers, adorned with laces and ribbons, already discolored by time.

Listening to Alborde's news, she questioned the validity of her life, noting the long inventory of dishonesty. Faced with the courage of those humble presenters, she thought herself a coward by comparison. Although she had lived according to her principles, she lacked the courage to demand the truth she deserved, pusillanimously giving Gonzalo the benefit of the doubt instead. She was careful not to judge others to avoid been judged, repeating to herself that every person would be measured according to his own measure; gradually her depression was turning into rage.

"How could I have been so self-destructive, to the point of invalidating my own instincts?"

Now she recognized that her children would always be her children, regardless of her marital status. She looked at herself as two different people, one spiritually fulfilled and the other tragically embittered by her habitual repression and inability to openly express her emotions. The fear of losing her family paralyzed her, not realizing the bad example of married life she was giving her children; she didn't know how to argue, silently running away from confrontation. And that sharper-than-a knife silence ripped her soul.

"Am I doing the same thing with my son? I don't know if Rogelio clearly knows what I expect from him as a son. Perhaps our relationship is so precarious for lack of clear and precise communication. I have to talk to Rogelio, my poor son!"

Rogelio probably didn't know the pain he caused his mother with his uncontrollable temper, insensitivity, and lack of diplomacy because that was the type of communication she had allowed throughout the years. At that moment, Rita questioned up to what point she was responsible for not having previously established specific boundaries, expectations, and a clear code of conduct.

While Rogelio truly suffered at the hands of Gonzalo and never had a healthy father-son relationship, Rita had allowed it, and she had to take responsibility for her actions as well as her inaction. She had to forgive herself and move on, doing all she could to maintain a healthy relationship with her children and forget about the past.

"I spent too much time intervening and protecting Rogelio. I didn't let him grow; I didn't let him lick his own wounds. Parents cannot solve all of their children's problems; they have to let them grow, encounter their own difficulties, trip over their own stones, without paving their way. Children have to grow and learn on their own.

"Rogelio has to discover and recognize what he needs and work to achieve it, and I have to let him grow. I can't continue running to help unsolicited, only to be offended by the lack of appreciation for what I have done. Dr. Martinez is right; this is a vicious cycle, predictable and sickening. It starts when I see the opportunity to feel useful to others. I do it all the time. I have to stop it if I don't want to feel used. When Rogelio needs something, he needs to find his own solution. I can be part of his life without being the answer to his problems."

She was listening to Alborde's citizens speak about their children's right to happiness, education, health, and social well-being, in essence the right to a stable and pleasant home, exactly what she fought so hard to keep for her children for so many years. She asked herself, "How long can a person stay mad at a loved one? Who is supposed to take the first step toward forgiveness? Life is so short and compounded by so many lessons learned along the way. I am sure Rogelio is suffering a great deal. After he offends me, he gets depressed. My poor son! He has so many emotional problems. He doesn't have peace in his heart!"

Rita started to feel anxious, exchanging her resentment for empathy, longing for the mental health and wellness of her son.

"He has suffered so much since childhood! I have to be more understanding. He didn't have a happy childhood and adolescence. Even Jesus was insensitive with his parents in his youth. Yes, yes, that's true. During the wedding in Cana when his mother said, 'Son, they have no wine,' Jesus' response was the same as Rogelio, 'Mother, it is not our business.'"

She smiled, making the analogy between Jesus and Rogelio. The last time they spoke, after a few moments of silence, she heard beeping on the line. Rogelio abruptly hung up the telephone on his own mother!

"He invalidates me as a mother with his contempt, and it is precisely Rogelio who owes me the most loyalty for having served as shield between him and his father, for having been such a difficult child to raise, in need of continuous attention. I remember the endless search for help, making so many appointments with psychologists. I have sacrificed more for him than for the rest of the children put together. Always overcompensating for Gonzalo's coldness, but mostly because Rogelio was the one who needed the most. Why am I resisting forgiving the people I love so much? I have everything that money can buy. Those parents in Alborde have to abandon their modest homes and resign themselves to living like gypsies out of their vehicles, mobile homes, and temporary shelters, enduring all sorts of vicissitudes to keep their family together. I am sure they live through very difficult moments. Nevertheless, they continue united, making enormous sacrifices to provide their children the best they can under the circumstances with love, with dedication, with forgiveness."

Rita started to enumerate the beautiful things in her life, the privilege bestowed on her, when entrusted with the care of four good and healthy children, the opportunity to leave her mark in each one of them, perpetuating her legacy. She was conscious of the honor it was to see her children construct their own future, graduating with honors in their respective disciplines, and becoming citizens of impeccable work ethic and professional values.

"The fact that one of my children continues needing my support is an added privilege; it's an honor! I have to stop whining. I am going to call Rogelio today to talk about the situation in Alborde. I am going to invite him to work with me and try to contribute to the well-being of other youngsters with real problems, problems that can be resolved with a little help, not problems invented to get attention as result of having everything."

She remembered her pride at the triumphs and achievements of her children, the result of assiduous work, and how she had dreaded the individual development that would eventually lead to their separation from her—the range of emotions evoked by that nucleus that constituted the very reason for her existence. Mostly, she evoked the beauty and exhilaration of that process called life.

Rita felt embarrassment for her previous thoughts of anger and defeat and decided not to waste any more time on resentment, making the decision to work with the children in Alborde. But first she had to earn the trust of those families that had suffered so much due to the stubbornness of the Mendoza family.

The one lesson Rita was learning after her divorce was to take responsibility and ownership of her own emotions, resisting the temptation to blame others, understanding that the only thing one can control in every situation is the way one responds. Just like a drug addict or an alcoholic, Rita was conscious of her tendency to become a victim, dwelling on pain and self-pity.

With the radio newscasts still in the background, she got up from her chair to immediately call Rogelio. Too much time had already been wasted without talking to Rogelio and seeing her grandson. After all, she and Rogelio had a loving relationship despite all the complications; they only needed to work at it a bit, at an adult level.

"That's it. I have continued treating Rogelio like a child. At his age, I have to switch the role of a mother for that of a friend. I have to work on this."

The storm had ended and the house had started to feel warm again. Rita rushed to use the telephone on the kitchen counter when the doorbell rang. For fear of losing the spontaneity of the moment, she decided to ignore the bell, but it sounded again, this time repeatedly and impatiently. She hung up. Perhaps she was not ready to speak to Rogelio after all, and the impertinence of the visitor was a sign from heaven to postpone the conversation.

Disturbed by the persistence of an inopportune visitor, Rita walked toward the door, grudgingly opening it. Rogelio was standing at her doorsteps, trembling under his drenched clothing. Mother and son embraced and between sobs started to talk at the same time.

"Did you hear what happened with the people from Alborde? Did you hear the presentation at the legislature?"

"Mom, please forgive me."

"I have thought of a social project with the people in Alborde I know you will love. Do you really love your mother?"

And that was how Rita Álamo de Mendoza and her son Rogelio started the project that changed the course of their lives in Alborde.

ENTERING THE
UNIVERSITY

Four years had passed since that winter day on which, as they walked through Alborde's olive groves, Grandpa Fello and Juan had spoken for the first time about the project that changed the course of the lives of hundreds of people. Although they initially faced all sorts of difficulties, the last few years had been the happiest for Juan and the Narvaez family, and very probably for most of the people in town.

Rafaelito, as Juan's youngest brother, Rafael, was affectionately called, started attending kindergarten, and when the inseparable friends, Antonio, José, and Juan stopped by his classroom to check on him, the children looked up to them, making them feel like adults and role models. They enjoyed the flattery and frequently visited the preschoolers to read them storybooks. The adolescents spent a great portion of their time on social service activities. They were natural leaders, used to playing that role in their town.

One of Rafaelito's favorite stories was one Jorge made up to entertain his sisters when they were children. The story was a compilation of adventures in the subterranean world of the rodents that, according to Jorge, definitely existed under the olive groves. Jorge claimed to be the only person who ever dared to visit the secret world.

The alleged entrance was hidden behind the gigantic roots of an old olive tree near his parents' home; each evening, a secret command would open the doors, allowing passage between the two worlds, and he vowed to never disclose the secret code. Every situation ever lived on the earth's surface was duplicated in the underlying world; the difference was underground inhabitants lived in peace and harmony, and the purpose of the replication exercise was to reach absolute perfection.

Wise rodents, supreme fighters for justice, inhabited the secret world instead of humans. They visited the world of humans every night to identify the doers of evil deeds and to analyze the effects of their bad actions with the purpose of learning from the human experience and never to reproduce the same type of inadequate behaviors in their world.

Each human being was modeled in the subterranean world in the form of an exemplary rodent. If a rodent did not learn how to repair the damage caused by his human counterpart, his world would immediately set on a course of imminent self-destruction. One of the main missions of each rodent was to inspire his human counterpart, passing on ideas for how to reach perfection and promptly resolve the problems they were experiencing on earth above. The rodents had to make all of this without allowing humans to discover their existence.

Each evening, during the years of his early childhood, Jorge had added a new chapter to the story, soon transforming the short fables into a robust legend the siblings latter narrated to their children, and Juan now shared with his little brother. When Juan arrived to Rafaelito's class, the children would all ask him to tell what happened in the underground world during the previous night, an opportunity Juan used to teach principles alluding to behaviors observed in the group. Antonio and José also contributed, aggrandizing the stories.

Alborde's Rehabilitation Committee had succeeded in securing from the Department of Education the construction and designation of operational budget for a vocational school; the building would be open by the end of June, on the exact date the three friends were going to graduate from high school.

The trio started to feel nostalgia for the period they sensed was going to be left behind. Enormous doors were opening before them, glimpsing multiple options that generated a paralyzing indecisiveness. Since they had grown up so quickly in so many aspects, forced to live under a magnifying glass, they got accustomed to public attention; thus it wasn't unusual that after concluding their secondary education, the three received recognition from different academic institutions and scholarship offers to facilitate their college education as well as room and board in the capital.

The names of Juan, Antonio, and José resonated in local and state governmental circles related to youth and community action. Through their work in the movement for Alborde's rehabilitation, the young men had gained recognition at the state and even national level through interviews published in newspapers and magazines reaching a national audience.

The three boys consistently showed a great capacity for dedication and cooperation, commonly foreign among people their age. They stood on the threshold of adult life with the weight of celebrity on their shoulders, a difficult burden to carry when trying to live a simple, unpresumptuous student life on campus.

There was always someone wanting to intrude on their lives, making false assumptions and asking imprudent questions that made them uncomfortable. But, on the positive side, they had the opportunity to recruit volunteers to work for their cause: young college students, well-trained idealists who would commit to work, first in Alborde and later in their respective communities, inspired by those small-town young men, filled with dreams and hopes, without perfidy, distrust, and the street wisdom that often contaminates young minds in big cities.

None of them had a normal adolescence. They dedicated their time to serious work for the well-being of others from the time they were thirteen years old and got involved in finding solutions to the social problems in their hometown. The adults often forgot that, although they were exceptional youngsters who had reached extraordinary goals, they were still only adolescents. But the boys didn't regret having lived so committed to their social cause or waste time longing for their childhood. They formed a formidable team, with unity of purpose, unpretentiously dedicated to the well-being of the youth in their town.

Nevertheless, the idea of leaving Alborde with so many expectations weighing on them made them feel insecure; they imagined gigantic molds preordained for each one of them that were very difficult to fit in.

Juan sensed that, like Don Quixote, he was expected to wield his sword against every adversity, and although he knew he had to learn to distinguish which battles were worth a fight and carefully choose each crusade, he felt obligated to spring into action at any request for help.

Juan carried in his wallet the letter Grandpa Fello gave him the day he received the first scholarship offer; his grandfather encouraged him to action. He had folded and unfolded the letter so many times it was about to tear at the edge of each crease:

> My dear Juan:
> Today, upon receiving the well-deserved scholarship to help cover your college tuition and expenses, the moment of your imminent departure becomes tangible, and I want to put in writing the thoughts that occupy my mind and share them with you, hoping they may guide you at the appropriate time. Don't forget the importance of the sense of identity of each social group. Starting with maintaining the individual identity of each family nucleus, we all have idiosyncrasies and individual attributes that shouldn't be lost during the process of coexistence when we are exposed to other groups and their consequent peculiarities.
> One of the factors that contributes to the sustainability and stability of a multicultural society is the harmonious coexistence of diverse groups with clear and solid convictions, committed to living under the same flag with mutual

respect and adherence to the norms that constitute the laws of the country. That is how it is possible for nations to exist inside of countries without undermining the stability of the same.

One must learn to coexist under only one constitution with its laws and decrees, respecting the traditions of all citizens without forcing their assimilation or allowing others to assimilate us, drifting like dry leaves on river currents, losing the identity that throughout many centuries has consolidated us as a nation, resisting enemies and multiple other adversities.

Imagine the human body: each organ is completely different form the other, but each works in perfect harmony to sustain only one body. If the heart suddenly decides it has to be and function like the liver, can you imagine the resulting chaos? The country has to follow the example of the human body, every citizen working to sustain it as if it all depended on him alone, knowing that real success depends on the sum total of each person's contributions for the common good.

If in your new life you observe a behavior, style, or criterion you start to consider better than what you have been taught and inherited—those values that have served you to become the man you are today—and you decide to adopt these new ways, do it only after carefully analyzing where it comes from, its origins, and the benefit it contributes to humanity. Do not allow anyone to pressure you to change your ideals only to ingratiate yourself with some particular group or adopt behaviors you have not analyzed carefully. Nor should you allow anyone to unilaterally affect the laws of your country, trampling upon the democratic process, imposing foreign criteria, usurping the system, or crushing the will of the citizens, the taxpayers' majority.

At the university, you will find people of anarchic tendencies that simply hate submitting to democratic order and authority; people who, lacking discernment, find pleasure in creating a chaotic and disorderly environment, to later be able to exercise their control appearing to be the problem-solvers of the entanglement they deliberately created.

Each generation experiences a version of the same situation. The academic elite manipulate their tacit authority over the students, using them as instruments of change to impose theories that only survive empirically inside a controlled classroom environment. They endanger society by mass producing partially informed militants while inhibiting the freedom of thought and expression of students who might disagree and yet become afraid to express their thoughts for fear of ridicule. Thus they impose on students their experimental theories. Consequently, many students turn against their parents' principles and become enemies of the country that provided them the opportunities and rights they enjoy, their liberty and freedom of speech.

I still remember some of my college friends parroting excerpts from Mao Tse-Tung's theory, citing the communist manifesto, and quoting speeches given by Stalin and Lenin only because they wanted to fit in when China was nothing more than a dream of fantastic adventures in the far east and the Soviet Union a mysterious empire wrapped in the silk of the czars, violently meandering over eternal snows that we all assumed covered the union of republics. In my youth, we found out about world events only through books, novels, newspapers, and magazines that were kept on coffee tables for many months, and even then, the professors and activists—without personal experience living in those countries—judged themselves irrefutable experts on the societies they wanted to promote at expense of ours. I cannot tell you how many times some of these professors made fun of my way of thinking, branding my principles archaic, even forcing me to leave the classroom for expressing my own thoughts.

Many professors promote the way of life of other societies after short visits and limited studies of their traditions and culture, idealizing what they have experienced because they didn't have to stay and function as natives in the systems they promote. So they conclude the foreign norms are better than ours without thinking that no system can be fully understood from the outside or with a dozen visits and that the traditions and idiosyncrasies of nations, like a riverbed, are not formed in one rainy season.

I invite you to listen to your professors with respect, to ponder on their lessons, always questioning the essence and intentions of their teachings. Ask others for different thoughts on the subjects; ask your teachers to promote participation in the democratic processes instead of showing hate or promoting ways to work against our system. Remember the poet who said, "Our grapes are sour, but they are our grapes."

Ask those who stand against the country that supports them the reasons why they nevertheless live in it. Show them that the system they attack is the same one that proclaims the laws protecting their civic right to express any idea, thought, or concept. Show them it is not wise to burn the ship in the middle of the ocean, not even to exterminate a plague.

There are many who come to this country for economic, political, or social reasons, and once they find safe haven here, when they come to enjoy the stability that this country provides, rather than defending it, instead engage in a quest to impose the same set of criteria that drove them to abandon their country of origin.

Lately, I have heard rhetoric of hate, destruction, and vengeance, news about activities that exhibit and tacitly promote denigration of the human dignity in many campuses around the nation—reasons why your departure worries me so greatly.

Universities have historically been conservatories of knowledge, a magnificent place to grow as intellectual human beings, to learn the latest advances in science. Universities have launched some of the greatest minds in history, but many take advantage of the university setting to indoctrinate idealistic and innocent young people like you, who often end up losing their way, squandered like spilled milk all over the table. Keep your eyes wide open; stay true to yourself and your principles. The opportunity to get a good education is a right, but to value that opportunity, consciously absorbing it and applying the knowledge acquired is a privilege. And that depends on each individual.

When people think they can do whatever they want without considering the impact of their actions on others, they are promoting disobedience to the established laws and implanting the seeds of anarchy. Always question the opinions expressed by anyone, be it wise men, professors, or students. Listen intelligently; ask why they believe to have the authority to change the core values that form the nation. What are their credentials as experts, and above all, what are their true intentions?

Generally, people criticize and call for change as a sort of mental gymnastics, just to hear themselves talk. I don't like anarchy. There are democratic processes and forums that allow and promote the participation of citizens in the processes of change. Although it is true that there are many obsolete laws and policies, the procedures for securing change in an orderly fashion have also been established. These procedures protect the citizenry from chaos, and we are responsible for supporting them and educating others about them. That is democracy; the rest is oligarchy or worse: anarchy. It worries me that you are leaving so soon to experience your independence.

I know you are of impeccable character; I trust your judgment and integrity. I am going to miss you, son!

Fello

That letter initiated a long correspondence between them that became a testimony of paternal love and an example for their descendants.

Although the state legislature had approved funding for the construction of a formal youth home with separate quarters for boys and girls that was almost ready to receive the certificate of occupancy, Grandpa Fello's home continued to be Alborde's favorite house and a meeting place for the seniors in town who continued gathering every afternoon to play their traditional games in the courtyard. This routine was beneficial for the elderly as well as for the youngsters; it gave them the opportunity to visit and shortened the generational distance that often alienated family members. The grandparents developed a healthy friendship with their grandchildren; they became strong role models and a reassuring link to the children's traveling parents. The adolescents, in turn, became encouragement, inspiration, and hope for their elders.

Grandpa Fello and Rita had daily meetings to discuss the needs of the children. They felt a great affinity and became inseparable friends. Rita was happy. She had bought a very big house in Alborde with the objective of turning it into a home for young girls and she dedicated herself to the meticulous administration of the project. She insisted on calling the house The Ladies' Residence, visibly enjoying being able to bestow her maternal instincts on those poor children in such need of affection and safety. The girls adored her. Rita was a phenomenal woman and terrific role model, completely dedicated to that social cause that in turn gave her strength and hope. People in Alborde started to call her Mama Rita.

Rogelio had moved to Alborde with his wife, Ana, and his two small children a couple of years before Rita was able to permanently stay there. People nicknamed him the Pioneer because during a long time prior to his move, no one ever emigrated to Alborde unless he or she married a person from town. Since his arrival, he had found an unusual peace that silenced his internal demons, allowing him to grow intellectually and spiritually. He was enjoying living in the heart of a town of modest and uncomplicated people, everyone focused on saving Alborde from devastation. It was easy for Rogelio to assimilate the culture of the place. Since childhood, he longed for a straightforward life with clear and tangible objectives.

When Rogelio arrived in Alborde, he purchased the main retailer, which was practically bankrupt, and worked hard to turn the business around, carrying new merchandise and personally guaranteeing lines of credit for the resident families. Initially, Ana was in charge of the store, but when it rapidly started to grow, they needed the services of a full-time accountant, so they hired the old bookkeeper, Silvano Mendez, who was happy to be reinstated to his old job in the store where he had worked most of his life and became part of an impressive business that contributed to the signs of rehabilitation in the local economy.

Since Rogelio got established in Alborde, his depression and aggressiveness had attenuated, his social graces had improved, and his abrupt character had mellowed out. He was tenacious and hard working; he had focused his strengths on the fundamental reason that had led him to live in Alborde. He dedicated his efforts to cultivate a friendship with the families in town, empathizing with their needs, tirelessly contributing whatever he could, especially collaborating with the Rehabilitation Committee.

It was precisely he who, becoming aware of the need for a home for girls, suggested to Rita she move to Alborde to assume a leadership role, pointing out that she was already contributing significantly to the restructuring and was the most suitable person to establish the house for young ladies. Rogelio eloquently expressed to his mother that he had found in Alborde the best environment he ever lived in, and he trusted he was going to live there for the rest of his life. Rogelio's enthusiasm convinced Rita to make the decision to sell everything she had in the big city and start a new life in the small community.

Rogelio was passionate about commerce, not as much for the money as for the challenge of achieving success under difficult circumstances in which everyone predicted failure. Gonzalo had completely opposed the decision made by Rita and Rogelio, but they ignored his disapproval.

When his paternal grandparents passed away, Rogelio inherited a great portion of land around Alborde and immediately decided to grant a property title to all the occupants who had legally applied for it, proving continuous productive occupation of the same. He committed, in turn, to actively work the rest of the olive groves shoulder-to-shoulder with the locals. With his frankness and generosity, Rogelio gained the complete trust of the residents of the region. Gradually the local economy started to turn around, with the need to hire people for cleaning and conditioning the land compelling many families to permanently return.

Rogelio and Rita cultivated a strong friendship with the Narváez family; they frequently got together to discuss Alborde's economic future and had concluded it was imperative to find another source of agricultural productivity besides the olives. The basic problem was that the olives occupied most of the land, and generally the trees were incompatible with the efficient planting of other crops. It became necessary to create a committee to investigate what other produce could be simultaneously planted alongside the olives, and when Juan expressed a desire to participate in the committee, Rogelio suggested he lead the investigation. From the time they started the rehabilitation project, Juan started to feel inclined to agriculture, and although he hadn't said anything to his father, he was seriously considering becoming an agricultural engineer instead of following in his father's footsteps as a lawyer.

The committee concluded that the investigation process would take at least three months. Rogelio and Juan traveled together to visit the School of Agricultural Sciences in the capital city, carrying test tubes filled with soil carefully collected and properly labeled, to order a scientific viability study of the land surrounding Alborde. They had also collected topographic and pluvial data for discussion among the scientists and expert professionals they were contracting at the university.

After only four weeks, they received a detailed productivity analysis report. The document established that practically any vegetable could successfully be planted in Alborde since they had a rich soil, ample rain periods, adequate drainage, and extensive land that was only waiting for the intervention of human hands to abundantly yield any crop.

Most people in Alborde knew from personal experience with their vegetable gardening that their land was appreciative and generous, but never before they had entertained the possibility of planting crops in between the olive trees because the constant irrigation required by most crops known to them could devastate these ancient trees. Thus the most interesting part of the study was the detailed report on farming white asparagus and artichoke, products that, according to the study, were not only compatible with the requirements and irrigation restrictions of the olive trees but were under such international demand their harvest yielded extraordinary income for specialty producers.

The news generated great excitement among Alborde's residents, who immediately held town meetings to discuss the magnitude of this opportunity and the level of participation required of each person. It was a long-term plan, demanding heavy investments and a new commitment from the group. The possibility of finding other products compatible with the olive tree was the long-awaited solution, potentially able to restore all sectors of the population; everyone had to have a stake in this project to secure its success. The project that started as an investigation now required an irrevocable commitment from the citizenry.

They divided the project into five phases:

1. A period of time dedicated to educating the public on all aspects of the program with instructions about people's roles, designation of administrative and labor functions, designation and prioritization of plots during each phase.

2. Organization and development of an agricultural cooperative including all citizens as active participants and stockholders

3. Planting and cultivation

4. Harvest and packing

5. Marketing and distribution

It was an ambitious project, promising economic development and long-term stability to Alborde's citizens. During the first phase, the objective was to consolidate the different pieces of land to start mixing the crop, allocate shares according to investment, identify financing sources, and above all work tirelessly to motivate each other.

Alborde started to progress gradually, first with the arrival of two commercial banks, followed by several purveyors of agricultural development equipment and products, a department store, and a distributor of heavy equipment.

Juan, Antonio, and José took and passed their college entrance exams and moved away in August. They went to live in a boarding house for students across a major plaza in the state capital; every afternoon the plaza came alive with all sorts of people leisurely walking after dining—well-dressed couples pushing baby carriages, businessmen with newspapers under their arms, and entire families including parents, grandparents, teenagers, and children riding their tricycles on the walkways.

The college students congregated in the plaza, drinking coffee and talking until late in the evenings. They were happy and frightened at the same time about their life in the city, and although they had planned to engage in all possible activities at the university, the three friends gravitated toward the same interests, consequently spending most of their free time together.

Juan went into agricultural engineering almost immediately. José signed up for social sciences with the intent of becoming a mathematics teacher, and Antonio entered the school of business administration.

They took advantage of any opportunity to visit Alborde, marveling at the progress they saw on each trip. Initially, the differences amounted to a fresh coat of paint on the houses, which for a long time had been a luxury reserved for the few well-off families in town. Later, it was the new commercial buildings and new landscaping, modern park benches, and beautiful covered structures and gazebos in the plazas. But the most impressive transformation was the attitude of the people displaying contagious enthusiasm and a new more evolved lexicon during conversations. Even the most unassuming residents spoke about macro and microeconomic processes, agricultural budgets, investments, and profits of over six figures, community projects, and teamwork—unheard of only a few years back when the poverty stricken people in town only spoke and thought about leaving Alborde to earn a modest pay or when they were going to receive the remittance from their migrant relative.

Carmen Rodríguez was a second year student in the school of liberal sciences; she was a melancholy girl from an underprivileged family living in a town even smaller than Alborde. Like the three friends, she attended school with the help of a merit-based scholarship, and she gravitated toward José from the moment she saw him the first week of class. She was a literary enthusiast and skillfully communicated her feelings through letters and poems frequently shared with José, solidifying a warmhearted friendship that lead to intimacy and confidences.

Juan and Antonio started to worry about the influence this girl exercised over José, considering Carmen melodramatic; that was until the day when, in her defense, José took the liberty of sharing with them a short segment of one of the essays written by the girl.

> Dear God,
> Here I am, alone in this world you created for the delight of humans, and I only find misery. Why is it that nothing I do is ever right or appreciated? Why? I have given to others everything they ever asked of me—my dreams my ambitions my friends my hopes—I have given all! How could it be that I am left empty-handed? That is not your divine promise!
>
> I don't even have the desire to hope and dream that motivated me long ago; at seventeen, my soul is empty. How is this possible?
>
> I believed the teachings of the church. I was taught love has no boundaries, no measures; then why do I feel this immense darkness inside? Why, then, in exchange for all my sacrifices, am I subject to atrocities at the hand of those who are supposed to care for me? I am been submerged in human misery; those feelings I had desperately tried to eradicate and forget weigh mercilessly on me. Please help me forgive those

who have hurt me; please help me forget those asphyxiating memories.

Dear God, omnipotent, omniscient, almighty God, you know the deepest thoughts hiding inside my mind, I confess to harboring confusion and resentment. Lord, you can penetrate the hearts of those who pray. Have mercy on mine, I beg of you.

Make my heart pure and my mind forgetful. Help me trust so I can give again. Let me lower the protective walls I have constructed around my heart. Help me find happiness, even if just a little, so I can help those in need, even if the price to pay is my own insignificant and miserable life. So be it!

I want to die, oh Lord!
I just want to go home.
The road is long and the provisions meager.
I want to die and reach your loving arms
To feel secure in heaven.
Father above,
People are everywhere;
Yet I am so alone.
I want to die and start again,
Some other time,
Engage in living free,
Leaving behind this darkness.
My body is only a prison
And death my only freedom
I will start my life
when I drift into heaven
Through the infinite blue
In your paternal care,
Finishing with myself
And all the things I dread.

I don't want tears on the day I die.
I have looked for death as a sanctuary of peace,
And perhaps death is simply

My only escape
From a life filled with wretchedness,
Seemingly tranquil.
I feel the blade of loneliness,
Living in isolation for so many years,
Violated, mistreated.
Doesn't anyone care?
Powerless, unprotected
An insatiable monster violating my body,
Using it as he pleases to satisfy his hunger,
Desecrating my life.
And no one cares. I want to die.

When they read those horrifying thoughts, they didn't know what to think; they felt guilty for having judged Carmen without taking into consideration she was in need of good friends.

That afternoon, when Carmen joined them at the plaza, both Juan and Antonio remained spellbound until long after midnight, listening to her account of the verbal, emotional, and physical abuse she had suffered in her family.

The family had lived crammed into two rooms at the maternal grandparents' house, inviting disrespect among the extended family members. Carmen had grown accustomed to being unable to separate reality from fiction, living the absurdity of moments too difficult to explain, buried in a sea of shame. Carmen confessed to the abuse of an alcoholic uncle, not going into great details, and the beating she endured for telling her mother about it, who, instead of protecting her, accused her daughter of creating more problems for the family and threatened to kick her out of the house if she continued with the outrageous accusations.

Carmen felt like one little piece in a giant puzzle she wanted to make disappear, but at the same time it constituted her history and she could not let go of it. She often contradicted the account of events, but the three friends understood she was sincere and the inconsistencies in her story were a product of the abuse she had experienced.

"I am on the verge of tears most of the time. In the depth of my soul I feel loneliness, and I can't find peace. Nevertheless, I remember some pleasant memories left behind long ago, when we had a modest house in our little town. It was modest, but it was ours. My only concern then was spending time with my family, with my brothers and my parents. We were like many others, a family working with dignity for our sustenance, a family in its own space, not piled up in someone else's place; that was a short period of time, and after that, I don't remember an instance of peace in my life.

"It was always like that, from my earliest childhood memories, always looking for peace, unable to find it. I learned to live sheltered in my own solitude, not allowing anyone in. My only satisfaction was in running away to my own imaginary world. I enjoyed watching the sunset over the mountains that surrounded my hometown. I always loved those mountains. I took long walks on the outskirts of town; it was lush, green, silent, and serene. I enjoyed the narrow cobblestones streets in the old part of town."

The three friends tried to relate to the stories Carmen shared, but the only resemblance between them was that Alborde was surrounded by the same mountain range.

"I didn't know how poor I was until my thirteenth birthday when my teacher organized a trip to the Museum of Science in the capital. Then I was able to observe how the rich people lived. I suppose I felt curiosity, not envy, but whatever that feeling was, it stayed with me; it wouldn't go away. I thought my parents had been irresponsible by bringing so many of us into the world, as if we were cats or dogs, at the mercy of whatever our luck could bring us, without the appropriate provisions to confront the adversities of life.

"When we went to sleep on piles of old bedspreads on the floor, hard and cold during the winter, I curled up like a shell to retain body heat, ruminating our scarcity. We lived in a wooden hovel that became illuminated at dawn as daylight filtered through the cracks in the walls. These crevices allowed the cold December drafts to sift quickly through, a breeze so much desired during the month of August. I struggled to find peace during those one-hundred-hour days, trying to convince myself there had to be something good about my life, something I was not seeing; for a long time I waited for a miracle.

"Perhaps I didn't find peace because I was a victim of the social class struggle from every imaginable angle. I reaped the benefits of corrupt policies, becoming one of those opportunistic girls who pretended to be something she was not to secure a scholarship to a Catholic school my family couldn't have ever afforded, unable to define a congruent reality for my life. I had to pay back the scholarship with domestic work at the convent.

"How naïve of me! I had so many dreams, trying to preserve all that for so long. Now all I see is a bitter, gloomy, and painful reality that still doesn't make sense. There were three social classes in my town: the miserable—servants, laborers, peddlers, etc.—the middle class with its different shades of possibilities, and the opportunistic politicians who would have liked to belong to the high class. In reality, having observed the different social ranks here in the city makes me conclude we didn't have an upper class in our town."

The three young men silently listened Carmen's account, feeling highly privileged and even more committed than ever to the principles they had upheld during their adolescence in Alborde.

"The miserable were those with distended bellies filled with parasites and a heart overflowing with hatred, a direct result of the injustices they experienced, sleeping in slums on the outskirts of town like dogs in the backyards of their masters. Their feelings oscillated between hate and gratefulness when they received the scraps, bones, and leftovers from the master's table. That is my group. Our sustenance is uncertain. We live in survival mode, only in the now. When I stop to think of it, I am embarrassed about indulging in better clothing, shoes, and my scholarship because I know injustice doesn't end, and I don't want to forget my origins, so maybe someday I can help correct that suffering. The fissure expands every day, along with the number of bare, hungry, and unsheltered children. With all my poverty, at least we had something to eat every day. And although many suffer and complain, in my town people aspiring to climb the social ladder still participate in parties and social activities; according to them, they are making an effort. Here, I think most of the students are rich like you."

Juan thought that, although Carmen's feelings were valid and profoundly felt, she was forgetting those who worked and struggled to make it to the top.

"Carmen, I understand your feelings; but we cannot spend our lives blaming others for our unhappiness; no one ever chooses where to be born, but we all can decide how to respond to adversity. Yes, there are injustices in the world, and we all have to wake up and fight against them to ensure everyone has the same level of opportunity; however, we cannot become steamrollers, capriciously leveling down society. I believe in equal opportunity, equal rights, and equal justice. But everyone has to work to reach his own goals and to preserve what is achieved."

"The majority belongs to a working class."

"And what is wrong with that?"

"What is wrong? We don't have any future; we live day-to-day, depending on a meager salary because our working class only has time to work. To what class do you think you belong?"

"To what class do I belong to? By your own description, I think I don't belong to any one of the classes you mentioned, although my parents and my parents' parents have always worked to earn their keep and there have been bad times and better times. My ancestors had been rich at times and poor at other times. Everything comes and goes; nothing is eternal. I think we need to forget about labels and start taking control of our lives, ensuring there is justice and equal opportunity during the times we are in control," José said.

"I am tired. I don't want to continue sharing so much human misery and indignity. In my town, I saw a middle class that spent their lives brownnosing, hanging on appearances, making believe they were rich, worshipping those in power, abandoning their sense of right and wrong to be able to keep up their pretenses."

"But just because some people in your town do this doesn't mean all those who are middle-class are opportunists," Juan said.

"The majority wants to be on top' it doesn't matter what price has to be paid, even drowning everyone at the bottom."

"But there are also those who work to overcome and stop being victims and recognize that everybody has to work as a team to be able to attain equality and social justice. In Alborde, we have lifted our collective heads to achieve what is best for all. Everyone has to learned to work toward the common good," said Antonio.

"What can be done when people are oppressed, when they are real victims of the system and the majority at the top does not care and instead victimizes those at the bottom, when people only work to survive without hope, without dreams, without incentives, because they know that no matter how hard they try, they can never get out of the vicious cycle?"

"Those who clearly see the problem have the responsibility to instigate change, utilizing the processes established by the law, spelled out in our constitution," Juan replied.

"And what do you do when there are no processes established?"

"Either one fights to institute the processes or resigns to remain victims of ignorance or inertia, refusing to recognize options for change," Jose responded.

"No, José, the people know that only the rich and powerful have access to security and safety in society. They know their dreams are subordinate to the favors they might receive from the privileged class in power, those who lend themselves to play the dirty game of politics."

"What about the conscience? Those with a conscience do not succumb to gifts and bribes; they neither do they accept positions that imply political compromise or sell their moral principles. Our parents belong to that group; they have lived their lives by strict rules, preserving an untarnished image for us, their children," Juan added.

"In my social class, that doesn't exist."

"Carmen, don't say that. Do not resign yourself to hopelessness. When I was little and my parents had to travel, following the rhythm of the crops, I often felt so disgraced. I didn't appreciate their sacrifices, and instead of recognizing their honesty and dedication to our family, I thought of them as pusillanimous. I didn't even know what to think about our socioeconomic condition because at the time I was only thinking about myself. When we start looking outside of ourselves, the horizons get bigger; we start to see the broader panorama. When you stop looking at one tree, you can enjoy the variety of the forest," José said.

"There are so many wrongs, so many changes to make. What about political corruption at all levels? When I think about our police, I am ashamed; they think they are a separate class. Just because they have a gun, they get away with whatever they want, abusing the unfortunate ones."

"Carmen, I think you are concentrating too much on being a victim. In every group, there are good and bad people, people that take part only for personal gain and those who really want to serve. You can't categorize everyone by the behavior of a few. I believe there are many more good people than bad ones, more citizens with a desire to serve society than wanting to serve themselves from society. There is a reason for everything that happens under the sun. There are natural laws and a reason behind every law. We tend to receive what we give every day. When we concentrate on the negative, we attract precisely that," Juan said.

"It is evident you come from a privileged family, Juan."

"Perhaps my family has been prosperous, Carmen, but each and every member of my family has always worked for a living. They do not spend their time playing and waiting for their dividends or rental income. One of my aunts is married to a police officer. Since I was a child, I have been reading every publication I ever came across about social justice and the laws of the country; Dad wanted me to be a lawyer with the hope we could work together in his law practice, but I always wanted to work the land of my ancestors. I made a commitment to the social fabric. With help from Antonio and José, I learned nothing is given to anyone for free. Furthermore, when we don't work toward accomplishing what we want, we can't appreciate what we get as we should. I believe that when we take responsibility for our actions and our inaction, that is when we start producing the changes we wish for. The next time you need the help of the police, would you instead trust in the protection of a drifter, one of those unfortunate people you describe as having felt oppressed by the police? Tell me, do you really think one of those vagrants will help you if you are defenseless in an alley? Or perhaps you think that if you see them in the act of robbery you can convince them to stop just because you believe in social justice?" Said Juan.

"What about their civil rights? What do you say about that?"

"I can only tell you that the rights one has not personally fought for are never truly appreciated. Even though it is true that police brutality exists, you must also think how a police officer feels when confronting the lawless element of society. A police officer is not superhuman; these men are simple human beings gambling their lives every day in a very dangerous job. They are family men, brothers, uncles, cousins, and friends with valid fears, endangering their lives in defense of public safety.

"Can you even begin to imagine the weight of public scrutiny on their backs? Each time a policeman leaves his house in the morning, he doesn't know if he will be alive to return home that evening because, whether one likes it or not, there are those who do not want to obey the laws of the land and, to make matters worse, there are people blindly defending the rights of the lawless instead of the rights of the law-abiding citizens because it is easier to feel like a victim than to make a decision to fight for the common good," Juan affirmed.

"It is clear that none of you have lived in poverty!"

"Poverty should not be an excuse for lack of discipline and public disorder. I understand your feelings, but we must overcome feelings to arrive at intelligent action, to achieve consensus and effectiveness," Antonio said. "We are suffering a devaluation of morals; we see it in the dissolution of the basic components of our social fabric. No one seems to stay faithful to the word of honor. Not even marriages are based on commitment to the commitment. There is a rampant propensity to personal pleasure that violates the law of sacrifice for the common good. Long ago, in the times of our grandparents, no one ever thought of asking, 'Are you happily married?' Our grandparents knew the word *happy* is only found in personal commitment. There is a myth of happiness around what is easy to obtain, self-gratifying, and guaranteed by society in the commercials. Instead of nurturing the commitment to contribute to a stable society with a solid moral and civic foundation, we blame others for what we don't have simply because we haven't attained it. I think selfishness is obliterating our concept of society; soon we will not have the slightest idea of what society is supposed to be like. I believe there is a new subculture seeking to level down society, to evade efforts implicit in the commitment to rise above our weakness," said Juan.

That evening, when they went to bed, none of the four friends was able to sleep. Juan got up and went to his desk to compose letters to his family.

Dear Grandpa Fello:
Today I thought a lot about you during a short discussion we had with Carmen, José's friend. I believe José is in love, and although Carmen seems to be a nice girl, I think she has socialist ideas, if not communist. Sometime ago I heard you say that during adolescence we are all socialists in one degree or another, thinking that society is responsible for the personal well-being of each individual in place of our parents. But if we continue believing everyone else to be responsible for what happens in our lives even after we are older, then we are simply unconscious and insensitive. In Carmen, I observe a mixture of impotence and socialism I hope she will soon be able to overcome, for her own good as well as for José's.

I wasn't able to sleep thinking about my childhood and adolescence that, thanks to you, were so special. I was thinking about Alborde's smells and flavors. I even longed for my parent's reprimands. I miss summer mornings in the old house, the dampness on my feet as I ran across the dew-covered grass at daybreak.

It is so special to remember the country home with you and Grandma. It is curious how one remembers certain things. I loved to have breakfast with the two of you, smelling the warm summer air that filtered through the kitchen windows.

Now that I am away, I am reassured in my memoires of you, images that seem so far away: drinking ginger, orange, and lemongrass tea, the aroma of the eucalyptus leaves you boiled on rainy days as a cure for the flu. A few days ago, we found a little Moroccan market with all sorts of herbal teas and spices and I bought a few for you. I remember you a lot, especially the trips walking back home in the afternoons; I think about your teachings, and I promise never to disappoint you!

But enough with the homesickness! I want to talk to you about Carmen and José. How I wish you could talk to her about her ideas and reflections about social classes. I would like to invite her to come to Alborde during our next break. I am organizing a group of students for an internship at our cooperative. Do you think it's a good idea to bring her? She doesn't want to go home during the summer; there is something wrong there; she had mentioned something about abuse, but she hasn't opened up completely.

Whenever you can, write back; tell me how the projects are coming along, about Miss Rita, and any other news you might have. How is Rafaelito doing? I hope you won't allow him to take my place in your heart; someone already told me that he has taken it upon himself to imitate me in almost everything we used to do together. I am only kidding! If there is something I want for him, it is that he learns to enjoy you as much as I did.

I miss you a lot and hope to see you soon.

Hugs,
Juan

Dear Dad,

It's been a long time since I've written you, and I don't want to allow much so time in between letters. It's incredible we are almost into the fourth semester of college! Soon it will be summer, so I want to mention a few ideas for the cooperative. Our social science professor, Don Rodrigo Diaz-Contreras has established a good relationship with us due to our activities in Alborde. This semester he allowed us to participate in extracurricular activities for extra credit. He treats José, Antonio, and me as a team; he asked us to prepare a series of talks for the students with the title "Visionary and Prudent Social Changes." I could have never have guessed that the situation in Alborde mirrors so many other towns across the country. Many students have approached us, asking about Alborde's experience, looking for ideas and solutions for their communities. I can't tell you how truly exciting it is to be able to serve others!

After we finish this series of presentations, we think it would be beneficial if we can start an internship at the cooperative in Alborde for those who are interested. This will give us low-cost help during summer vacation and provide the students important experience in organizing a practical and efficient cooperative. The only thing we have to provide is room and board and a small stipend since most of the students interested in the internship come from families of limited economic means; their families sacrifice a great deal so they can go to college. Besides, it is a social contribution for the benefit of many communities across the nation.

I want to take advantage of this letter to express something I should have told you long ago. I infinitely appreciate the sacrifices you and Mom made to properly support and educate our family. It is as years go by and we see the misfortune of many that we realize the gifts, the sacrifices, and the dedication of our parents.

I never openly thanked you for your support in Alborde's rehabilitation project. When we are little and immature, we think we are owed everything we receive, without thinking about the sacrifices of our parents and without appreciating what is given to us.

It is not until we face the reality that no one is owed anything without working for it and that only God gives his grace undeservingly and without any effort on our part that we start to be grateful, starting with the hot water for our bath, the clean plate for our food, the roof over our heads, and the clean clothes in our drawers.

When we have to live on a budget in college and the stipend is short, leaving us hungry for extra food we can't afford, then when we remember how many times we complained about been forced to finish our vegetables and soup.

You are a great father; you instilled in each of your children an unbreakable love for humanity, an unquestionable respect for the dignity of each human being, and an irrevocable sense of justice. I could go on and on with a long list of your attributes, first as a father and now as a friend.

With you and Grandpa Fello, I learned that the true values of life, the real treasures, have to be cultivated, not purchased, that we only own what we can freely give. What we have given others is the only thing we can take to our graves when we die. Today, from the bottom of my soul, I want to thank you and recognize your teachings.

I think of you every time I explore the mind of each individual I meet along the way, hoping to find the friend you assured us resides inside each person treated with dignity and respect.

Today, I want to tell you that your teachings and life ethics are invaluable and that I miss you a lot.

Hugs and kisses,
Juan

The essays and poems Carmen wrote started to circulate among the group of friends and ended up influencing many students who, inspired by the social context of the writings, initiated a movement to revive the old university newspaper, *The Student Gazette*, and started publishing it weekly with opinions, essays, open letters, and poems.

THE CRUMBLING WORLD

By Lucy G.

Staring through your shadowed eyes
that hold behind their gloss
A crumbling world of fantasies
and growing sense of loss
From this world the joy has bled,
the light has gone away
And a pervasive sense of persecution
haunts each corner every day
Where elves and fairies used to dance
below the willow tree
darkness has swept over
and has caused them all to flee
As I look into your eyes
And realize its fate,
Let me save your crumbling world
Before it is too late

I PROMISE

By Lucy G.

I see you behind the window
I see you protected and hiding inside
I see you behind half smiles and the tears
I know you've been through this before
I know you don't want to love, anymore
Mom, I think that
if I could only get you
Outside of this horror
Then maybe, our lives
Can be normal again
If only you would let me in
If only you'd show me the pain that you are in
If only you'd let me step in
I promise he'll never hurt you again

and the fears and tears
You hold close to heart
Will soon fade
And the circle of hope
That was present before
Will protect us forever
I promise he'll never hurt you again
If only you would let me step in
If only you'd show me the pain that you're in

LOOKING INTO THE EYES OF AN ANGEL

By Roxy G. M.
Dedicated to my loving mother

The little world that took me years to build
is slowly crumbling
The support fails from under me and
I go plummeting into darkness
The light looks like a little firefly
Flying farther and farther away until
I can see it no more
My hair wraps around my face
until I see only darkness
I am falling faster and faster
until the cold floor slaps me hard on the back
like a mother punishing her child
Immense pain in my head
Slowly I pick up some supplies to build
my way back to the top, back to the light
that I miss so much
I am a whisper
I am a shadow
My breath echoes through the darkness
and I feel the cold marble walls,
of death and depression
I lay my head down to rest

Not knowing if I'll ever wake up
The splinters in my hands have numbed my fingers
I am slipping away until a hand
Reaches through the darkness
I hold on to it willingly and
smile into the face of an angel!
This angel holds me she takes out
the splinters from my hands the sadness of my soul
And since someone must have them,
she embraces the wound
to keep me from experiencing the pain
Her face glowing like a distant star
I rest my head upon her tender lap
I close my eyes
Hearing her humming softly in the back of my mind
She has always been there for me
and she will always be
A shiver runs through me
As I recall the coldness of the walls my self-imprisonment
But all that is gone she is here all that is gone
I know I should say something to her, but she knows it
She's an angel
She's my savior
She's the light that watches over me
She is the lamb inside the lion
And the innocence inside of us all

MY ABYSS

Anonymous

There was an abyss
in the middle of my chest
cold, empty, in darkness
my life devoid of joy and
simply passing by me
Suddenly, there was, you
for a moment in time

that abyss disappeared
the void was filled by ecstasy
my spirit with gladness
and my soul was appeased
for a moment in time
I felt the touch of God
through the hands of a
human!
I experienced God's warmth
through the warmth of your
body!
You surrounded my life
with unexpected kindness
your light fully dispelling
the sad and profound darkness
and I became alive
for a moment in time
beauty passion communion,
Fulfilling sense of oneness
Then I opened my eyes
there is an abyss
in the middle of my chest

YOUR SILENCE MY LOVE

Anonymous

Silence, your sword, rips
apart the fiber of my soul.
Silence emasculates my dignity
desecrating the most intimate
emotions—even in my sleep.
Silence cruelty in the most
sophisticated form
it is the fear of giving
only saving for self
Forever expecting famine and scarcity.
it breeds resentment

procreates distrust and
there is loneliness
Amid the multitudes.
I hold
Promissory notes of memories
good times left so far behind
vast emptiness in the most inner depth,
Able to think yet maimed by the inability to dream
forever in my mouth the acid taste of your betrayal, and
I swear not to let anyone hurt me again
is this what wisdom is about?
How I want to be ignorant!
Primal uninhibited naked
loving hurts,
the price to pay for a moment
of innocence and joy
is torture yet,
I want to feel the steel
through my flesh,
experience the emotion that
Holds the hand of pain
Bleeding to death
I want to love again

IN LOVE

Anonymous

I call your name
And the cosmic immensity
can't compare to the ecstasy or my soul in expectation
I hear your voice
And a million bells
Begin a song of joy
That somehow
Surrounds planet earth
Reverberating to the vastness of the universe
I see you

Truth, understanding, and compassion
Materialize before my eyes
Reassuring my spirit of promises
Of good days ahead
You touch me
I experience in my flesh
in my soul
The sacredness of man
I begin to understand
the extent of eternity
I feel love

TO LIVE OR DIE

Anonymous

I do not want to live to be one hundred
I yearn to be the breeze that gently rocks the flowers,
I want to embrace the planet
I want to be the wind,
gliding the sails that venture into sea
I want to lift the kites tied down
by a string to little children's hands,
to make them happy
to let them dream
to let them fly
I want to embrace
the centenarian tree,
softly caressing its exhausted branches
and become one with its tender new leaves
I want to be the silver springs
playfully leaping down to the valleys
I want to be the torrential rains during the month of May
I want to be intertwined with the rays of
sunshine that wake up the city
I want to be the mysterious moonlight kissing the fields in the midst of night

I want to be the veil that gently cov-
ers the mountains in December
The sensuous dew over the ocean of daf-
fodils in the wake of April mornings
I want to be the seasons that never
learned the paradox of time
Forgive me, Lord,
But don't let me live to be one hundred

OUR FATHER

Anonymous

Our Father, who art in heaven,
I feel so lonely deep inside my soul
As I realize how petty this world is
I run to you in search of peace and love
Races, betrayals, egocentric maniacs
I cannot understand this untrustworthy people
Indignant with a system so pregnant with injustice
I feel utterly impotent, doing nothing at all
Moreover, I don't want to be part of the human
race, at all levels denigrating each other
I recall your scriptures, where you tell us incessantly
"By my care and my love, being my chil-
dren you are brothers"
Hundreds of helpless humans are dying in this world
As a result of hunger, desolation, and lies
As we take up fake collections, only to appear conscious
And proclaim with fat bellies "What
good Christians we are"
And the concepts of peace and war seriously scare me
I'm trying to comprehend it, though I don't understand
When in one hand, so proudly, some hold the holy Bible
And with the other petitions to approve a nuclear war
I am worried about the disappearing conscience
Hearing the monologues of many Christian Leaders
Preaching a lust for money,

claiming to know the Scriptures
But not caring at all for the rest of your people
I have seen with amazement, in anger, and despair
How a temple is built to the good god of money
My spirit recoils, sinking in disappointment
And going home to you is all I really want.

THE COOPERATIVE
IN ALBORDE

The establishment of a cooperative in Alborde for the purpose of planting, harvesting, and packaging their agricultural production brought a new institution that revitalized the local economy and created a wide variety of employment opportunities for professionals, technicians, and laborers, in addition to starting a migratory current toward the town, which started to look more and more like a vibrant city.

The fundamental structure of the co-op defined the participation of its workers as co-owners in the business. A participatory scheme that established Alborde's transformational organization was developed. Each employee was committed to work in the cooperative with a nominal salary, defined and designated according to profits, without exceeding a predetermined sum corresponding to the responsibilities of each position. A maximum of eight hours of labor per day was defined as a workday for all employees. Besides, all shareholders had to volunteer as needed in any department of the cooperative, without additional pay, which was often necessary during the developmental phase. A system for tracking the time invested by each participant was instituted for future payment.

As a direct result of the activities of the cooperative, a technical school opened in Alborde, authorized by the department of education to issue certificates and diplomas in administrative and technological fields. The cooperative administration complex was impressive; it was a series of interconnected buildings with advanced and modern facilities, solvent and debt free. They managed to develop an organization with impeccable credit. Later, the co-op administrators initiated a series of mortgage transactions that allowed the creation of their own credit association, expediting the new institution's banking transactions, and consequently setting in motion an economic boom in their town.

In the outskirts of Alborde, near the youth residence—and precisely to facilitate the participation of young men and women—they started the construction of a cold storage plant for the sorting and storage of their produce. The construction was located next to an old abandoned structure, boarded up for many years and built as a municipal social hall, suitable for splendid parties and formal receptions, very popular during Alborde's glory days, and now a silent testimony of long-gone grand times.

Because it was a big and well-constructed structure, they decided to use portions of the building for offices and employee training halls. Enormous freezers with thick plastic strips that also served as doors were installed to keep the refrigerated areas cool while facilitating the traffic of produce that traveled from one area to the other on conveyor belts in continuous motion. The produce, temporarily packed in the fields in plastic containers cushioned with a foamy lining, was transported to the processing plant in modern refrigerated trucks.

Save a small few changes to expedite the delivery process, the produce was still received at the processing plant using the same system. It arrived in an open area where it was manually placed on a conveyor belt that took the produce to an area where it was carefully inspected and washed using an automated pipe system.

Once clean and inspected by a quality control team, the vegetables were classified and separated according to final product: processing for canning and pickling, fresh packaging, and quick-freeze.

In a hall of tall ceilings ventilated with giant industrial fans fixed into the lateral walls, the produce destined for fresh market consumption—olives, artichokes, asparagus, and other vegetables—were packed in attractive protective wrapping that, without touching, allowed consumers to inspect them. The packaging, created by their merchandising division, was appealing, lending a competitive edge to their product at a national level and, according to industrial experts, preventing bacterial contamination of produce during distribution.

A department or experimental kitchen was created in the co-op for the confection and creation of table-ready products. This department was in charge of developing recipes incorporating the different vegetables of Alborde, including preserves, gourmet products, and delicacies of the area in high demand in the national market, such as artichoke hearts in olive oil, olive tapenades for appetizers, sweet pepper mélange, stuffed olives, white asparagus in water or olive oil, and other specialties.

When the co-op started to function, the older people concentrated on doing manual labor in the fields while the packing house was filled with women and young people covered from top to bottom in white gowns, wearing hair nets to prevent contamination of the product. Now the employees in the processing plant were men and women of all ages. Applicants were always welcome and many jobs were available in Alborde's cooperative.

During the winter break of his second year in college, Juan participated in the first ever planting of white asparagus and artichoke, functioning as agricultural expert. Parallel alternate lines were formed in between the olives trees, laying the foundation for the future of Alborde.

The first planting season was a remarkable event for the residents of Alborde, who, for many years prior, had started to diversify their family orchards to get acquainted with the peculiarities of the new crop. Since the process of Alborde's rehabilitation had started, the residents had been asked to experiment with the planting of crops that were in high demand and find out which products were suitable for packing, freezing, or processing. They started this practice to later apply their acquired knowledge at a larger scale in the cooperative.

The planning committee started offering a series of classes taught by agricultural experts hired from some of the most successful agricultural production plants from around the country. During these sessions, the farmers extensively learned about the production of asparagus and artichokes, verifying old farming theories and applying new techniques. They learned how to develop and use advanced irrigation systems instead of traditional approaches, such as humidity and continuous drop irrigation that, though essential in the industrial production of most vegetables, would damage the olive trees if used excessively.

Alborde's farmers knew that water saturation in clay-like soil like theirs was particularly damaging to the roots of the olive tree, which needed air and controlled humidity. During the agricultural classes and in the laboratories that developed around town, they learned ways to foster the favorable coexistence of asparagus and artichoke with the many varietals of olives typical of their zone: manzanilla, gordal, and verdial. Asparagus and artichoke flourished in clay-like soil with controlled humidity, making their cultivation feasible in conjunction with the olive trees.

Since both asparagus and artichoke had to be picked by hand, the olives were not damaged during their harvest. Besides optimizing the harvesting processes, it was possible to yield several harvests throughout the year without any detectable deterioration or damage to the old trees. They had discovered an ideal symbiosis for the benefit of Alborde's people.

Strategically, they positioned sensors to detect and control the levels of humidity in the olive fields with extraordinary results. Alborde could finally see a dazzling light at the end of the dark tunnel in which it had been trapped for so many decades.

The most interesting aspect of Alborde's experience is that the participants were in agreement and in full understanding of their commitment to the remarkable project. They embarked on the development of a formal business plan, assigning administrative and labor duties according to the capability of each individual member of the group. Curiously, there was no damaging resistance from or rivalry among the workers of the cooperative.

In the articles of incorporation, it was stipulated that in the event of disagreements among members, they would be immediately addressed and resolved through mediation, discussing the complaint before a mediation committee until a harmonious and equitable agreement was reached between the affected parties. Members of the mediation committee were selected by direct vote.

They defined all the elements of the plan, describing each of the steps and their resulting implications, classifying the short, medium, and long-term consequences; ensuring they were in a position to take on the challenges. All citizens committed to transparency in the processes. Each job opening at the cooperative would be published along with a well-defined list of competencies, required knowledge, and experience necessary to qualify for the position.

They contracted Don Gonzalo Calderón, an executive expert on the development of agricultural business enterprises, from the northern part of the country to direct operations, and he was given the title of chief executive officer. Don Calderón insisted in contracting the services of a highly respected and nationally acclaimed marketing company to promote and sell their products in a wider, more competitive market.

Gonzalo Calderón was an entrepreneur, a hard-working individual who focused his efforts on the formulation of a training plan for laborers, shaping educational coalitions and strategic partnerships with agricultural giants outside the country. He had the vision to share and exchange knowledge by swapping executives and workers for limited periods, bringing a fresh set of eyes to the equation, and even sharing training tools. Gonzalo Calderón's plans became a working model for the agricultural industry, and this also helped to promote Alborde's produce internationally.

He also devised a reporting system that transformed the sharing of organizational information into an educational and employee training opportunity.

Each week, every department nominated one of its employees for public recognition; companywide activities took place on a monthly basis, recognizing those nominees and promoting pride in the achievement of excellence at work.

The different workgroups of Alborde's Rehabilitation Committee met frequently. They were the ones who defined the resources of the group, identifying appropriate collaterals for loan applications on behalf of the new cooperative. A capital investment model was structured and shares were distributed among its members in direct proportion to the sum of individual investments.

A participation plan was designed for those workers without investment capital that consisted of corporate shares to be paid upon retirement. This measure turned out to be highly motivating to the employees, who, conscious of the opportunities afforded them, wanted to maximize their investment in the team; they were willing to work and personally sacrifice as much as they could to reach the goals and objectives established as a group.

They had advanced a great deal; nonetheless, they needed to build strong protective walls to withstand external pressures and stay within their predetermined work plan, committing to a rigorous rules of order for all meetings and discussions of the cooperative. These workers knew they could achieve success through their efforts and were not willing to squander their investment; they collectively decided not to ever again be victimized by other people or circumstances.

The cooperative earned the support of several members of the state legislature, and this sparked the interest of some regional banking institutions, later getting the attention of investment capital groups. The investment capital institutions sent their experts to conduct feasibility studies and to investigate the phenomenal changes taking place in Alborde, as before making any investment recommendations regarding the emerging industry, they were required to ensure that it posed no unreasonable risks.

Another factor in favor of Alborde's new project was that it was taking place at the right time, precisely at the moment international trade widened, at the dawn of the globalization movement.

Don Gonzalo Calderón was a widely respected national figure. His transfer to Alborde and faith in the new industry lent credibility to the project. However, the idea of product diversification had emerged intuitively at the onset of Alborde's rehabilitation committee. They were finally able to create new employment opportunities for Alborde's citizens, facilitating their permanency in town under Don Calderón, who, with his professional team, was instrumental in the detection and quantification of existing competitive threats, guiding the group of citizens to carefully analyze the challenges to come up with control strategies, risk reduction, and exit strategies as a team in full agreement.

In only a few years, Alborde's citizens turned into protagonists of their own lives and community development. At the heart of a basic organization, they got used to taking control in their areas of responsibility and ownership of their actions.

It was difficult at first for the workers to straddle the fence between making decisions as a group and following the leadership of the professional executives in the corporation. At the beginning, they all wanted to give their opinion at every step and about every subject. Don Calderón patiently guided the members of the cooperative to help them understand the executive powers bestowed on the directors and managers, teaching them to wait for the quarterly reports and open meetings. He trained them on how to participate in the discussions within the established framework and took responsibility for the decisions made by his executive team, conferring power to the workers as well to the investors and members of the cooperative.

A grading system was established to train cooperative members in an orderly participatory process. With this development, the citizens continued being owners of the process while learning how to delegate corporate decisions to the executives, trusting in the integrity of the processes and final results. They democratically elected people to be in charge of planning, to learn the inside rules dominating the agricultural product market at a national level, the legal aspects, trade, and promotion of said products.

Each member of the organization was attuned to the general plan, contributing with personal opinions and proposing solutions beneficial to all, not defined by personal agendas and self-interest. They met regularly to discuss the advances and constructively analyze mistakes.

Although they worked intensely within the municipal governmental frame, exploring ways to achieve their goals and produce the desired changes necessary for establishing the new local industry and the structuring of an individual remuneration system for the shareholders and active workers, everyone agreed that this was an autonomous project belonging to Alborde's citizens on a quest for efficiency and economic independence.

The cooperative brought an infusion of capital to all citizens and educational opportunities for the youth. Don Calderón organized a summer internship program for college students and a year-round internship program to attract new professionals to the area. During the first years, a good group of students accompanied Juan, José, and Antonio to participate in the summer internship at the packinghouse, and almost every one of them returned to Alborde permanently after graduation.

The internship program for students continued to thrive, teaching participants about the value of a strong work ethic while presenting a realistic view of their job prospects. Many recent college graduates think they are prepared for the workforce, immediately eligible for executive positions with significant salaries without having worked a day in their respective fields or gradually rising through the ranks of an organization. Even worse, many expect to get the job without any practical experience, which is often more valuable than a diploma in the practical execution of functions.

The internships also helped the novices in learning how to deal with difficulties at work, how to judiciously manage what appeared to be injustice, to understand that honest work was never degrading, no matter how humble it might appear, to be responsible for their actions, and to constructively learn from their own mistakes in the real world. A person who participates in any type of internship becomes a better and more efficient employee than one who wins an appointment straight out of college without practical work experience.

Carmen was one of the first participants in the program and she stayed at the Ladies' Residence during her summer internship. She worked at the co-op during the day and in the afternoons contributed to the housework as required. Rita took care to cultivate a beautiful friendship with the girls who lived in the house. Since Carmen was in need of so much understanding and longed for affection, she rapidly started to share her feelings with that woman who had left behind a high-class social life to give herself completely to the adolescents in need.

Initially, Carmen regarded Rita with suspicion, disbelieving the stories José told her about Rita, about her life and her social work; Carmen thought no one ever gave anything without personal interest or possible gain. But as she started to know Rita, she became interested in her community work. Carmen often heard Rita say that life is not necessarily fair and the sooner we learn this, the sooner we can start to deal with adversity with positivism without becoming or feeling like victims. Rita was renowned for her pearls of wisdom; she employed an arsenal of saying that remained fixed in the minds of the young people who listened to her: "It is easier to forgive than to live chained by rancor or to cry indignantly instead of learning how to ask for forgiveness." "It's better to arrive late than never." "It's better to take precautions unnecessarily than to be caught by the storm unprotected." "In turbulent seas, a good fishermen can find his catch" and many other clever adages.

During long conversations with Rita, Carmen complained about having lived a sorrowful, underprivileged life in a hopeless environment, and Rita said, "It is capricious and narcissistic to think that everything that happens around us is happening to us; it is absurd to think there is an invisible entity whose only purpose is making our lives miserable. When it rains, we can't think it is raining just to annoy us, neither we can assume that is not fair to have to change our plans due to the rain. Doesn't it sound ridiculous? We have to learn to be flexible when confronting adversity; we have to take ownership of our own actions or inactions and learn from our personal experiences; there is our opportunity!

"We are not responsible for our feelings; however, we are totally responsible for the actions we take based on those emotions and for our attitude toward them Also, it is not right to judge others for the actions of their ancestors, demanding retribution for what others did long ago even though we have to learn from our history to avoid repeating it. We must learn how to leave our past in the past where it belongs. A significant part of the process of maturing is to finally realize we are not the axis on which the universe revolves."

When Carmen told Rita her poverty-stricken life story, her sadness, and the physical and sexual abuse endured at the hands of a drunken uncle, her mother's oldest brother, she spoke with hatred toward humanity, revealing pain, anger, and resentment, especially because her parents didn't protect her when she told them about the maltreatment and sexual abuse. Carmen's parents didn't believe her and were confused by the charges made by the girl; they didn't know how to respond or appropriately intervene. The maternal family accused Carmen of misinterpreting the uncle's demonstrations of affection and slandering her benefactor. She was called ungrateful and disrespectful toward the one who provided a roof over their heads and food on the table for the entire family.

Rita listened to Carmen's account of events, her eyes lost in the distance. It wasn't the first time she had heard stories such as this one. Many years back, she had been a volunteer in a youth shelter in the capital, a safe haven for abused and deprived young girls, and she said to Carmen, "It is certainly inexcusable that you had to endure living under such deplorable conditions, but in reality, you can't change your past. You are no longer under the danger of abuse, and although it was an injustice and the price of your freedom was extremely high, you have been able to overcome it. Next year you will receive your university diploma; you'll be free to rebuild your life anywhere you choose. What is within your reach and what you can do right now is make the decision to leave that chapter of your life behind you. You need to learn how to completely enjoy your present, never allowing the story to be repeated.

"You need to commit to building a future filled with hopes, dreams, and aspirations; to learn from your experiences, the good as well as the bad, and embrace them; they made who you are. Often what is perceived as negative experiences turn out to be the most solid foundation over which one can build positive outcomes. The horrible experience of abuse you endured could very well serve you in a positive way, to be able to understand those suffering abuse, for example. You could serve in a home for abused adolescents because you understand what they suffered in a way others could not. There is such an enormous need for sensitive and caring people in this world, people like you. I believe your suffering has made you more sensitive, more understanding of other people's suffering. Most people don't concern themselves with the self-esteem and feelings of others. That is why each person has to work on building his or her own sense of worth. Each has to define what is important or not, with clear goals and objectives. Only you can define the purpose of your life, what is important to you, and make a commitment to diligently work at it until it is reached, completely independent from the actions and opinions of others."

Carmen listened to Rita without uttering a sound, tightening her lips and considering Rita's words insensitive and condescending, simply callused. Without even waiting for Rita to finish her conversation, Carmen abruptly got up, leaving the room in the middle of one of Rita's sentences, running to her room to cry inconsolably, filled with indignation. Later, when Carmen returned to the group before dinner, Rita discretely called her aside and said, "Carmen, don't believe for a second I don't understand you. I don't want you to have the impression that I am invalidating your thoughts and feelings; earlier I expressed my point of view in a constructive way. You are deeply hurt, but I know from personal experience that one can't live an entire life in anger and resentment against humanity. It is counterproductive and paralyzing. We all have options. Each time we opt for negative feelings, we relive the hurtful past, unconsciously relinquishing the beautiful possibilities the present time is giving us.

"When you chose to retire to your room this afternoon, you missed the opportunity to share some fun time with your housemates; you missed a beautiful sunset; you missed the opportunity to build new and positive experiences with others. Think about this. You choose to continue giving complete power over your present to the person who hurt you so deeply long ago. Each time you relive those moments of abuse, you are allowing him to hurt you again. The only antidote to your pain is total forgiveness; you must forgive those who offend you, not for their benefit and convenience, but instead for your own. You must learn to leave behind the memories that torment you. Bitterness is spiritually and physically damaging.

"I met Lucille in my adolescence; she became a great friend and mentor. I learned a great deal from her many lessons. She told me about a situation with Nelly, the aunt of her deceased husband, who managed to remove Lucille from the family's will after her husband died, taking away her right to a beautiful house Nelly was positioned to occupy as only living surviving member of the family. Young and inexperienced, I was astounded listening to the story and by the actions of a lady I had believed to be a person of integrity; besides, I had been taught to show respect to any individual according to his or her age. I was impressed because Lucille always treated Aunt Nelly with love and respect without ever making any reference to the incident that had happened many years before. I asked Lucille why she had never confronted Nelly, claiming the part that was legally hers. Lucille responded, 'If Nelly can live with what she did and enjoy the house and other benefits without remorse, I can live without anything else. I feel pity for Nelly. I would not want to bear the weight of this type of action on my conscience.' Not a day goes by that I do not remember that conversation with Lucille for one reason or another. Rich and poor, men and women, blacks and whites, we are all born naked, covered in blood, hungry, and with an indomitable instinct to survive. Even if it looks like many are born with their life settled for them, with the proverbial silver spoon in their mouth, money, social position, and other conditions don't guarantee happiness; it is our attitude that takes us to happiness or to misfortune.

"We all have options; each one of us unilaterally decides how to react when confronting the challenges and adversity of life; that is the fundamental difference between one person and another, between a happy person and an unfortunate soul, between a successful individual and one who considers himself a failure."

Rita paused for a moment.

"I am going to offer you something to help you start afresh. I want to pay for attorneys and court expenses to bring your assailant to justice and give closure to your ordeal, although it happened so long ago that perhaps the statute of limitations on this crime has passed."

"What I really want is to kill him with my own hands, making him pay for what he did to me. I am disgusted with my own body. I can't stand it when someone gets close to me or tries to hold me and caress me. Only God knows how many others he hurt in the same way. You know what? This is the first time I think that dirty old man could have easily done the same thing to other little girls in town. I always thought he only raped me."

"Let's talk to Dr. Narváez about this. However, if I were in your place, I would choose to forgive, forget, and continue on forward, cheerfully taking advantage of the opportunities life is giving us each and every day. That is the best way to dismiss that horrible man, disempowering him from exerting any influence whatsoever over your present.

"Carmen, regardless of what might happen during the trial, try to eliminate the negative from your heart so you can finally find peace. With such a thick web of distrust and resentment, you are disallowing the flow of light into your soul. Beware; you can turn into an embittered woman for the rest of your life. Only you have the power to choose what you become."

After saying this, Rita embraced her tenderly, and Carmen received the embrace, thinking about her own mother and how much she would want to be able to get close to her; it had been so long, she forgot what it was to feel any type of protection from a mother figure.

Carmen cried on Rita's shoulders for a long while, but this time shedding purifying tears, feeling like a little child again. This compassionate woman was willing to protect the little girl hidden inside Carmen, a child raped, humiliated, frail and defenseless for so many years. And right there and then, Carmen made up her mind. She decided to take this uncle to court with the purpose of stopping any further abuse. After that, she would never have to think again about the day when a despicable, unashamed drunk who was supposed to protect her ripped away her innocence.

During the following weeks, Carmen noticed a radical change in the content of her writings; in fact, she noticed a remarkable new way of processing her thoughts; a soothing tranquility nested in her soul, softly touching and spreading its wings in every word she uttered.

During the internship, Carmen received a note from her family communicating the death of her father, and although she decided not to attend the funeral, still terrified by thoughts of confronting her past face-to-face, she incessantly wrote about her father in her diary.

On my father's death:

I have lost you again, this time permanently, and although sadness reigns in every corner of my soul, I can't cry. I have spent so many years feeling sorry for myself; I lost the last opportunity to thank you for the life you gave us and for the endless sacrifices you had to make for your children.

Now, when I can't express to you how much I always loved you and how much I have missed you, when I cannot tell you how sorry I am for spending my life wallowing in resentment, having dug such a deep emotional and physical fissure between me and my family, now I wish I could embrace you, hear your voice once more.

Dad, I am ripped apart by the remorse of having said hurtful, ignorant words against the modest home you provided us and for having rubbed in your face so many times the poverty we endured. Who am I to demand from you or to blame you? Sons and daughters don't have the right to demand from their parents what they can't provide!

Perhaps it was precisely for having so many children that we were so poor, and you and Mom loved us and gave us everything you had. You and Mom always said that God sends each child along with what he or she needs, and I saw both of you joyfully awaiting the arrival of each new baby.

I often heard people in town say that you and Mom lived a comfortable life when you married and before you had any children. I was told that you and Mom were very popular and enjoyed a happy social life with your friends, unconcerned about scarcity. I can't believe I acted with such self-righteousness, with my presumptuous sense of entitlement, judging you both. I had the audacity to look down on both of you! The insolence to judge precisely those who had given up everything for our well being. I insulted the two people to whom I owed my life and all my respect! High is the price one must pay for immaturity and arrogance!

I feel so guilty for not having been there with you during your last moments alive, for not having given a eulogy at your funeral. Cowardly, I didn't want to confront your death or my inequities. Even worse, my selfishness stops me from going home to support Mom and my brothers.

I wish I could tell you I recognize your efforts and I have never been worthy of your unselfish love and commitment to the family. I have been a resentful brat, filled with envy, a beggar for affection, unwilling to do anything to earn it; it is now when I begin to understand that no one can ask for what one is incapable of giving to others.

Dad, I want to tell you that I recognize you gave yourself to us completely, not withholding a thing. As a tribute to your memory, I will dedicate every effort to improve the condition of our family, the family you created and dedicated your life to; I will follow through the way it is expected from a loyal daughter and a good sister. I humbly receive your legacy of honest work, humanism, and sense of justice; from now on, I promise to value each and every day, living it enthusiastically as if it were my first and with the solemnity of the last.

I hope you can forgive me for my actions of the past! I kiss your forehead with love.

Good-bye, Dad.

After her father's death, Carmen spent most of her free time with the elders in town, trying to understand and absorb the principles that shaped the characters of her three dear friends; she found refuge in the unassuming wisdom of the grandparents. She learned that before asking for something, one has to give, that before demanding anything from anyone, one has to know how to sacrifice all for someone else. In the crucible of volunteerism she found an answer to her questions about social justice, understanding that in the real world people cannot receive what they have not earned, not only because it is wrong and unfair to everyone else, but because no one appreciates what is received without making any effort to attain it.

She saw the absurdity of the false pride that so wrongly separated her from her roots and finally abandoned her victim complex. Seeing the farmers work together as a team, shoulder to shoulder, she absorbed the components of success: organization, respect, and work.

Carmen started to think about her siblings frequently, often wondering how much they must suffer the absence of their father and decided she should promptly do something to help her family. So Carmen made the decision to return to her town once the internship was completed. But before doing this, she had to contact her mother and settle things with her. During the following weeks she wrote many letters addressed to her mother, letters that ended in piles of crumpled paper in the trashcan until she finally achieving a draft that became a formal letter sent by special delivery.

Dear Mom,

First of all, I want to implore your forgiveness for having failed you not only as daughter, but also as a decent human being eager to express her condolences at a time of an incalculable loss, the death of your husband, my father.

There is no possible excuse to diminish the impertinence of my silence. I was not ready to face my past and forge my own future. However, if you allow me, I want to return home imploring your mercy, to serve you in the manner you deserve, and fulfill my duty of contributing to the family with whatever you wish and need.

These recent years have helped me grow and see clearly, beyond the lens of caprices. Sometimes I feel alienated from society while other times I think I could live anywhere in the world, but in the bottom of my heart, all I want is to reintegrate myself into our family. I want to go home at the end of this academic year.

Perhaps back in my own town I could find the opportunity to develop some of my childhood dreams, but above all, returning home I want to give back to our family part of what you and Dad invested in me. Maybe someday we can even talk about Uncle Manuel; I know he died a few days after dad passed away, but right now all I want is to forget him.

I want to return before it is too late to do anything for you and the family, as I should. I don't want to spend my youth trying to adapt to another city, a different group of people, and a new environment, renouncing my duties as a daughter and the opportunity to improve my own community, the town where I was born.

I have behaved like an ungrateful teenager. I long for my childhood, which was taken from me too soon, and I refuse to accept changes. I feel so anxious! I fear that after finishing my career, I will be nothing more than a half-professional and half-farmer, when what I really want to be is an advocate for social change. My perception on life continues to be unrealistic, often clashing with the modern life of the capital, although my desire for social justice and activism are more accepted in this overwhelming metropolis. I want to return to my town, to my family, to heal wounds, and to bridge the gap between us.

I miss Dad so much! The certainty that I will never see him again has made his image perfect to me, and, although I know that nobody is perfect, he has become a legend in my memory. I know you and Dad made enormous sacrifices so I could study; I was so ungrateful! Always thinking I deserved the scholarships I got in elementary, middle, and high school; but after Dad died I learned from the nuns that both of you exchanged school fees for long hours of maintenance and cleaning work at the school. I feel so low! The two of you allowed me to believe I had earned the scholarships on my own merit!

You both taught us that money is nothing more than a tool to achieve something else, and I really like your definition of money. It gives a fresh perspective on making money; it prevents us from making money a goal in itself. You worked tirelessly and lived every second of your life for your family. I appreciate this now. Thank you, Mom! When I return soon, I will help you carry the load. You will be able to rest a little and take the vacation you have yearned for and spoken of my entire life.

I hope you are open to receiving me, to let me back into your heart, and let me show you how much I respect you and admire you now. I want your forgiveness.

Your daughter,
Carmen

When Dr. Narváez initiated legal proceedings against Manuel Rosario, Carmen's uncle, the simple act of setting in motion the judicial process acted as a catalyst that redefined the value scale of the young woman. Although the timing of the legal action was unfortunate, too late to bring justice to Carmen since her uncle had passed away from hepatic cirrhosis a few days after her father had died, Carmen was finally able to close a chapter in her life she never again wanted to revisit.

She enthusiastically reunited with her college friends and for the first time in her life started to take pleasure in doing small things, nonacademic activities, with her friends. Carmen embraced life fully; she stopped comparing her situation to others and consciously avoided animosity, recognizing it had become a flaw in her personality.

Carmen looked at the events from a different perspective, committed to generous social contribution without preconditions. Recognizing her weaknesses, she tirelessly worked to overcome hostility that had limited her in the past. When the internship was nearly finished, Rita asked Carmen to address the group of students leaving Alborde, ready to go back to their respective lives. During that farewell dinner she spoke to the group spontaneously, straight from her heart.

"Dear parents, grandparents, adoptive family, co-workers and friends, when I had the opportunity to enter the university with a scholarship from the Cultural Institute, I believed the world owed me retribution for the social and economic conditions of my family. It didn't occur to me I should be thankful for the generosity and the distinction bestowed on my person by the institution.

"On campus, I spent most of time trying to hide my humble roots, accumulating rancor against those who, according to my understanding, received everything on a silver platter simply for being born into a wealthy family.

"Only God knows how many positive experiences I missed by embracing that attitude of offended prima donna. I refused to see my schoolmates for what they were—adolescents like me, trying to learn how to be adults, training to be productive in life according to their respective dreams, goals, vocations, and desire for self-improvement, human beings trying to contribute to the society in which we live. I never even tried to see the magnificent human being dwelling in each person or to discover their inner beauty and recognize their capacity to reach their potential.

"I thought of myself as the image of justice with scales and measuring stick in each hand, keeping the bandages on my eyes, not to blindly enforce justice but instead to avoid finding the truth; I was always quantifying my handicaps, comparing them to the apparent superior advantage of the privileged. I missed the friendship of every human being I judged more successful, more graceful or more privileged. Looking back, I can say that I harbored and fed only resentment and envy in my heart without identifying it as such at the time.

"I built a wall around me and only allowed inside those I believed to be disadvantaged, those I considered to be equal or worse off than me. It was such a false sense of humility! I simply wanted to see everyone below me, riding on my high horse of righteousness!

"Today, I want to thank those who judged me as severely as I deserved, those who, knowing my flaws, still chose to include me in their circle of friends. Thank you, José, Antonio, Juan. I want to tell all of you that these three friends changed my life completely; their straightforward and sincere attitude captivated my attention from the beginning.

"First it was José. I started to observe him during class; he was open and receptive with everyone. Then I met Juan and later Antonio in the study groups. I noticed they were very alike, perhaps due to the good food in Alborde."

A round of applause interrupted Carmen's speech.

"I paid attention to their conversations and the way they conducted themselves in and out of class; although I understood their dedication to community activities and their interest in the well-being of the community of students, I remained suspicious. I was expecting to find the real José any moment. I believed no one was capable of giving anything without expecting something in return. Little by little, a friendship was born and with it trust and respect for José and his inseparable friends. A small fissure started opening in my heart, allowing their noble dreams and desires for self-improvement to filter in."

Tears began to choke Carmen's words.

"I never thought anyone could influence my life the way you have done during this time together and the sense of service I have found in Alborde. The day Juan spoke to me about coming here for this internship, I agreed only because I didn't want to go home and also because I needed the scholarship for the summer. Mama Rita, Grandpa Fello, Don Jorge, Doña Susana, and all of you my dear friends have given me a new purpose in life. You have helped me recuperate my family, a family I embrace today with genuine sense of pride, hoping they are able to forgive my petulance. I have learned that to be able to determine our path and clearly identify our goal, we can never forget where we come from. Thank you, many times thank you."

A roaring applause filled the air. One by one, the members of the audience rose from their seats in standing ovation to Carmen's words, most of them with tears in their eyes. That week, the local newspaper published a children's story written by Carmen dedicated to Juan, Antonio, and José:

THE COLOR OF THE SOUL

The color yellow resided deep in the magic universe, the most perfect shade of yellow that ever existed. This color lived happily, lighting everything up with her complete spectrum of tones; that was until one day when the rain released a drop that changed into prism, unfolding her yellow shade into a prodigious rainbow. When Yellow realized there were other colors, she started to feel awfully lonely.

And that evening, when the wishing star appeared in the sky, Yellow asked it for a partner. And the star that inhabited in the depths of the dark infinite universe, where all colors disappear, felt sorry for Yellow and decided to send her, as companion, the deepest blue from the most remote corners of space.

Together, Yellow and Blue rhythmically moved to the sounds of the dance that imagined light and gave birth to all colors perceived only by humans. It was an amazingly powerful event, charged with mystifying energy. Yellow and Blue merged as one, and the color Green was born with the first lights of dawn.

When Yellow saw they had both turned into a magnificent emerald green, one and the same, Yellow sensed she would never be lonely again. And for a long, long time, they lived uncommonly happy, gladly expressing their new splendid color to the world.

Sometimes they emanated yellow tonalities while other times they displayed deep strokes of different shades of blue. Those who noticed their presence admired the new green, and experts tried to decipher their essence, unable to define it. They were fascinated by the multifaceted tones of green, resulting from the generous, unselfish contribution of the primary colors.

All was going great until one day when Blue decided to turn back to his original color, determined to take a different and separate road from his Yellow. Yellow was saddened; she had gotten used to being many shades of green, and yellow started to cry inconsolably, thinking about the absence of her Blue. And she cried bitterly for a long, long time until dawn when she languidly lifted her head; she discovered in amazement her teardrops merrily splashing on the ground, unfolding the light of dawn into magnificent multicolored bundles, pushing darkness away.

And instead of loneliness, her world was filled with joy. By herself she was able to give life to all colors, and the more she devoted of her own essence, the more revitalized her indomitable color became, and more colors came to life— soft tones of yellow, orange, red, violet, and blue—and she felt utterly happy in the transformation that was only possible after conquering fear under the prism of pain.

And to this day, from the beginning of time, that light continues to express itself through every human being willing to overcome adversity. We see those rays of light in the performance of good deeds and in the array of goodwill born in the hearts of those who appreciate the gifts they have been given. That light fills our souls when we recognize the innate value of each human being. And we dwell inside the light, in the simplicity of unselfish giving, which transforms any person into an enlightened human being.

José received a letter from Carmen in the mail.

My dearest José,
Loving companion, friend, and counselor, by the time you receive this letter, I will be back in La Hoya, trying to rebuild my relationship with my family. I hope you can find forgiveness in your heart for my furtive departure from town; if I had spoken with you, I would not have been able to keep the promise I made to myself when Dad passed away. I had sworn to return home.

Because I love you, I want to set you free. You don't deserve to have to carry on your shoulders the complicated burden I am at this time of my life. Although I must confess I will love you till the day I die and beyond.

I know when you finish your degree you will return to Alborde, the town that forged your ideals and profound convictions. There, you will attain the fulfillment of your dreams. It was so beautiful to spend time with you and get to know the people of your hometown! Thanks to you, I have found the way back home. But I am going to miss you more than I can ever express with words; words seem so empty and inadequate!

The years we shared—it seems like a lifetime—have pushed us to become adults in a hurry, and as such, being the eldest sibling, I fully understand I must help Mom and the family. If I don't do it now, crushed by the weight of my own guilt, I will never be able to form a family of my own.

You are a great man, and I want you to reach your maximum potential. Some poet said that love is like a butterfly, and if we want to preserve it, we have to hold it with wide-open hands to avoid damaging her wings. I firmly believe that staying together would be a dreadful emotional weight on you that will inevitably end up damaging your wings—the wings I know with certainty will carry you to the highest levels of achievement. It is not right to add my burdens to your life. You promised to marry me, but you are too young to tie your sails to my pier without ever having ventured to sea.

I pray to God our paths cross again someday, enabling us to embrace and rest in the certainty of our commitment to each other's happiness, a commitment forged in the fire of this pure and inextinguishable love that today brings me to the decision that I should renounce your promises of love and care. I know I will never find another man like you.

Forgive me, José! I love you with all my heart.

Carmen

NEW LEADERSHIP
IN ALBORDE

The graduation ceremony of the three friends, attended by parents, grandparents, uncles, aunts, cousins, and many friends, took place on a Wednesday, and they immediately prepared to return to the jobs they had been developing during their vacation breaks in Alborde, which awaited them with much to be done.

Since Alicia was preparing to start college in the fall, Jorge and Susana decided to stay in the capital a few extra days to familiarize her with the city. Juan took advantage of the additional time to show Grandpa Fello some of the sites he had described to him in the letters they frequently exchanged, especially the coffee shop across from the old boarding house that had become a favorite student meeting place for his group and a shelter and rehabilitation center for runaway youth where Juan had served as volunteer for a couple of years. The center was a nonprofit organization primarily funded by private grants and donations and limited government funding.

Fello was interested in the organizational structure of the group and arranged a meeting with the administrator and a few board members to exchange innovative ideas, especially pertaining to the optimization of resources and fundraising activities in the private sector.

This visit turned out to be very productive since the shelter was well organized with access to modern resources, enjoying worldwide recognition and financial support. They knew how to capitalize on the resources available to nonprofit organizations. Fello seized the opportunity to learn, taking notes on every detail, including addresses and telephone numbers of international organizations working on behalf of the rights of minors. He learned that these organizations held conferences around the world with the precise purpose of exchanging experiences, ideas, information, and access to resources.

Alicia, on the other hand, was anxious to tour the university and speak with the counselors in charge of admissions. Although certain she was going to be a lawyer, she wanted to learn about other disciplines, reasoning that widening her educational foundation would improve her prospects, advancing her capacity to serve the community later on.

While Juan was her role model, Jorge remained her idol. Since early in her childhood, Alicia had developed an exceptional relationship with her father, considering him her best friend. She wanted to prepare academically to be able to work side-by-side with her father. She knew she was going to inherit Jorge's law practice one day together with it his legacy of service in town. Since high school, she had worked with her father in the afternoons, helping with research assignments and organizing files. Alicia learned Jorge's organizational methods, a virtue that propelled her to excellence in her class and to prominence on the national debate and math teams.

Alicia was recognized in student debate circles, having won dozen of medals and trophies in national and international competitions; she was one of the best students in her school, famous for being able to debate any subject at any time. Her investigative methods were impeccable; Alicia could passionately support the opposing extremes of any argument presented to her. During one of the national competitions attended with her school team, Alicia had prepared to oppose the death penalty; she compiled all publications related to the penalty both nationally and internationally, the current rulings on the topic, legal penal precedents, and all sorts of supporting material to sustain her argument; however, the team designated to defend the opposing argument was unable to attend the tournament at the last moment. When Alicia found out that no other team in the competition had prepared to defend the death penalty, she offered to take on the argument against her own team. Alicia insisted on continuing with the program as planned, defending exactly the opposite of what she had prepared for. The professor finally agreed to allow her to proceed. She ferociously confronted a procession of opponents, unquestionably wining the argument, astounding the attending judges and teachers. During the trip back home, the teacher asked Alicia how she was able to prepare so swiftly to defend something so diametrically opposed to her views.

"Dad trained me; and he is the best instructor of oratory and debate. Besides, for some reason, debate comes naturally to me when I prepare to defend any point of view. The first thing I do is to place myself in my opponents' shoes and take their position. I investigate any and everything that can be used to support the opposing argument and systematically attack their foundation. That is what Dad has taught me to do. He says that if we don't understand the essence of the zeal in our adversary, we will never find the enthusiasm to strengthen our arguments. This works great for me; I am always ready to defend both sides of the argument, the opposing point of view, but my position is based in moral convictions, based in the values and legacy of our parents."

Alicia was an excellent orator as well, recognized in Alborde and its surroundings for her theatrical abilities in the recitation of poetry; she was frequently invited to local radio and television stations to read poetry. During her adolescence, along with her sister, cousins, and some of her classmates, she founded a poetry choir group they christened with the name Apollo XIV, in honor of the god of poetry in Greek mythology, the NASA space program that had just placed a man on the moon that Alicia admired so much, and the fourteen youngsters comprising the original group. That little group served not only as an outlet for artistic expression, but little by little it turned into the voice and forum of adolescents denouncing some of the social problems of their time. Later, many young people joined Apollo XIV, bringing their own unedited poems for recital, often expressing innovative ideas and revealing their social concerns. During the performances at local and regional events, each member of the troupe contributed to the artistic production with impromptu sounds of tambourines, guitars, or any other instrument at hand.

A direct inheritance form the Greeks, choral poetry was an extraordinarily beautiful forum for the expression of feelings among young people at that time. Groups recited poems about love, melancholy, hope, exploring social issues, and the entire scope of emotions that bring passion into human hearts. It is a shame that the communication style popular among the youth of today is often insolent and vulgar, disrespectful to women and traditional values using language that annihilates the sublime that has elevated the human spirit for ages.

YOUTH

Wake up to life!
Perpetual, exultant young men
and joyous graceful women,
Hear the beckoning of the winds
and the ocean waves,
the calling of the swallows
as they gently open their wings
to engage in a desperate flight
knowing they will never be able to return
they are calling you
Yours are the lights of the coming days
A voracious need for love and peace
All belongs to you:
flowers, meadows,
smiles, olive branches
and longing songs

Life is wide open to you
Bursting with optimism,
Knowing one day you will bring to pass
The dreams you created when you were a child,
hopes and aspirations
of our humankind.
Awaken to life!
Your elders are calling
upon you
Whispering as they fade
into the gentle night
To place in your hands
the blazing sacred torch
in which the fire of love
and sense of duty burns.
Do not you put out the flame of that torch:
it is life, your legacy
of your ancestor's love
Raise your head with pride;
sing your new song,
Understand that destiny rests in your hands:
You and only you
hold the future of civilization
You and only you
can keep that flame alive

EMPTINESS

A moment like any other
An instant in which one looks
without seeing a thing
Carrying inside heavy burdens of sadness,
upon thinking
that in the vast plains of life
Days continue to fall like small grains of sand,
that can hold deep meaning for the soul
or just as well be worthless and lost
among all other days

And the smell of dust
already tired of rolling around the globe
confuses me
Along with the noise of motors
and the incessant traffic
that wounds our senses
creating a hostile
environment
Favorable for nothing
and even the breeze
believed to bring relief
seems unnatural
The noises of this and that group
Voices and sounds
assault our ears,
nailed into our brains,
permeating the subconscious mind
in perpetual contamination
no one can rest!
Humankind preoccupation of self
dreadfully egotist
incapable of going beyond
what is strictly personal.
And the multitude shouts a
refrain among all men
people no longer want to be considered ordinary people
and there are so few extraordinary ones!
And a mixture of human and automaton
Wanders about the streets
absorbing the uncouth beauty of the cities
The wild pulsation of nature is
wretchedly contaminated
demeaning pleasures,
intoxication by excess of amusement hurts us deeply!
And pages of our calendars continue
to fall one-by-one
in the vast plains of life
and they remain entangled,

> meaningless, forever useless
> lost in eternity
> nonetheless irreplaceable

On the other hand, Sofía was more interested in biology. She spent most of her free time collecting samples of insects and worms, deliberately disgusting the women in the family when she approached them with her finds in hand. From the time she was a small child, Sofía had spoken about wanting to be a medical doctor. Her first pet was a hamster her parents gave her on a trip to the countryside; unfortunately it died in the claws of a cat and, to the surprise of her parents, Sofía did not cry. Instead, she kept insisting on opening the womb of the hamster to see with her own eyes what the little animal had inside his guts. Susana suggested asking the biology teacher to do it in class, and her schoolmates were horrified with the idea. But the teacher accepted the proposition and froze the hamster, taking advantage of the opportunity to expand the study of rodents for more than a week. The episode spread around Alborde faster than an oil fire, and Sofía obtained a high level of popularity among the boys her age in the school, although she lost some of the female friends in her class for a time until they finally forgot the whole controversial incident.

After Juan's graduation ceremony, the only thing that interested Sofía was to camp at the Museum of Natural Sciences. The first day she went there with Rafaelito, who refused to return because he didn't find the dinosaurs and elephants he expected to find in the building; however, Sofia returned by herself each of the consecutive days, carefully studying every detail of each exhibit.

After satisfying the formalities of graduation ceremonies, greeting professors, thanking mentors, and so forth, the families of the three graduates met at a bistro near the university, very popular among students, to celebrate the event. The specialty of the restaurant was breaded octopus and fried fresh sardine appetizers. They there for several hours amid toast after toast, savoring the many different dishes and speaking with graduates and classmates that came in and out of the establishment. It was near dusk when the group of friends started their unhurried walk toward the hostel where they were staying, stopping at different taverns to again toast to the success of their sons each time they met one of their friends until they finally arrived at the lodge in the center of town.

Antonio's parents and grandparents were in heaven. They had been saving money for several months for the purpose of taking this trip leisurely and without economic worries, and although they were a big family, they were not counting pennies during the long-awaited festivities, insisting on inviting all their friends to eat and drink in celebration of their son, the new business administrator.

Antonio's brothers looked up to him with admiration while his elders were filled with pride and satisfaction. Who could have thought only a few years back that their family's destiny was going to take such a favorable change? Grandpa Domingo could not have imagined, not even in his most remote dreams, that his grandson was going to graduate with honors from one of the most prestigious universities on the continent.

While watching the joyous exchanges among the youngsters in the group, Domingo's thoughts traveled back to the day when a thirteen-year-old boy pointed the way to change to Alborde's elders, and he silently said a thankful prayer for having had sufficient humility to listen to Juan and Fello at the gazebo in the park years before. It occurred to him that if it hadn't been for this, his son and grandchildren would still be traveling as migrant workers, laboring in some else's ranches around the country. At that point in time, they were small businessmen filled with hopes, reaping the fruit of their labor. He made a mental note on how imperative it was to continue encouraging and strengthening the leadership skills in these young graduates before they got too deeply involved in their routines, burying their noses in daily responsibilities to the point where they would forget the call to leadership they had received, which, thanks to their tenacity, propelled them to achieve the radical changes Alborde was enjoying.

The evening was moving, and although José felt somewhat saddened by Carmen's absence during the celebration, there wasn't even one discordant note in the conversation; nobody made a single comment about her. The subject monopolizing the conversation was the marketing of Alborde's products in the national market. While they walked by the many windows that aligned the thoroughfare, children and adults alike pointed and identified some product similar to the ones they produced at the cooperative, making qualitative comparisons and speculating on how to apply the novelties discovered in the big city to their products. In those moments, the three families felt like a single unit under the protective wings of the three grandfathers.

José's parents observed their son with pride, somewhat concerned about his emotional state. And although they understood his heartbrokenness, to some extent they were happy the engagement with Carmen hadn't taken place. The family had warmed up to Carmen during her stay in Alborde and recognized her undeniable qualities and leadership potential; however, José's parents also identified her conflicted nature, understanding she needed a great deal of soul searching to find herself before she could happily unite her life to another.

José had always been a well-intentioned and solemn individual, now deeply in love with Carmen and profoundly hurt by the abrupt end of the relationship. Refusing to accept the situation, he maintained contact with her for several months, as if nothing had happened. He wrote long, heartfelt letters to Carmen and went to visit her several times after the internship. During these visits her family welcomed José affectionately; he developed a good relationship with her mother and brothers, corroborating the reasons why she so needed the restitution of her family and her own spiritual recovery.

José incessantly tried to persuade Carmen to continue in their relationship despite the physical distance, but she insisted on setting him free, allowing time for her to rebuild her relationship with her family. He was unable to convince her to return to Alborde to work with him at the cooperative.

Carmen's family lived in the most austere poverty in a large, dilapidated two-level adobe structure on the outskirts of her small town. The bottom floor was a large storage area with access from the street, protected by a large rustic wooden door with barbed-wire on top, where two cows, three pigs, two donkeys, ten sheep, eight goats, fifteen chickens, thirty rabbits, six ducks, and dozens doves were sheltered at night, all bred for domestic consumption. The heat generated by these animals helped to moderate the temperature of the upper flat during the winter months.

The family dwelling consisted of a small room that simultaneously served as dining room and living room. Upon entering on the left-hand side there was a tiny room separated by rudimentary curtains and surrounded by plain cabinets without doors where dishes, serving plates, kitchen utensils, and scant food were stored.

At the far left corner in back of the room stood a round table made of unpolished wood facing a small balcony cloistered by rusted iron bars; narrow double doors, each with four glass squares encrusted on the upper part, were held to the worn-out doorframe by iron hinges and precariously held each other with a pair of crossbars. The table was half covered by a white tablecloth embroidered in cross-stitch with fringes on the edges, besieged by seven narrow back chairs of unmatched cushions, which constituted the magnetic center of the room, toward which every visitor gravitated. The table was topped with an artesian white and blue ceramic bowl where the vegetables and fruits gathered daily for consumption were placed.

Embedded in the middle of the back wall that separated the living area from the sleeping quarters was a huge wood-burning fireplace that served as both cooking and heating system. At the far right of the same wall a narrow door gave way to a short hall leading to a small bathroom and two bedrooms, one for the boys and the other for the girls in the family.

The interior of the house was covered with recurrent layers of white lime renewed weekly as a method of cleaning. On the walls of the sitting room they had placed a few handcrafted ceramic plates and two posters, one announcing the musical play *Jesus Christ Superstar* with Camilo Cesto and Ángela Carrasco and the other advertising a bullfight during the regional festivities, displaying one of the famous photographs of the renowned bullfighter Dominguin. This constituted the only wall decoration of the humble home.

The windows facing the narrow stone paved alleys of the neighborhood were imprisoned by iron bars to which clung red clay flowerpots brimming with flowering geraniums, their branches carelessly pouring cascades of exuberant green freckled with colorful bouquets.

The access to the second floor was a series of narrow steps that ended on a precarious foyer just at the entrance door, which was covered by small roof of copper tiles. On both sides of that atrium, a copious climbing jasmine embraced the structure, infusing the evening air.

Immediately after finishing her political science studies, Carmen went on to be the provider of her family, working in the department of elections in the municipal government of La Hoya.

A few years later, taking advantage of the experience acquired and pursuing her desire for public service, Carmen became a candidate for director of Department of Elections in her province, cementing with her dedication and enthusiasm an illustrious career in public service that empowered and encouraged citizens to become participants in the public processes. Carmen revolutionized the electoral processes, culminating in reforms that strengthened the voice of the taxpayer.

In her functions as director of the Department of Elections, she established campaigns to educate the public on participatory rights and civic involvement; she established reasonable indictment processes, simple ways of denouncing elections fraud, and ordinances to ensure access of the disabled to the polls. One of her most innovative achievements was the establishment and promotion of the absentee ballot, facilitating inclusion for many people that, for different reasons, could not be present to vote on election day, losing their opportunity to make their voices heard.

José continued to work on his job as accountant at the cooperative, but everyone sensed that if Carmen didn't make the decision to return to him, he was going to leave town at some point in his life. For a long time they both refused to establish romantic relationships with other people, and time inevitably took it upon itself to erase their memories.

A year later, José left his job at the cooperative to assume the administrative direction of the Salesian schools in Alborde without abandoning his activities on the board of directors and his volunteerism. He became the first layperson director of a school in the congregation. Since only priests and nuns were allowed to teach in Salesian classrooms other than kindergarten, the decline in religious vocation led to a shortage of professors and a consequent decline of the schools.

The first executive decision made by José, as he looked for ways to modernize the schools and improve their results, was the establishment of coeducation, eliminating the old same-sex tradition, challenging the Salesian educational methodology. His innovative direction reverberated throughout the congregation, earning him a reputation for astuteness and sagacity. Soon, José was promoted to prefect of the institution, covering a wide territory, assigned to traveling to the different schools to evaluate and prescribe specific directives for improving managerial and didactic institutional effectiveness.

When they returned to Alborde after graduation, Don Domingo took the opportunity to gather the new graduates to share his thoughts, ideas, and aspirations regarding the future of their new generation of professionals and leaders.

"Sons, you just received the diplomas that certify you as proficient in your professional fields. You have achieved more than anyone in Alborde, including parents and grandparents, could have possibly imagined for themselves. The time has come to recognize our limitations and place the leadership of our town in your hands."

"But what are you saying, Grandpa?" Antonio asked.

"Antonio, we are not getting any younger, and although we have achieved an extraordinary unity of purpose among the people in Alborde, not everyone is found within the frame of altruism. The veteran professional politicians in the municipal council continue on with their old tricks. They cling to power because the only thing they know how to do is politics, in the worse sense of the word, that's all. The popular belief is that it is better to have a politician with the pockets already half filled because he already took advantage of his position than one with empty pockets eager to fill them up as quickly as possible at our expense, taking advantage of his political position.

"We cannot continue with the old way of thinking, arms crossed, looking in the other direction to avoid confronting reality. The time has come to establish a new kind of leadership instead of just talking about what is wrong with government. We must demand from our representatives and leaders a style of governance based on dignity and respect, what is right for the people instead of what is right for their agendas, a government for the people and by the people."

"Don Domingo, what happened to make you view things so dismally?" José asked.

"José, you are always such an idealist, so naïve. It is not about seeing things in a negative light; it is about confronting our reality. We do not have evaluation processes in place so people can evaluate the work of the politicians, and most people are too busy or misinformed to investigate on their own.

"Our politicians believe they own the positions they were elected for. Haven't you heard the media say a candidate is running for Mr. So-and-so's congressional seat instead of saying the candidate is running for the people of Alborde's congressional seat? In my lifetime, I have seen politicians leave the seat to their sons, relatives, and friends as if it were a personal inheritance!

"I have seen politicians at all levels of government protected by their peers after committing improprieties, allowed to continue on serving in their posts as if nothing had happened. I have seeing congress pass laws, placing themselves above the people of the country, against what is directly specified in the constitution. We currently have thieves and liars occupying high offices in our country, and that is unacceptable!

"Our elected offices belong to people of impeccable character, not to charlatans with the ability to speak in front of people or into television cameras as primary qualifications. The situations we witness in government would never be accepted in the private sector. A popular expression goes, 'If you fool me once, shame on you; if you fool me twice, shame on me.'

"I don't understand how we got this far down. We have people of dubious backgrounds at every level of government; many were prosecuted but have evaded their sentences by misusing power and political influence. However, any other citizen under the same circumstances would have been forced to face the consequences of his actions, more than likely losing his job and freedom.

"We even have brothers and sisters, husbands and wives in congress representing different districts when obviously one of them does not live in the district he or she claims to represent.

"Elected officials continue to violate the laws they are supposed to uphold with impunity because public servants only work to serve themselves, not to serve the public.

"They have formed a special elite separate from the general population; they work at protecting their own interests and each other to ensure permanence. No one dares to confront them on behalf of the people! Each year, people in congress designate a salary increase for themselves even though they have failed to accomplish what they were hired to do. I could go on and on, denouncing a series of punishable acts committed by our elected officials, but that is not what I want to discuss with you today.

"At this time, we have an unprecedented group of young graduates from all social strata experienced in political action, young people who love their town. You are Alborde's future. We must start changing the political directive of our country, starting with our own community. After accomplishing this, we will continue with the province, the state, and our national government."

" Don Domingo, that is a big project, a long-term project," Juan said.

"And since when do you fear big projects? The first time I heard you speak about the problems of our town, I admired your enthusiasm and idealism. Juan, I know you now have an enormous burden on your shoulders; however, don't let the weight of responsibilities impair your judgment. Let's come together and commit to renewing our political system. Let's go back to the constitution of our founding fathers; let's reinstate integrity, honesty, and truth as qualifications for public offices; let's expect the best and demand the highest level of service from our elected officials; let's stop lowering the bar, settling for the lowest common denominator! We can commit to start at a small scale, inside the smallest cell of democracy, in our municipal government."

"You are right,. Don Domingo. Our town has a simple form of government with six council members, one mayor, and a few elected positions aside from the judicial power, with judges and sheriffs designated by the governor of the province. The next level of elected officials consists of two representatives to the provincial government, and the third level is a delegate in the house of representatives and another in the senate. The first thing we should do is educate our citizens about the functions of each one of the positions we can vote on. We should establish an evaluation system, qualifying and quantifying the performance of each elected official, the same way we do at the cooperative. This way, the people can know if the elected officials are doing their jobs as they should, going straight to the facts."

"Bravo, Juan! Does this mean you are in agreement with my proposal?"

"Only a thoughtless person would dare to contradict the validity of your argument and what you pointed out to us! What I believe is that before we engage in trying to replace the politicians in power, we are obligated to educate the citizenry so each individual is able to form his or her own opinion from a well-informed perspective without being indoctrinated by any political party, personal interest, or demagogue."

Antonio remained deep in thought; he enjoyed seeing his grandfather exercising a leadership role. After listening for a while, he said, "I have an idea! The three of us could start a local radio talk program to discuss the issues in an open forum. We can ask the listeners to send letters or to call us on the telephone, providing their opinions, which in turn can be used as themes for the programs, or asking questions that we find experts to answers. All issues would be discussed openly and fairly. Without question, we can turn the program into that educational tool we have been talking about, into a classroom without walls."

"That is a great idea! We can invite guests who are specialists on different issues and disseminate their knowledge directly among our citizens," said José.

"We can dedicate the entire time to one issue and open the microphone to the common citizen, who always feels dismissed and shut out of the discussion. Anyone would be allowed to come to the radio station and participate in the dialogue," added Antonio.

"That would be chaotic! The correct thing to do is to establish a process by which those interested in expressing their opinions could do so by sending a request ahead of time. This way we could have some order and control over the discussion without mixing the issues," said Juan.

"I don't know about so much control," wondered Antonio. "However, we could advertise the issues to be discussed ahead of time. Well, in any case, we are getting ahead of ourselves. The first thing to do is to talk to the owner of the radio station, Don Gabino Aldabín. He has always been open to new ideas, especially when it comes to education and political action.

Remember when we talked about the cooperative? He was one of our first allies, mentioning the benefits of cooperative actions and organized efforts."

That was how the idea for their radio program that revolutionized the youth in Alborde was born. A version of the same program is still aired in the southern part of the country, promoting activism that leads to tangible results. The program has gone through many philosophical phases and formats through the years, but remains an active component of their local society.

The radio broadcast was soon syndicated, gaining a national audience. The three friends committed to be producers, writers, and hosts of the program, *Usted y Nosotros (You and Us)*, as volunteers without pay. Sometimes it was co-hosted by all three friends while other times the host was whoever was available.

During the inaugural program, which all three hosted together, each of them presented a different theme; Juan emitted the famous phrase that went on to be the theme and name of the program.

"There are two kinds of people: those who complain because bad things always happen to them and those who do something to make good things happen to all. We want to belong to the second group, and to that end, we commit ourselves to create a broadcast featuring honest analysis of the issues and tireless civic action because everything depends on you and us."

The radio station was electrified by the discussion and the frank exposition of issues; the only two telephone lines at the station remained busy throughout the entire hour of the radio broadcast, which was immediately increased to two at the request of Don Gabino. When they finished the first program, they found that a group of young people had congregated at the radio station door because they hadn't been able to get through on the phone and wanted to express their opinions to the friends.

The commercial director at the station and Don Gabino instantly realized the enormous potential of the program and rushed to ensure the longevity of the concept. The program would be transmitted Monday through Friday during the midday break. Don Gabino committed to cover all production and programming expenses; he even offered to share profits generated by commercials. However, the three friends begged him not to turn the program into a commercial circus, asking the director to agree to sell only three minutes at the start of the program and three minutes at the end and to donate to the youth homes in Alborde the share of the advertising revenue offered to them by Don Gabino.

The program aired for a few months, during which Alborde received it with much anticipation, thus increasing the popularity of the radio station throughout the province. Later, the station directors came up with the idea of transmitting from a mobile unit, moving around the different neighborhoods in Alborde and surrounding area villages. They started using a white moving truck with humongous red letters announcing the station and radio program. This way, they started opening the microphones to listeners in their own territories and began transmitting from otherwise inaccessible places—schools, hospitals, and even from the cooperative, the week when the program was going to talk about civic organization, building consensus, and community activities.

The radio program concept allowed them to cross borders and restricted spaces, shortening distances and going beyond social classes. They initiated a peaceful social revolution based on constructive ideas, intelligent discussions, dialogue, and, above all, a genuine desire to build consensus based in hope. Each program was defined at the start by an issue that established the parameters of the discussion.

"We cannot say we want an esoteric change. When we speak of change, we must define what it is that we want to change and with what we propose to replace it. We must define the essence of the situation, specifically enumerating the improvements we are capable of producing and the cost of the proposed changes. Let's talk about the process of change, just you and us."

Each topic prompted a wave of endless discussions within and beyond the broadcast. The program reverberated in local pubs and cafés, at work, and at all levels of the local community.

"Where are we heading? We are getting ourselves deeper and deeper into a cattle culture. We are allowing outside stimuli and special interests to drag us into a current, defined by the whims of marketing executives without evaluating the product shoved down our throats, without asking why the masses are galloping in one or another direction. We invite you to analyze the capacity of groups to investigate who is pulling the strings of the marionette and how to break the spell of the mass media. We invite you to a dialogue, just you and us."

In subsequent program discussions, they presented other public interest issues. To engage the audience, they invited direct requests for program themes; the listeners suggested many diverse issues, and the producers of the program conducted formal and informal surveys to identify the most pressing issues of the community. *You and Us* soon became one of the most popular national radio programs.

Almost ten years of such social activism had passed when, frustrated by the inaction, inefficiency, and inefficacy of the politicians representing their district, Juan finally decided to take the bull by the horns, fully entering into the local political arena. He had carefully considered the issue for some time before taking the steps that eventually placed him at the helm of Alborde's municipal government. A few years before that, he had married Maria del Pilar Corominas, a young attorney friend of Alicia whom he had met during the summer break of her second year of law school, when Pilar was visiting with Alicia and the family. They had fallen in love the moment they met, starting an informal relationship during that summer that gradually strengthened during the girls' subsequent winter, spring, and summer break visits. When Alicia returned to Alborde as a young law graduate, Maria del Pilar partnered with her, establishing their law practice in Jorge's office, changing the old bronze plate at the door for a new one that read, "Narváez, Narváez, Corominas & Associates."

At the insistence of Jorge and Susana, they organized a beautiful family gathering celebrating the engagement between Juan and Maria del Pilar, which led after a few months to a wedding ceremony, moderate and without excesses, organized by the parents of the bride in the capital city where their entire family lived. Even so, the wedding was attended by distinguished and prominent social figures and it was reported in the local media as a social event of relevance.

Juan did not make his decision to run for office without due consideration. He met with Jorge and Fello to speak about his candidacy at length, and they reached the conclusion that running for the position of mayor of Alborde was the most logical resolution if they really wanted to produce essential changes in the way business was conducted at the municipal level.

Maria del Pilar was in total agreement and completely supportive. They were expecting their first child and wanted to secure the best environment for their family; which included the responsible growth of Alborde.

They started the political campaign by establishing that they would show respect for all candidates, without exception. None of them wanted to be involved in a campaign filled with grandstanding, marked by irresponsible statements in poor taste that usually left out the essence of any honest and transparent candidacy. After all, the will of the people was to elect a person of integrity, committed to transparency, capable of discerning the best solution for their constituents, on their own or with the help of professionals that had been proven worthy of public trust.

Juan established a task force to plan his campaign, designating experts in the areas of fundraising, marketing, project management, and public policy. They committed to managing the campaign with utmost integrity, creating a fiscally solid and a trustworthy organization, refusing contributions that suggested the influence of lobbyists, intermediaries, and special interests, alien to the welfare of the community.

They also determined to form public participation groups in each electoral precinct to gather directly from the voters their opinions, worries, and expectations regarding public positions and Juan's potential administration.

The marketing committee printed placards with the slogan, "Juan Narváez Martinez: Real and Effective Representation," and pamphlets that delineated Juan's proposal for office: Transparent representation that advocates municipal autonomy, fortifying the administrative structure and civic participation, where the mayor and councilmen vow to remain accessible to the people they represent, attentive to their needs, proactive in solving problems, and wedded to fiscal responsibility.

They also distributed evaluation forms, including descriptions of each of the elected political positions, accompanied by a list of competencies required to be able to carry out the functions of each; these forms became a hallmark of Juan's administration.

The campaign lasted six months and, during this first of Juan's elections, more than twenty years ago, Juan was elected mayor of Alborde with seventy-five percent of the votes and an approval rating oscillating between eighty and eighty-five percent.

According to Alborde's municipal records, Juan distinguished himself for organizing the creation of a far-reaching economic development project, built on an educational and participatory foundation, emphasizing fiscal effectiveness and the responsibility of the electorate.

Another of Juan's popular projects in the area of economic development was the creation of the Hospitality Academy, where the most refined culinary artists and hospitality experts of the country were trained. The academy attracted young people and new families, leading to exponential growth, making Alborde without a doubt one of the most prosperous towns in the southern region of the country.

"One of the municipal ordinances I pushed with special conviction and dedication," explained Juan, "was the process of selecting names for public places: parks, hospitals, roads, governmental buildings, libraries, etc. Since I was a child, it irritated me to see that many buildings were named after politicians, people that, apart from being an elected official, didn't contribute anything special to the community and nevertheless benefited from perpetuating their names in the subconscious minds of the voters by affixing their names to prominent structures. Early in life, I realized politicians manipulated the system to get their names on monuments, pretending they had received the honor through popular vote, when, in reality, whoever voted in favor of the decision was manipulating the electorate, and, of course, waiting for their turn to get their own name on a monument.

"The sad thing is that most voters vote for the name that sounds most familiar, without scrutinizing the résumé and paying attention to the character of the person they are voting into office to speak for us in this representative democracy.

"It can be argued that political apathy reflects public trust in the political processes and the elected officials, but as we have seen in Alborde, it actually evidences a diametrically opposite condition. We succeeded in enacting a state law that provides:

"( ) No public structure shall bear the name of a living politician or private citizen, unless the individual has paid for all the expenses of construction and management of said public structure. Baptizing a building in honor of a person should be a posthumous homage that local citizens want to bestow in memory of impeccable men and women. It cannot be a political decision made by a few who, one way or another, can derive benefit from such action. In every case, when a building or monument officially bears the name of a citizen, said name must have been subjected to an official process of rigorous scrutiny that certifies an impeccable past behind the name; therefore, when our children ask who the person is and why he or she deserves the distinction of having their name perpetuated in a building designated for public use, anyone could proudly speak about the honoree, recognizing them as commendable role model to all those listening to their life story."

THE FUTURE IS
IN OUR HANDS

I met Juan when he was fifty-three years old, having already served for two decades as mayor of Alborde. I was fascinated with the idea of speaking to a mayor who had generated such a sensation at an international level, touted as an exemplary model in Ibero-American municipal spheres, and whose administration was directly linked to the transformation of a dying town into one of the most prosperous cities in the country.

I arrived in Alborde on the first morning train and was surprised by the congestion of the morning rush hour, especially the great number of luxury vehicles, such as Land Rovers and Mercedes-Benz, contrasting with the small to midsize fuel-efficient vehicles popular in the rest of the country. The old train station was in the process of being restored to its original splendor. As I approached the information kiosk to ask for directions to the municipal palace, I noticed an efficient customer-centered management style supported by modern, top-of-the-line installations. A young woman wearing a dark navy blue uniform, long pants, and jacket over a white and red striped shirt, politely gave me instructions while lively gesturing animatedly with her hands. "You don't need a taxi; the municipal building is in the center of town nearby. You only have to walk about three blocks north, exiting through the main entrance. Take the street that terminates at the train station to your right. When you get to the light at the central plaza, you will see to your right an old building surrounded by gardens just in front of the cathedral. There is no way you can get lost; you will easily identify it because there is a big clock on its bronze dome that can be seen from almost everywhere in the downtown area."

I thanked her for the directions and promptly left the station, carrying my big purse and business briefcase containing a pocket recorder, a notebook in which I kept my travel log, a small bag of toiletries, a change of clothes, and a woolen shawl, just in case I ended up having to spend the night in Alborde.

Those were the last days of May, and it was still cold. The frigid air penetrated my clothing and I tried to cover myself a little more. With my right hand, I crossed the front of my jacket while struggling to keep the strap of my purse from falling off of my shoulder. I noticed that everyone else was in short sleeves and coatless. I tried to raise my left arm, in which I carried my briefcase, to look at the time and I realized I had almost two hours until the interview with Juan. Looking around the park absentmindedly, I sat down on a stone bench at the entrance of the municipal gardens across the park with the intention of organizing my thoughts. I searched inside my briefcase until I found my navy blue shawl and immediately wrapped my shoulders with it; the color of the shawl clashed with the greenish tones of my attire, but I gave it no importance; the cold weather had won over elegance.

Many trees were in bloom, and I got distracted by the different flowers, trying to tell them apart, wondering if they were cherries, apples, or peaches. Nature was showing off, displaying the most elaborate array of colors imaginable in the gardens at the plaza. I focused on the palette of recently invented shades of green covering the treetops that bordered the avenue. I was captivated by their discreet beauty and, recalling my old inclination to floriculture, started reciting the names of different botanical species. Some seemed to be birches, maples, and cedars. I thought about taking my camera out of the bag, but I remembered that, as usual, I had forgotten the battery charger back at the hotel, rendering the camera useless. Frustrated with myself, I thought that perhaps I could find someone at the municipality willing to snap a couple of photos of me with the mayor to send to me by email.

Men and women dressed smartly in business attire, umbrellas in hand, had started to march in front of me, a silent omen of the impending May rainfall. I looked at the sky to check if it had become cloudy, but thick intertwined branches impeded my view. I thought that, if it started to rain, I could find shelter in any of the cafés around the central park.

The endless rows of apartment buildings outlining the downtown area caught my attention; this was not the town I had imagined when I was told about Alborde's municipal experience.

I debated a few moments whether to go for some coffee in the plaza or show up for the interview at the mayor's office ahead of time. Looking at the municipal palace, I noticed its enormous clock at the same height as the bells of the cathedral. It was a centenary clock lodged in the enormous bronze dome, oxidized green over time, its Roman numerals clearly visible from a distance. When the hands of the clock reached the top of the hour, the bells rang in agreement to the rhythm of an old popular song.

I opted to show up at the office of Mayor Juan José Narváez Martínez ahead of time. After collecting my bag from the bench, I paused an instant to enjoy the old building's ornate cornice with classical sphinxes that crowned six Roman columns framing the facade of city hall. I climbed the few steps that ended at the atrium of the building. It was an open foyer surrounded by wide stained glass windows displaying allegoric images designed by teachers and students of the school of arts and crafts.

On both sides of the rectangle of marbled floors, ample staircases announced the existence of a second floor where other dependences were located, including public assembly rooms and offices of the mayor and council members. It was an environment at once stern and diaphanous. Sitting on her chair behind the information desk, a receptionist congenially invited me to continue to the upper floor sitting room, indicating she would announce my arrival to the assistant to the mayor.

I climbed the beautiful white marble steps, worn down exactly at the center, holding on to the cedar handrail with my right hand and thoroughly inspecting the stained glass windows scenes. I entered into a simple waiting room that was elegantly furnished. Three cushioned armchairs covered with light brown pillows where six people could comfortably sit surrounded a square table about one meter and a half in length displaying magazines and informational pamphlets. The pale lime green walls enhanced the clarity of the environment, reflecting multicolored rays of light refracted by the stained glass windows. There was no one else there, and I calmly sat down, waiting for my scheduled time.

I heard a light sound at the door and a uniformed young woman entered the room, pushing a tray cart with a service of coffee and shortbreads. She politely asked if I would like to have coffee with milk and sugar and, before I could answer, proceeded to serve it and extend to me the steaming cup. Without asking anything else, she immediately placed on the table a small plate with some bite-sized cookies nested in a linen napkin along with some sugar packets, artificial sweeteners, and a small ceramic container with milk. Although I did not want to eat, I didn't dare to reject the offer, nor did she allow me the opportunity to do so. I craved the coffee, which I eagerly started to drink, enjoying its fragrance, flavor, and comforting warmth.

I was filled with curiosity and the anticipation I had built up in the days leading up to the interview. It had been difficult to get an interview with Juan since he was in high demand in municipal circles, maintaining his radio and television broadcasts, and often invited to speak at municipal conferences and presentations. I relished the opportunity to meet with Juan, to explore Alborde's past and learn from the process of modernization of a town that had made history. I reviewed in my mind the long list of questions I had prepared. I retrieved my notepad to check on some comments and amend the list.

No more than twenty minutes had passed when Juan's figure appeared at the doorway on the wall at the far end of the parlor. Contrasting with the attitude I had observed in other public figures in the different countries I had visited, Juan was straightforward and unassuming, abstaining from formalities that could distance him from the citizens he represented. He despised grandiloquence, avoiding what he considered insubstantial social acts, leaving the council members to officiate inaugurations, fairs, and festivals, and centering his attention in civic participation activities and situations where his presence was actually necessary.

He was tall and thin with light brown hair sprinkled with white strands of experience. He looked directly into my eyes, inviting to total transparency; he approached me, offering his right hand with a firm grip.

"How was your trip? It's a shame you didn't tell us the time of your arrival. If I had known, someone from the municipality could have gone to greet you. Come on. Let's go into my office."

His presence emanated harmony and security; he moved about unpresumptuously. Some called him enigmatic; but he struck me as a straightforward man without duplicities, which in itself was foreign to the political environment.

"I didn't want to cause any troubles. Besides, I wasn't sure about the train schedule."

We sat on a pair of heavy cushioned chairs in front of his desk, and he asked me if I wanted coffee; when I said no, he offered me water and stood up close to the intercom to ask for it; promptly, the same uniformed girl arrived with her cart, bringing a few bottles of water with clear glasses and some napkins.

"Tell me what aspects of Alborde's experience interest you."

"I was briefly told about the former circumstances of Alborde, about the changes that have taken place in the city over the past three decades. I am interested in knowing everything I can. I am interested in the entire story."

"You want to know the entire history? It's long and complex. Do you work in a municipality in America?"

"No, but during my entire professional life, since my adolescence, I have worked in activities related to the local community and municipal action. I have collaborated with the media: print, radio, and television. Later in life, that activism and unstructured social action turned into my profession. I ended up specializing in community affairs at a local television station. But let's not waste your time talking about me. I know your time is limited, Mr. Mayor."

"Please don't call me mister; everyone calls me by my first name."

"Thank you. Besides taking notes, I would like to record our interview so I don't miss any details. Do you mind?"

"Of course it doesn't bother me."

"I want you to tell me how the transformation movement started; everything from the very beginning."

That day, after talking to Juan for over two hours, he offered to take me on a tour of the city, showing me the most important places representative of the progress that had taken place over the previous three decades.

Understandably proud, Juan showed me the vocational school, introducing me to several teachers, a few of those old university classmates who had moved to Alborde at the encouragement of him and his friends.

It was an immense warehouse-type building. Three levels of classrooms were installed in the center of the building, surrounded by multicolor windows. Most technical professions were taught at the institute under the expert guidance of nationally recognized masters. Mercedes-Benz sponsored the ultramodern automotive mechanic school, and most graduates could count on a secure future at the famous auto maker's factories around the nation. The stained glass windows of the art school were recognized throughout the country; they had been able to place a line of windows and lamps in an international chain of high-class interior design stores, achieving fiscal autonomy. Plus, the most prestigious designers around the nation used the services of the school to produce their exclusive designs.

Alborde's technical school of arts had achieved such recognition that it was precisely there where the aspiring instructors would go to receive their training to teach at other technical schools around the country.

Juan told me that, when he returned to Alborde after his academic training, he stayed there working at the cooperative and busy with the Youth Home, along with his father and grandfather. He recalled the events nostalgically, recalling memories of transcendental moments in his life, with his eyes lost at a distant point on the horizon.

"I made the decision to stay in Alborde just like Antonio and José. Although later on Jose, after achieving the professional goals he had set for himself with the Salesians, left Alborde to live in La Hoya, Carmen's town. José always enjoyed challenges; he started to feel restless, thinking he had finished his contribution to the educational program here. He was always able to visualize life in clear and specific chapters, each with its respective process of creation, implementation, and conclusion, and the unfinished relationship with Carmen was a magnet toward which he gravitated. In La Hoya, he first worked as professor and then as advisor in the public school system. A few years later, he started the political career that elevated him to the national senate, where he still is one of the most effective officials, serving with dignity, integrity, and respect so seldom seen."

"I love the story of your group of friends for many reasons. I feel affinity with your group because I also studied with the Salesians. Is their school still operating in Alborde? Do they still keep the Salesian Seminary here? I would love to visit the school. You know, it's an old tradition among Salesian alumni."

"The old schools have changed. When they switched to a coed student body, they closed the girls' school, Maria Auxiliadora, and modernized the boys' school where they united the student bodies. They kept the name St. Juan Bosco. It's not the same. I still find it strange to see girls in our old classrooms. The congregation moved its headquarters, along with the seminary, to other cities, separate from the schools. The elementary, middle, and secondary schools are administered by a secular team under the direction of the national board of education; it is not the same."

"It makes me choke up. I am nostalgic for the Salesian life of my youth . Tell me, what happened with Carmen?"

"Ah! That is a long story. I don't think we have time to go into it in detail and risk leaving you with the wrong impression of those two beloved friends. Although José never married Carmen, they still maintain a constant, solid friendship. They each collaborate with the other, defending many social causes, each in their own way. They are often seen in the newspapers and televised evening news; she constantly challenging the system, participating in public protests and other activities at the National Elections Committee—it is her style and who she is—and José appears signing agreements, making public statements, and legislating in his function as representative of the people with utmost and flawless dignity; he is a great man."

I could not stop asking questions; the process that produced such a model of representative democracy intrigued me. I wanted to know how they had achieved a transparent local administration with a mayor who enjoyed the highest level of public approval, having to reluctantly run for office, time after time, at the insistence of the citizenry.

When it was time for lunch, Juan cancelled his scheduled commitments for the rest of the day and invited me to tour the city, during which he recounted in detail the history of his town and the enduring engagement of its citizenry, insisting he had done nothing extraordinary and that the key to Alborde's progress lay in the outstanding inhabitants of the city and their irrevocable commitment to participation in the political and decision-making processes.

"When Alborde's citizens made a commitment to change the depraved attitude of the elected officials who acted as if they were owners and masters of their positions rather than emissaries of the will and interest of the electorate, we faced a difficult challenge, similar to David and Goliath—the political giant taking advantage of their elected positions and the suffering people putting up with the abusive situation until the day when we finally realized, first, that we own our options and, second, that government is not an abstract, obscure, and foreign figure. We are the government; the elected officers represent our will and must govern in our best interests.

"Although everything is not perfect here, during the process of coming to an awareness of the problems, the citizenry was able appreciate the power of their vote and exercised the right to demand from our elected officials appropriate performance of the job they are elected to perform, to do what is right for the people and not what is convenient to execute their personal agendas or perpetuate their political positions, and to be proactive in governmental processes.

"Society is a living organism, constantly changing. What has really been special in Alborde is that we have been able to reach a consensus on most issues despite our tremendous differences.

"United, we asked ourselves, 'What type of city do we want?' and we committed to achieving a prosperous town in which our children and grandchildren can work, own a home, have access to education, and culture, good parks, efficient public services, and equal opportunities, understanding that there is no guarantee of equal outcome. In short, we're a modern city, always understanding we must pay for services received one way or another.

"To stimulate participatory democracy, we formed citizens' groups to deal with public issues based on geographical area or personal interest. The element of education regarding personal responsibility was an important factor in our success."

"And what issues were resolved with these measures?"

"It was a radical change in people's mentality. All issues pertaining to the municipality and the region at large were included in the proposals. The voters have the last word, and the elected officials must learn to respect it and validate it—an inconceivable idea in the past. We proposed governmental structures correlated to population number, electoral reforms to limit the number of years each elected official can serve in that particular position, including legislators and senators, open books at all levels, compensation plans for elected officials, budgetary structures to control arbitrary spending in the municipalities, new municipal tax obligations, and democratic tax control systems, in addition to transparent process implementation methods to safeguard against government corruption. .."

"What kind of government was in place prior to this transformation?"

"It was a democratic government in theory, but plagued with many forms of corruption and old worrisome patterns. We had to fight the legislative and executive powers for municipal autonomy. Although the municipality is recognized as the cornerstone of democracy, it has traditionally been treated as Cinderella within central governmental structures. Municipal budgets used to depend—and in many countries still do depend—on the whim of a provincial governmental body and the charity of those in power. Thirty years ago, the state was the main actor in municipal politics, exercising legislative and economic power over it. City hall did not have autonomy. We had to show the citizens that a municipal organization is similar to that of a small state, compounded by immediacy and an obligation to render services that demand reliability and continuity in their execution."

"I have seen these problems in the municipalities I have visited in many countries," I replied. "A lack of basic knowledge about the duties and rights of the citizenry prevails; the paternalistic mentality of dependency is nourished, enabling politicians to control the masses with irrelevant and unsustainable gifts."

"The concepts of government appear abstract to the ordinary citizen because politicians complicate the language with their governmental jargon; they purposely use their gobbledygook to conceal the practical and essential meaning of the laws while at the same time inserting for their own benefit in the same regulations escape strategies and loopholes. That is why, at the moment that legislators cast their ballots, voters can't understand the actual meaning of what they are voting on. We demanded the use of concise and clear language on the ballot and in all municipal ordinances, proposals, and communications, and we accomplished it. We are still trying to achieve it at a national level. The elitists in government take advantage of contrivances to convince regular citizens they are incapable of understanding the laws, the processes, and procedures, thus needing the politicians and his lawyers for their interpretation and to make the right decisions. Nothing could be farther from the truth. I have been able to experience the profound wisdom of Alborde's elderly; many of them didn't complete secondary school, but their common sense and practical experience is a force to be reckoned with. This has been influential in our local processes. We respect our elders and we consult then for guidance. Experience cannot be learned in books.

"I learned from our elders about the practical side of economic principles: not to spend more than I earn; to save a portion of my earnings every month; to budget my home expenses, limiting them to no more than a third of my total income; to openly recognize when I don't know or understand something; to refrain from reacting out of anger; to consult with those who know more than me and with my loved ones before making drastic decisions; to make a list of basic points in an argument before engaging in any disagreement; to think before pronouncing words that can be offensive to others, especially to our loved ones. In short, I learned that years of experience can teach us much more than simply memorizing theories. Above all, I learned that if we don't learn from our history, we repeat our mistakes.

"Another important point is that we established executive continuity. Before, after each election, all municipals workers used to be fired and replaced by friends of the newly elected body; now we all know the municipal administration cannot be changed along with the new city council and mayor. It would kill continuity and efficiency at the taxpayers' expense. The educational campaign continues. We emphasize that motivation for public service should not be based on desire for power, influence, or personal profit; lack of desire to serve is what unmistakably carries us to a system of political patronage."

"Juan, it is difficult to encourage altruism in a society corroded by skepticism for a long time. The citizenry has grown accustomed to the duplicity of their politicians and has suffered grave consequences under inept and sinister administrations."

"It is true, but if the people don't get involved, they relinquish their right to demand integrity from those in government. It is not enough to simply criticize our government during social gatherings. We have to stop governmental parasites at all levels of government.

"We need to be able generate sources of production to achieve budgetary surplus conducive to service improvement and long-term prosperity. People must be conscious of the fact that we have to pay for services one way or another; we either pay through our taxes or as direct users of specific services such as water, energy, sewer, telephone, and waste disposal.

"Regarding public expectation, and at the risk of sounding naïve, I dare to say that should the media impose on themselves a campaign to report positive things, showcasing the accomplishments and constructive improvements of our collective lives, in a few weeks we would see positive changes in our society, beginning with the consumer confidence index and the economic outlook. The continuous awareness of a negative reality ends up visibly affecting our actions. It is like quantum physics."

Juan spoke with complete conviction, with an enthusiasm that could only come from absolute certainty.

The first stop on our tour was Alborde's Youth Home, where I noticed a marked transformation in his voice and demeanor. With great sadness, he told me that his grandfather, Fello, had passed away five years ago.

"One afternoon, I waited for Grandpa Fello at the plaza. He always liked to walk in the afternoons, and we had agreed to meet at his favorite café. Noticing his delay, I called the residence, and someone told me he was still taking his afternoon nap. I decided to drive the short distance to the house, thinking he needed more rest. I idled a few minutes talking to some of the kids, waiting until Grandpa awakened. After a few moments,

I noticed he was taking too long in coming out of his bedroom and I went to see how he was doing. I found him on his bed, head resting on his left arm; I called him, but he didn't answer. I ran to his side; he was cold. I stood immobilized with a piercing pain in my chest. I feel the same pain every time I remember that moment, thinking that if I had arrived a little earlier to his room, I would have been able to do something to prevent his death. The doctors assured me it was inevitable because he had suffered a massive heart attack. Grandpa Fello died in his sleep with the windows of his room open to the mountain range, toward where the fields of olives extended in a tireless march. The peaceful expression that illuminated his face when I found him mitigated my feelings of guilt. I understood that he had finally joined my beloved grandmother. His funeral was a national affair; hundreds of people whose lives had been directly or indirectly touched by the works of Grandpa Fello attended the funeral. At the insistence of the young residents of the home, the wake took place in their library, surrounded by candles in a constant vigil and floral tributes from friends and strangers from all the corners of the country. Grandfather's body was on view for two days to allow time for the arrival of graduates and other people who requested an opportunity to pay their last respects to the founder of the home that served as refuge to so many youths.

"The display of respect and admiration bestowed on my grandfather during his wake made us see the impact a productive and generous life has on mankind. Instead of a funeral, the boys organized a celebration of Grandpa Fello's life. Following a wagon pulled by white horses carrying the coffin, the funeral procession walked the four kilometers that separated the house from the cemetery. An endless sequence of men and women of all ages lined both sides of the way, honoring my grandfather, holding flowers and candles. During the religious services, we all cried inconsolably for our loss, although instead of lamenting his death, we tried to celebrate Grandpa's extraordinary life.

"Around the entire province, flags were lowered to half-staff, and the day of his death was declared a day of mourning in the province. The youngsters circulated a petition to name the youth residency and Alborde's main avenue in his honor. Fello had donated his home as patrimony to Alborde's Rehabilitation Movement with specific clauses prohibiting its sale. As you can see, the concept of the youth home had evolved according to the needs of our youths. However, it continues to serve as a nonprofit student residence where the concepts of civic engagement and personal responsibility are taught."

The small castle had been restored to its original splendor, and the aroma of orange blossoms impregnated the May air. In the gardens, I observed a few youngsters sitting on the lawn, some only taking in the sun, some reading, and others conversing in small groups. Juan asked if I was interested in seeing the interior of the dwelling, immediately adding that he had photos and pamphlets detailing the philosophy and history of the shelter and suggesting that we move on with the tour to make time to see the cooperative and other places of interest. I concurred, thinking the last train returning to the capital left before ten that night. As we passed a beautiful dwelling surrounded by spacious gardens, he said, "That big home is the Ladies' Residence; after Grandpa Fello died, Rita became president of the board of directors and administrator of both youth homes; she continues to play a very important role in the lives of Alborde's youth; since her arrival in town, she has lived in the same home. Rita and her son, Rogelio, have been the main benefactors of the charitable projects of the region. They are generous people of impeccable character and behavior. If you have time, you should talk to Rita; you will enjoy hearing the stories straight from her own mouth. Given your interest in civic involvement, if you want to witness total commitment to a cause, you have to meet to Rita. We can meet with her at the end of our city tour."

Enthusiastically, Juan pointed to the different cooperatives, indicating their productivity index, their capacity for generating jobs, and other statistics. We went by the Roman aqueduct and he mentioned that on the other side of the avenue, behind a growth of trees, they had built a boarding house and popular inn that offered tour guides familiar with different archeological sites preserved by the municipality. He emphasized that the people of Alborde truly valued the archaeological treasures of the zone, and he was proud of it.

"Antonio continued developing his prolific career in administration. A few years after receiving his degree in business administration, he was invited to apply for a scholarship offered by international organizations, and he left Alborde to work on a masters in business administration at Harvard University. Following extensive and notable publications, having the option to settle in any city in the world, Antonio returned to Alborde to raise his family in the town he had loved and fought for since childhood. Today, he is the executive director at the helm of the cooperative's conglomerate; he has taken our companies public, successfully trading on Wall Street. Thanks to Antonio, we have achieved extraordinary financial success. The glass building at the end of the lot houses the cooperative offices. Antonio is traveling this week, invited to be the keynote speaker at the agricultural produce international conference; that's why I'm not taking you to meet him. Would you like to tour the packing house?"

It was evident that the three friends maintained strong unifying ties and similar values despite the unexpected turns their lives had taken. We entered the building and were warmly received by employees, openly expressing respect and affection for Juan. The tour started in the vegetable unloading area.

"What are the most urgent concerns of the municipality, the province, and the nation?" I asked.

"With few exceptions, the problems are about the same at all levels; we cannot untie the nation from the province and the province from the municipality. Everyone is concerned with the economy, safety, social security, health, access to a home, education, etc. The list is long, but it all points to responsibility, starting with the citizens, the private sector, and government in that order."

We were walking the halls of the cooperative, often pausing for Juan to point out details of the operation; Juan stopped a moment, as if regrouping his thoughts, and continued, "In the last three decades, I have seen an inexplicable decline of the moral principles that have sustained our nation throughout history. It is worth making a distinction between a sovereign country and a nation of people, although it might seem I am going off the point. I want to share with you a thought that deeply worries me. Even though I am against unnecessary government intervention, I must add that I believe the decadence of values and personal responsibility that is the fundamental cause of our national problems is compounded by deregulation in three important areas: communications, insurance, and civil aeronautics. The chaos we experience in these three areas affects the progress and welfare of the nation and its citizens.

"First, the lack of ethics and control in the media is a national problem because their big outfits are misinforming and misleading the citizenry. Editorial opinions are introduced as facts, and yellow journalism proliferates. Unfortunately, people depend on the media as source of information. Years ago, the Federal Communications Commission penalized radio and television stations and news outfits when they leaked false or questionable facts without verifying their sources. The FCC penalized the transmission of vulgar and indecent acts over the public airways. Now, the stations are not held accountable for anything; they are burning integrity, honesty, and civic responsibility on the altar of freedom of expression, leaving pandemonium in their place.

"Second, each time a company breaks its commitment to their investors and clients, it affects us all. Unilaterally, the insurance companies have revoked their responsibilities to their customers. They wager with impunity, and no one stands up to them in favor of the citizens. Big executives embezzle from the companies they are responsible for while elected officials look the other way, and the people end up paying for the extravagance of a few. If the executives were responsible for publicly justifying the bonuses they give themselves and were forced to return every penny they took if a company failed, we would not be experiencing the financial debacle we are suffering today.

"And third, when the airlines were regulated, they operated reasonably. Airlines were not allowed to charge abusive or erratic fares beyond the maximum mileage permitted, according to the Federal Aeronautic Administration. Nowadays, same as with the insurance industry, the taxpayer is left defenseless, without recourse. Information, insurance, and air transport are essential necessities of modern society, and they should operate under strict rules and continuous scrutiny mindful of people's rights. If we could succeed in establishing a sense of responsibility—vertically and horizontally—problems could be resolved more easily and would not proliferate. I believe everything is made complicated to intimidate citizens from participating in the decision-making processes."

"I agree with what you say. The lack of integrity and responsibility of the media has deeply disillusioned me. I personally experienced it. I suffered from the reckless actions of decadent executives who rescind the media's responsibility to inform and educate, exchanging it for easy income, transmitting corrupt programs that stimulate the herd mentality. It is not by accident. They are conscious of the power the media exercises over the masses, and they choose to squander the opportunity to air good programming. The executives settle for the easiest and cheapest choice that yields the greatest profit, producing crude entertainment that satisfies the popular hunger for instant gratification. . It is easier to lower the bar than to elevate the masses. This is what led me to abandon my television career."

"It seems like you enjoy your municipal work, don't you? I don't know if it is the same in your country, but here the politicians use the word *change* to agitate. We hear them talking about change without elaborating on what is it they propose to change. Citizen participation in the process of changes is imperative. In Alborde, we decided to form neighborhood groups to discuss the issues regularly and produce deliberate, transparent change. We learned to identify what types of changes were necessary, defining whether we were talking about changes in expenditure, costs, income, processes, or procedures, although at times it is a crisis rather than deliberate planning that propels the short-term changes. However, one should not wait for a crisis to emphasize the need for restructuring in the fiber and content of national, state, and municipal politics."

We had arrived at a small gift shop displaying products made at the cooperative; they had set up stations where one could sample some of their products. At Juan's encouragement, I purchased a variety of items: a paste made of sweet red peppers and an assortment of different types of olives, cheeses, and Serrano ham all packed for export. The attendant assured me I would not have any problems with customs inspectors upon returning to my country. Juan invited me to have lunch at the Institute of Culinary Arts.

It was an old castle converted into a hostel where the students could practice the different aspects of the hospitality industry. Juan said the school was so widely recognized that, during high season for tourism, a reservation had to be made several days in advance and it was often not possible to get a table. They served each meal following the strict etiquette each student had to learn as part of the academic requirements of the hospitality institute. It was an exquisite experience; the menu was extensive with four entrées, plus dessert, each accompanied by the appropriate wine suggested by the student under the watchful attention of the instructors.

During lunch, Juan introduced me to the director of the institute, who enthusiastically spoke about the philosophy of the institute and his personal goals and objectives to help students achieve maximum performance and success. We shared many ideas on education and professional growth, and I agreed to contact the officials at my local culinary arts school back home to explore the possibility of a student and professor exchange between the institutions, following the guidelines suggested by Sister Cities International, a nonprofit organization in which I had been active for over fifteen years.

Before leaving the restaurant, the director gave me a reusable bag filled with informational pamphlets, a beautiful commemorative key chain featuring a bronze symbol of the hostel, and a notepad bearing the logo of the restaurant. I thanked him for the gesture and placed some of the products I had purchased in the linen bag. We said our good-byes and, as we walked toward the vehicle, Juan announced that we still had time to visit the Ladies' Residence and meet Rita. He had communicated with her during lunch and she was expecting us.

"I know you are a very busy man. I truly appreciate your time, your kindness, and this fantastic and unexpected tour of Alborde. I thank you for making the time to talk to me, for agreeing to the interview; it was so much more than I expected! I thank you for your transparency, your candor, and the exceptional meal, which was quite an experience! I appreciate that you personally took me to those places that mean so much to you, silent witnesses of Alborde's history. I have enjoyed every moment. I will never forget what I have lived today."

"It has been a pleasure. I am proud of our people. As you were able to see with the experiences in the hospitality institute, we have learned that the public servant must be open to learning from the people and must be committed to investigation to improve his service to the constituency, open to introducing courageous and innovative ideas that rise above partisan dogmas and political cycles, designed specifically to serve the interests of the communities they represent. Years ago, we recognized that tourism was essential, so we engaged in developing the industry to prosper our local economy and increase our revenues. We had to evolve and take into consideration all segments of the population. That is how many projects were born."

During the visit, I continuously thought of my father. Like Jorge Narváez, he was an attorney upholding high values and ideals. Dad believed in democracy and consistently served his community, loyal to his commitments and principles.

"Today, I have remembered my father a great deal," I said. "He was a dreamer, he believed in democracy and taught us that laws and procedures only exist to serve mankind; man was not created to be a servant of the systems and laws created by men. Dad professed that every law must be clear and logical, with plausible intentions and easy to understand; we have no use for ambiguous laws. He used to say that, when citizens have to become contortionists to be able to follow the established laws, that is when the need for change arises."

"Yes, frequently ideals clash with procedures and the temptation is to lower the expectations of citizens and the quality of services. But we shouldn't give up our ideals to accommodate procedures. As well, governmental entities maintain archaic and inefficient processes that stifle institutional advancement and modernization, thus negatively impacting the citizenry. Government officials build upon old structures, mandates, and regulations without bothering to analyze and understand the relevancy of the existing norms, without making laws logically according to the needs of the citizenry."

"We do count upon organized investigative groups that conduct scientific studies and publicize their findings," I said. "However, when problems are at a national level, it is difficult to produce any relevant change in the short term. Alborde's experience confirms that truly effective changes take place at the municipal level. Do you have any message or special recommendation for our youth?"

"I would love to see the restoration of mandatory military service immediately after high school, a very special type of service, giving our youth the opportunity to transition into adulthood while serving their country for a period of two years. What I propose is to have them serve at all levels of government, including law enforcement. I envision an army of volunteers receiving a merit-base stipend, with all their living expenses covered. Only those who opt to stay in the military as a career would be sent into a conflict zone. Military service instills the discipline and character lacking in today's youth. I recommend our youth to get involved in the democratic processes and in the development of local, state, and national policies with passion. Youth must become conscious of their civic responsibilities and duties. It is better to be penalized for mistakes made in taking action than to be guilty of inaction, negligently allowing the decay of our communities. Every decision we make affects the future of our children and grandchildren. Our descendants will pay the consequences for us.

"There are many schools of thought regarding civic engagement; what is indisputable is the need for citizens to participate and build consensus, to elect people of integrity committed to the improvement of our society—candidates sufficiently humble to know they don't have all the answers and sufficiently wise to listen to the voices of the people that elected them. Furthermore, fulfillment of the functions of elected officials cannot be left up to individual judgment or luck; we have to define clear parameters of expectations and outline consequences for failure to respond accordingly. We must implement an evaluation system for each elected post to allow people to directly evaluate the performance of elected public servants. Now that we have so many means at our disposal, including instant access to public forums in the Internet, the idea becomes more relevant. It would even be practical to have a true direct democracy."

"I have seen you are very popular and that you have tried to retire from public life several times, but Alborde's citizens have not let you do it. You enjoy public recognition and approval. Even so, looking into our past, there is always something we wish we could have done differently, something we regret. Is there one decision in your political life that you wish you had made differently?"

We had left the cooperative on the way to the home for girls. Juan was driving slowly, pointing out the many places of interest along the way and interjecting comments in the conversation. After a long pause, he confessed, "If I had a corn seed for every mistake I have made throughout my life, I would need a granary. I have agreed to serve as mayor during five consecutive terms because no one wanted to run for this office, but I don't like the idea of been mayor for life. It is not consistent with democratic principles.

"Three years ago, we initiated an educational campaign asking the youth to become involved in the process of identifying someone interested in the municipal issues and the position of mayor."

I noticed that the prospect of remaining as mayor made him uncomfortable; he became silent for a few moments. Fearing that I might have offended him with the tone of my question, I had started to think of ways to reformulate it to break the silence when he suddenly continued, "The worst decision of my life was postponing my incorporation into local politics for so many years. After our graduation from the university, I believed I could change my surroundings from the private perspective. I had delineated a draft of my life, designating myself a nonpolitical role, outside any political parties, without thinking that abstinence from a political posture is a form of politics in and of itself. I also believed all politicians were corrupt and that, if I participated in any way, I would inevitably become as corrupt as any of them. As time went by, I understood that politics are what citizens want it to be, and if it is basically dirty, it is precisely because honest citizens don't want to be involved. Good citizens refuse to participate because they are frustrated with the apparent impenetrability and recalcitrance of the system. But I also realized that, if we are truly committed to honesty, we must surround ourselves with people of integrity, knowledgeable people who are able to counsel and help us in establishing specific long- and short-term goals, willing to point out our mistakes and demand our integrity, holding us responsible at all times. Every citizen must participate in politics at one level or another."

"You are right! It is easier to be a bystander than a protagonist. People want change, yet they do not know how to define change. In addition, politicians have taken upon themselves to make the system as complicated as possible, incomprehensible. Tell me, Juan, what was the best choice of your career?"

As I waited for the answer, I looked straight into his eyes, and he responded almost immediately.

"I think it was precisely entering politics after acquiring executive experience, waiting until the concepts stopped been pages, chapters and quotes from books, and turned into personal experiences. When my wife announced we were expecting our first child, I felt the pressing need to improve our surroundings; I became a candidate and wanted to be mayor of Alborde for my daughter. Learning I was going to be a father prepared me to effectively make a commitment to action. I conceived life in its many dimensions at once, not framed by dogmas dictated by political parties or the opportunity to have power over others, but because I wanted to make the world a better place for my child."

Juan parked his car in front of Rita's house. It was a lovely big house surrounded by meticulously manicured gardens with blooming shrubs and trees and flowerbeds packed with gladiolus, lilies, irises, narcissus, and tulips. We stepped out of the car and walked the short way to the front of the house; a young girl in her teens opened the door and welcomed me with a warm embrace. Juan gave her a kiss on each cheek and told her Rita was expecting us.

It was Ana, Rogelio's granddaughter and a classmate of Juan's children. She invited us to follow her to the library, where the distinguished lady was waiting, and we trailed Ana through a short hallway up to the study room. Every wall within view was covered by a coat of soft peach paint, and the tall windows were dressed with cream-colored French lace curtains, gracefully flowing with the breeze that entered the room through the half-opened panels. The estate, tastefully decorated in the nostalgic Victorian style, exhibited a delicate sobriety. Fresh flowers neatly placed in transparent crystal vases adorned shelves, tables, and desks. Captivated by the harmonious combination of colors and styles, I felt in the embrace of those walls an unusual sense of peace, and wished I could remain there for a long time.

Rita was seated behind a Florentine desk adorned with soft golden inlays on a cushioned chair of thick copper-colored pillows in front of an ample window that beckoned the splendor of spring into the room. Ana entered first, hurrying to embrace and kiss her great-grandmother, followed by Juan, who affectionately kissed her cheeks, relaying a short synopsis of my visit and the experiences of the day. Rita looked at me tenderly, and I instantly understood why everyone loved her.

There wasn't a single filament of wickedness in her. She was a refined and elegant woman. I calculated she was at least eighty years old. Her white hair, sparsely streaked with darker locks, tied in a simple tuft at the nape of the neck, revealed a once light brown mane. The afternoon glow gently brushed her back, producing a yellowish, almost celestial halo. Rita tried to stand up, pressing both hands against the desk.

"Don't get up, Rita, we are among friends. All we want is say hello and talk a little with you. Our visitor is very interested in Alborde's transformation. I told her that, without personally meeting with you, no one could know the real history of our town."

"You are a flattering politician, Juanjo!"

Smiling, Rita affectionately pinched both of Juan's cheeks. Frustrated with my lack of preparation, I wished again for my camera so that I could capture that incredibly tender moment. What kind of reporter have I turned into? To make matters worse, although I had recorded most of the conversation with Juan during the day, even before lunch I had already run out of the cassettes I had taken for the trip, and was too embarrassed to ask anyone to take me to a local store to purchase more. Juan ignored Rita's comment.

"How is your back problem? Getting any better?"

"Give me your arm, Juan. I want to sit with both of you. I do not like to receive my friends sitting behind a desk. One only talks to debt collectors from behind a desk."

She smiled again as she rose from her chair, and the three of us walked toward the comfortable seats covered with rich, copper-toned brocade silk. We engaged in a friendly conversation and after a while Juan said he had some commitments that needed his immediate attention, promising to return for me later and take me to the train station. I said I didn't want to inconvenience them, imposing on their time, and Rita affably invited me to spend the rest of the afternoon with her, saying, "I love to speak about Alborde and the social, economic, and political experience here; today I have all the time in the world at your disposal. Don't worry. Go ahead, Juan. The last train leaves at ten tonight; I will personally ensure someone takes our guest to the station."

Juan apologized again, citing the reasons why they were unable to cancel the aforementioned activities that forced him to leave.

"You have to return with enough time to meet Alborde's celebrities; they are key people in our town, and our circle of friends. Remember, we have several open internship positions. I would love for you to return to Alborde to do research in the municipality and stay longer this time. When you return, you will stay with our family. My house is your house," said Juan.

I got up and embraced Juan tightly. My eyes filled with tears, touched by his sentiment. It felt like saying good-bye to an old childhood friend, and I was embarrassed by my emotional display, unacceptable in a woman accustomed to conducting television interviews and regularly addressing emotional issues under the watchful gaze of the cameras. Blushing, I apologized for my outburst.

"You don't have to feel embarrassed, lady! You are genuine and I also feel as if we have known each other for a long time. The invitation I have extended is sincere, not simple politeness. You can return to visit with us any time you want."

We said good-bye, and Ana accompanied Juan to the door. I stood by until they left the library and Rita tapped a few times on the sofa, inviting me to sit down.

From the moment I saw her sitting in front of the window, I spiritually connected with Rita. The moment we found ourselves alone, the sadness of my farewell to Juan took us away from the municipal issue and drew us to the personal aspects of the lives of Alborde's activists.

Rita transported us to her youth and the years after her marriage during which she became part of a very important family in the capital. She talked about the experience of educating a family built on solid values, about her personal frustration in the face of vanity, and the superficial aspects of the society in which she had to live, the bitterness she endured, and how she was finally able to break her ties to all that. She revealed deep sorrows yet trapped within her, sharing details only spoken between women.

Rita was the image of the perfect grandmother; sweet and perceptive, she inspired trust, and when she opened her heart by sharing family intimacies with me, I was able to understand the spiritual, moral, and civic investment of the founding group, how this exemplary team had coalesced and inspired an entire town—young and old alike—to civic action and commitment.

We talked for several hours. Rita described details of her arrival to Alborde and the lives of the families that headed the movement for the rehabilitation of Alborde, insisting on the stardom of the Narváez family, especially Juan and Fello.

She shared very personal details of her private life, which she asked me not to divulge to others out of respect for the families involved.

"There were many factors that invigorated Juan's proposal. The town was then very small. The lives of all residents were affected by the lack of employment; besides, Fello and the entire Narváez family were highly respected. I witnessed the coming together of three generations in pursuit of a common cause and, although Fello and Jorge had very strong ideas, at times contradictory, they never dissented in public. I remember the first formal campaign initiated with the purpose of educating the citizens about development as a form of investment, a very complicated issue given the lack of trust in public administrations.

"At that time, it was important to make people understand the difference between 'interventionist policies for economic growth' and 'liberation' or free-market policies so people could participate from an educated perspective and separate themselves from political paternalism. It was a difficult process. The decisive moment in Alborde's trajectory was when the citizens were able to visualize government as their direct representative and not as an obscure entity controlling them. The motto of the campaign was 'at the fringes no more'. We decided to firmly stand up and face the governing authorities and never again live at the mercy of others. We were determined to eliminate the manipulative tools used by politicians; to get involved with passion, to support each proposal until it was instituted, or fight against it with conviction until it was off the table. We decided to stop leaving unresolved issues looming over us. That lack of decisiveness is what bogs down public system. It was fascinating to see the change in attitude of the common citizen regarding the tax system once they felt part of the process. When it became clear to people that taxes collected are intended to pay the cost of municipal works and that budgets should be completely transparent and open to inspection, the people of Alborde decided to become entrepreneurs in their own government and started asking legitimate questions regarding viability and administration such as, 'Is this project essential for the well-being of our people? Does it make sense to make the investment now or at some point in the future?' Since then, the citizens of Alborde willfully pay their share of taxes and do not mind temporarily increasing their tax contribution if that means an improvement in service or specific projects democratically agreed upon. The citizenry became conscious of the cost of services administered by the municipality: transportation, police, fire protection, solid waste, sewer, water, energy, schools, hospitals, etc. Our citizens are well informed about their duties and their rights and have learned to educate themselves and participate in local, state, and national politics."

Ana returned to the library, and Rita asked her to see about preparing something to eat. I immediately told her not to worry about me because I soon had to leave for the station. She insisted I join them for dinner before leaving, arguing that if I ate before boarding the train, I could get a comfortable seat and sleep for the entire trip. She tried to stand up again, and I offered her my right arm to lean on. We walked toward the desk and she sat in her chair, whispering an expression of relief.

"The problem with old people is that, although we feel young at heart, we cannot recapture our youthful strength."

She lowered her head, carefully looking for something in the drawers. Without uttering a word, she brought out several large yellow envelopes, placing them on the desk. After closing the last drawer, she raised her head, solemnly stating, "Since Juan called me this afternoon, talking about your visit and the conversations you were having, I sensed this was going to be a very special meeting. I was filled with emotion upon learning of your interest in Alborde's experience and your desire to document it. After we met, you gained my trust. My arrival in Alborde was a miracle in itself. I was newly divorced, living in a society in which rebuilding a life after divorce is difficult for any woman. I had subconsciously surrendered to self-pity and prejudices. I always thought there are only two ways of living: one either adds or subtracts. When we are open to receive each day with enthusiasm and gratefulness, we enjoy one more day, but when we don't appreciate life and refuse to fully embrace it, we have one less day of life, sinking into bitter pessimism and lacking vision. We reject the most precious of treasures: life.

"Alborde's rehabilitation movement saved my life, when I decided to join the group. Since my arrival here, I have kept a daily account of events, writing down personal experiences and observations. I want to share this with you today. Here in my diary you will find an account of events from a very personal perspective, chronicles, newspaper clippings, and other documents. I know you will share our experiences with young people in other countries, and I believe you will do it with an understanding of the great effort and commitment the people of Alborde invested in their town. Tell the world that Juan is every young man and woman in any town, and Fello is each and every grandparent concerned about the future of his grandchildren. Let everyone know that Alborde is any town in any country around the world, that each concerned citizen can alter and improve the future of his town; encourage people to make their voices heard. We, the people, are the government."

I was astounded and I couldn't think of a word to say and adequately express my feelings. I could not accept the responsibility of keeping Rita's family heirlooms.

"Please promise me you are going to tell our story, sharing the principles that defined the destiny of Juan's town. This envelope contains all sorts of documents pertaining to the cooperative. In this other you will find the bylaws of both youth homes, including the original document that outlined a disciplinary code of conduct and a clear and concise declaration on moral and civic principles to teach our residents. It was written by Alborde's rehabilitation founding group. And this other one contains very personal notes, letters, keepsake items that mean the world to me. I know that, after reading this, you will extract what is needed to tell the complete story of Alborde. I know you will value the information I am giving you now."

I collapsed on the sofa, holding onto the bundle of documents, and began to read Rita's diary, unable to stop myself, not for even an instant. I understood how a determined person could change the destiny of his town and a group of citizens educated in their rights and duties could transform their nation. I felt it was a privilege to know and share my day with people capable of giving their lives for a worthy cause, dedicated to resolving their common issues.

From the time of my childhood, I had heard my father define urbanization as the transformation of cities based on respect for the right of each citizen; in Alborde, I had just found the perfect model of that definition.

Every human being is either a building block or an agent of destruction. There is no middle ground when it comes to integrity; each individual must contribute to the community where he lives. The fundamental basis of a coherent society is respect: respect for oneself, for the family, for the community, and the nation.

I have also found people completely alien to the values upheld in their community. They are mostly bitter, cynical, and deeply unhappy; they remain reluctant to take charge of their responsibilities, but very willing to claim their rights.

No one should live in a place he doesn't respect or love. No person can live productively on the fringes of collective life; it contradicts the very definition of society.

Irreverence, disrespect, bellicosity, or passive aggressiveness impede personal growth and prevent the healthy integration of the individual into his community. Jorge says we must continue with our efforts to integrate every citizen into our project, at least to educate the public about their rights. Each citizen owes it to himself to be integrated into his community.

I don't know what to think about those who are always unhappy and dissatisfied; they resist every suggestion and idea. Nothing is ever right. I am tired of them! They embody an oppositional spirit. Nothing satisfies them; they should try to find another community to live in, another town where they can be happy living with people of similar values.

There's so much to do and only twenty-four hours in the day.

In those yellowing pages I found the essential tools to reorganize a society, and I suddenly felt the need to passionately live a purposeful life, enjoying every moment of meaningful action. Alborde's people learned to love their town in the face of the possibility of losing it; Rita learned to love Alborde when she found a place to serve people who truly needed her and appreciated her gifts.

Today, during the meeting of the Organization Committee, I was able to confirm that, when we don't love the life we have, it's due to lack of purpose. The only requirement to be happy is to look outside of ourselves, to find ways of serving others, people in need. We all can produce spectacular changes in our surroundings because each one of us has something special to give to others, and when we identify that special gift and start giving it, we find the purpose of our lives.

I thought of my community and the many tools at our disposal that we take for granted. Their message was clear.

If a person can't respect our society and refuses to contribute with positive actions, he must move on and find a community where he or she can be fully integrated, embracing the collective ideals and principles. To become a responsible citizen, every individual needs to live in a community where he or she can be fully integrated and committed to contribute with awareness and a sense of purpose. A respectable person shouldn't settle for an opportunistic life, enjoying the benefits society provides, with indifference, unwilling to make sacrifices and commitments; that is biting the hand that feeds you."

In many of her entries, Rita mentioned Jorge and how cultured he was:

Jorge asks me not to be impatient. He says that all political processes are slow, and we have to keep our focus on helping people understand the laws and their rights

There is a significant difference between what the laws (normative) are and the way in which they are executed (procedures).

I want immediate changes and to be able to open my house to all those young girls in need.

I like that Rogelio has dedicated himself to creating new job opportunities for the people here. Who would have imagined the work my son has accomplished in this town?

I thank God every day for having granted us a new life here in Alborde.

"Dinner is served."

I lifted my head when I heard Ana's voice. It was nine thirty and Rita had fallen asleep, reclining in the seat next to me. I didn't have time to eat now. I was afraid to miss the last train of the night. I touched Rita's arms softly to awaken her and, surprised, she opened her eyes, saying, "Sorry. Was I snoring?"

"No, no, Rita. It is already nine thirty, and I have to leave."

"But aren't you going to eat with us? At least take something with you."

"I am sorry. I don't have much time."

I placed the papers back in their respective envelopes to return to Rita, but she insisted on letting me take the package with me and return it to her when I had finished reading the story of Alborde. I felt a pit in my stomach when I hugged Rita good-bye, my eyes welling with tears. I took out my blue scarf and wrapped it around her shoulders.

"I want to give you my scarf as keepsake so that you will remember me; it was hand-woven in Guatema. I promise to return these documents to you the moment I finish reading your notes. I will send the package via certified mail to ensure it gets here safely."

Looking at her wristwatch, Ana said she was going to take me to the train station. The moment I crossed the exterior doorway, I was unable to control my tears; digging in my purse for the little package with tissues, I concentrated on regaining my composure.

We reached the station in less than fifteen minutes. Ana said she wanted to stay with me until departure of the train, and although I thanked her for her kind gesture, I insisted that she return to have dinner with her grandmother.

There were many people at the station. I walked among the passengers approaching the exit ramp, looking for a place to sit and wait for the arrival of my train; my arms were full as I carried the briefcase, the bag filled of gifts, the package of documents Rita had given me, and my handbag. I saw an empty seat and I rushed to take it. A young woman with a little girl on her lap and a young boy in his teens sat on either side of the chair. I asked if they were using it; shaking his head, the young man indicated the seat was free as he moved next to the woman, inviting me to sit where he had just been. I thanked him for his chivalrous gesture and settled into the seat, reviewing the day's events in my mind.

The visit to Alborde and the meeting with its leaders had ignited my thoughts about the meaning of power and duties of citizens in their sociopolitical environment. The concept of personal responsibility had been brewing within me for many years, becoming a personal philosophy. The experiences of the day had made me reflect upon my own life. I had spent too much time during my youth convinced of my impotence and being a victim of circumstances, perceiving economic, political, and social limitations as insurmountable barriers. I had squandered much of my life thinking I was condemned to live within the parameters set by others without fully taking responsibility for changing my situation.

Alborde showed me that obstacles are merely challenges that can bring out the best human qualities if we recognize them as opportunities for growth. Our attitude toward life is a personal decision. We are all in the same race with its consequent obstacles, and each of us has the choice to view it as our road to success or as a path to torture and suffering.

Right there at the train station, I promised myself that I would revisit the dogmas and myths that had previously dictated the rhythm of my footsteps. We all have options, even when it appears we have no choice; whatever we do is our choice, even when what we choose is against our will. And the simple realization of this principle gave me a sense of power I had never experienced before.

The municipality of Alborde practices an effective style of pragmatic participatory democracy, the product of an organic process of civic awareness, but it was the call to service of a young man and a town committed to civic responsibility that transformed that city into a legend throughout Ibero-America.

The bells chimed a sweet melody at the top of the hour. I tried to take one last look at the cathedral tower, but the roof of the station's corridor obstructed the view and I couldn't see the tower or its bouncing bells as I absentmindedly started humming their tune.

The train was delayed by a few minutes, and I immediately rushed to board the car right after the first call, positioning myself in my assigned seat next to a window. Now I was able to clearly see the entire bell tower, part of the cathedral, and the clock above city hall. I rested my forehead against the window, deeply inhaling the cold night air; diffusing the buildings behind a foggy circle in which I drew the letter A with my index finger, trying already to preserve in my memory the enchanting images of Alborde.

Melancholy nested in my soul. Lazily, the train began to advance, gradually accelerating its pace. Soon it rhythmically rocked the swaying cabin as it intoned its characteristic lullaby, singing the gentle hills to sleep. Little by little, Alborde receded in the distance, transformed into a cluster of lights that was soon lost in the starry night far beyond the mountains.

ORGANIZATIONS OF INTEREST

Ibero-American Union of Municipalists
(*Unión Iberoamericana de Municipalistas* [UIM])
World Migrations Organization
National Taxpayer Union
Townhall.com